SEATON POINT

NOVEL

A SPARE CHANGE BOOK

WYG

SEATON POINT

A novel

By Rob Colson, Martin Cooper, Ted Curtis, Robert Dellar, Keith Mallinson, Emma McElwee and Lucy Williams.

First edition, 1998.

ISBN 0-9525744-1-1

Published by Spare Change Books, Box 26, 136-138 Kingsland High Street, Hackney, London E8 2SN.

Thanks to Julie Hathaway for desktop publishing.

Front cover art by Keith Mallinson. Seaton Point lager by Martin Cooper.

Distribution thanks to AK: PO Box 40682, San Francisco, CA 94149-0682 USA/ AK: PO Box 12766, Edinburgh EH8 9YE, Scotland/ Jon Active, BM Active, London WC1N 3XX.

Printed in Great Britain.

SEATON POINT

A NOVEL
By

Rob Colson, Martin Cooper, Ted Curtis, Robert Dellar,
Keith Mallinson, Emma McElwee And Lucy Williams

SPARE CHANGE BOOKS

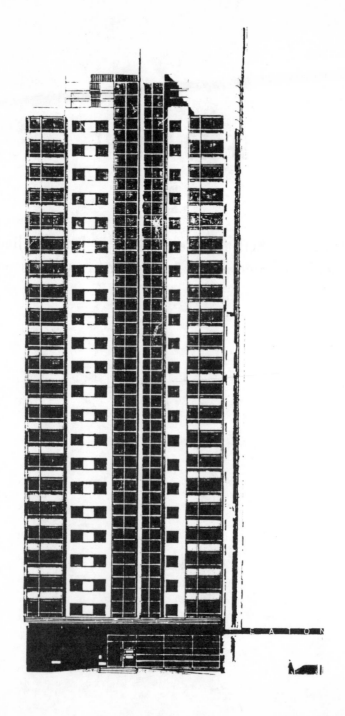

INTRODUCTION

The joint-novel project which came to be known as Seaton Point has come out in the face of cultural hostility to such undertakings. In the ever more Americanised 'shrink culture' of the global village, introspection and the journey towards the isolated understanding of oneself are the standard fare. Quite apart from the fact that many, maybe most of the world's population pondering the source of its next meal has never even seen a computer let alone participated in the life of the global village, it is forgotten that the modern novel of single authorship came into being only in the modern era.

This fact is buried under a facade of individual vision. When finally written down, oral folklore such as the Odyssey is allocated a single creator – the mythical Homer – in order for it to be understood by those of limited outlook. Thenceforth, the work is immutable, it is killed as an evolving story: to add to it now would be to invite accusations of presumptuousness from outraged classical 'scholars'. We are a corrective to such cultural imperialism. In this work, the process is transparent and we lay no exclusive claim to it. But we do lay claim to our culture. We are not postmodern or ironic or any of that self-indulgent Western nonsense. We mean it.

All seven authors contributed to Spare Change's punk anthology Gobbing, Pogoing and Gratuitous Bad Language, which for some of us was our first time in paperback. We each brought with us our own very different life experiences and varying degrees of accomplishment in a wide range of cultural pursuits – art, music, storytelling and drinking being the main ones; a potential well of resources which could together produce more than any individual member working alone. The spontaneous explosion into our collective consciousness of one great idea – a multi-author novel pooling efforts in the spirit of communal struggle – did not occur; Robert Dellar thought of it first. When Robert called us all together on that fateful day in 1996, these lofty goals were beyond most of our horizons. The comforting thought that the work involved in writing a novel would be divided by seven and the support provided by group work were the immediate attractions. As the work came in and we flew with each other's creations, it was clear that the thing was much more than this.

We have created an urban myth, an inner-city tale of magic, mayhem and gratuitous sex scenes. Occasionally beautiful, mostly repulsive, the characters and plot came into being and from seven minds was born one novel. Far from hindering the text as each different bit is taken on by a different voice, the contrasting styles complement and enrich each other, as in traditional storytelling where a body of countless imaginations is added to in each rendition. We do not seek to disguise the multi-authorship: there is no conscious attempt to harmonise conflicting styles. The tensions and conflicts are central to the novel, the catalyst through which many of us have produced some of our best work – it was the only way that such an enterprise could have succeeded. This is a living work which we feel compelled to disseminate to the wider world.

We know what the establishment will make of this book. Martin Amis will not like it. Good. We don't like his books either and our sex scenes are better. The residents of the Nightingale Estate are outraged, Mary Whitehouse has been called out of retirement and the blasphemy lawbook is being dusted off. We do not care. This book is not about the power struggles of the great and good. It is about the survival struggles of the not so great and the downright bad. It is only after wallowing in the mud that we realise how dirty we already were.

March 1998, London.

The six towers of the Nightingale estate stood guard over Hackney Downs like monolith concrete sentinels waiting for something to happen. You felt, as with the stone heads of Easter Island, as if they must have always been there, but the estate had only been built in the briefly optimistic post-hippie era of the early 1970's when it had seemed that the good times might go on forever, at least in the isolated and cocaine-addled minds of the architects. It incorporated 987 separate dwellings, 88 per cent of which were situated in blocks of at least six stories.

But there were more stories than this: pulsing through the heart of the Nightingale, underneath St. Terry's pentecostal church of the seventh apocalypse and Seaton Point – one of the half-dozen 22-floor high tower blocks – ran a principal leyline for the south-east of England. And directly beneath Seaton Point itself lay the prehistoric site of the thirteenth bunghole, into which demons from hell had been pushed and sealed by St. Terry himself during the evil psychic doom-wars of 6,000 BC.

It appeared that most people had conveniently forgotten this important aspect of local history and you probably wouldn't read about it in the "historic walks" guide available from the library on Mare Street, but the demons were still down there regardless, still waiting. Waiting for something to happen.

SEATON POINT

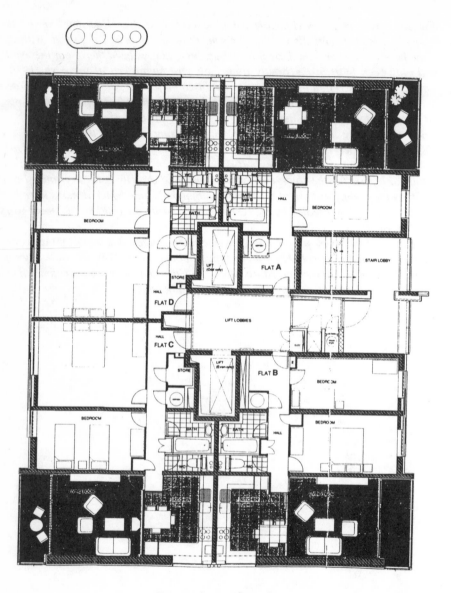

Proposed upper floor plan

1 The mirror was large, ornate, dusty and slightly cracked. The reflection was fake: distorted, disturbed, warped. Lee Christo's face was caked in powder pink, his eyes were smacked with glitter blue, his lips were lush with cherry red and his lashes heavy with silver. He could have been Cinderella, but this impression was spoiled by the smeared, charcoal black eyeliner which had burrowed itself into crows' feet, and by the large Diamonte earrings which he ripped from their holes and threw onto the brick floor, scattering tiny, fake diamonds into every conceivable nook and cranny. They twinkled from their black pits as spotlights caught their faceted surfaces.

It was 3 AM. Lee could have been Sleeping Beauty, if it hadn't been for the hyperactive expression in his green eyes and the tormented anger creeping its way across his slender face. He tore off his long, white-haired wig and threw it in the direction of the television, where it gently came to rest on top of a slumbering feline.

He desperately lit up a cigarette for fear that he might cry, and stood up, kicking off his purple patent six-inch stilettos as he did so. He'd laddered his fifth pair of fishnets in two months, and his purple lame dress was split in four different places, two of which weren't intentional. He ran slender, bony fingers tipped with long, fake red nails through black, jelled-back hair, whilst inhaling heavily – the smoke, the nicotine. A poison to add to the poison already languishing in his veins.

He could have been in a fairy tale, were it not for the cold, spartan atmosphere which hung over the concrete and chipped paint. The old pipes gurgled as he left the room and walked hurriedly along endless dimly lit corridors.

The small room in the cellar was illuminated by one solitary candle. Lee entered slowly and felt cautious, as if life still persisted within the damp, mildewed walls. He inhaled the familiar odour deep into his lungs – the sweet, sickly smell of death.

Could he look at her – would he dare?

But after all, he'd dared to drain every last drop of blood from Poppy's body; dared to absorb her last faltering breath.

A tall, willowy figure whose shadow danced over the stone walls as the flame from the candle flickered in the considerable draught from the open doorway, Lee walked slowly over to the open casket.

She could have been Snow White – if he had been the prince, to kiss her pale lips and rouse her from the heavy sleep; to lift the curse of the wicked witch and liberate her from the glass coffin. She was like a brittle porcelain doll, with the complexion of milk: lifeless, cold and dead. Poppy had long black lashes and veiled, closed eyes. A loose-fitting, multi-coloured dress fashioned out of many different fabrics swathed a beautiful, soft, rotting body.

Tears saturated with mascara and eyeliner dribbled from Lee's eyes, forming rivulets gouged through pink, powdered cheeks, and dripped their way relentlessly over the face of the woman he loved. He was not the prince of fairy tales but of darkness; of a hell filled with bitter dreams and insatiable desires. A drag queen of unforgiving, merciless nights. Lost in endless time – the undead, living life on the outside of existence. A life metamorphosing into the shriek of the bat, the howl of the wolf, the disease of the rat, the vision of vapour, the tarnish of the queen Tululah Climax. The torment of the man.

Lee stroked Poppy's silken hair gently and ran his hands over her breasts, reminiscing back to the times when they'd heaved with life. Her pink flesh had glowed and she had known his secret. She had embraced him; they'd kissed and ended up having sex on the floor whilst the ten o'clock news serenaded them. She'd wanted him, wanted to become him, unaware of the sacrifice involved. Sex was an absorption in passion and confrontation, each fixated on the other's mind and drinking the fluids of bodies entwined. Within the hour, they were both blissfully drunk. Hot, sticky sweat dampened their skin and hair. Little had been said, but much communicated with movement alone.

His mind was pregnant with memories. He had to learn to let go, a skill he had not yet perfected for all his lifetimes of trying. The feelings that now overwhelmed him were hard to bear – they were extremely painful, extremely human. He kissed her lips softly for the last time, lingering on the sensation of cold damp skin against cold damp skin. Death ran deep in her veins, as it did in his.

His mouth left her whilst his heart remained. He dragged the heavy lid across the coffin, engulfing Poppy in eternal darkness. The candle continued to flicker in the ice chill, but he felt nothing of the cold, only the pain of longing and of loss.

Sealing the lid reluctantly, Lee was left alone with his tears, and the tormenting knowledge that he could never join her. He blew out the flame gently and left the room.

"Goodbye my precious love," he whispered. "Forgive me."

Once back in his boudoir he lit a cigarette, turned on the TV and sat down on the huge, blood-red sofa. He gazed lifelessly at a tedious American film, the images of which meant nothing to him; the story line was trivial compared to the power he harboured. Hollywood annoyed him. It was all about commodities, commercialism and standardisation: stifling creativity and strangling the essence of the human soul. It was destructive in a way that he could never be.

He extinguished his cigarette, picked up a bottle of cheap vodka and swigged back its remaining contents in one go. He would slumber when the sun rose. When he awoke he would take the one he loved up onto the downs in her coffin. There at midnight he'd set fire to the casket and the corpse. As the orange flames rose into a deep purple and black sky, Lee Christo would raise a glass of warm, fresh blood to the pearl moon and drink a toast in remembrance of his Poppy.

2 Like a great many people, Iolanthe only really knew for certain the four walls: silver walls, twinkling and glittering their cold, dull, vacuous viciousness back at him. Dimpled and dappled, dull stained immaculate; and to his right the buttons set therein; and above them, of all things a short clear tube.

Three times daily a slightly viscous pink goo would ooze from the tube: yoghurt. With time, in order to keep himself going, he learned to anticipate the coming of the yoghurt with its accompanying low and monotonous hum that he now barely noticed; but time was a nameless and intangible thing that he had no real concept of. There were no fruit pieces in the yoghurt. Fruit pieces might have blocked the tube. At times, he thought that this perhaps indicated some mild manner of design at work here. There wasn't a whole lot else to think about, sitting there in the lift.

The lift travelled; the lift travelled constantly and it travelled vertically. The only times when it ever paused were when it changed its trajectory: from up to down or from down to up. Iolanthe could only tell which might be which from a slight and momentary change of pressure either at the top of his head or in the soles of his feet. This occurred about once a minute with seemingly unerring regularity. Up and down, down and up. The whole world seemed to be a safe and predictable place and there was no danger anywhere. Life seemed good to him unless he began to think, so he staved that off, he made himself beat it back for as long and as long as possible, although occasionally it came.

When it did come, it was usually during the hours of darkness and so it kept him from his sleep, not that he really needed to sleep all that much. The overhead strip-light in the lift flickered out at what appeared to be the same time every 1,200 changes in lift direction. And then, having urinated out the yoghurt by-products into a corner, he lay down, curled up on the floor and waited. He would drift off somewhere and, just as suddenly, the light up above would wake him again and he would almost feel drowsily refreshed. His piss was always gone from the corner by then, apparently having leaked away to someplace else – where, he knew not; and only the vaguest of blemishes remained.

But it was all very samey, something of a treadmill. He felt sure that there ought to be something else. Was he married at all? Did he have a house, a nice car and satisfying job or career, any children? It was all a mystery. What would it actually be like to have all or any of these things, to walk in the streets or the woods and smell the air, or to hear the birds sing and the soulless, destitute lost souls of nowhere wail inconsolably?

He pictured it for a moment: the Ford XR3i in the drive behind the bleached white picket fence, the children fighting sweetly and his ordinary wife waving an ordinary knotted handkerchief at him and mopping her eyes as he left for work one bright spring morning with the sun just getting up there into the brightest blue and cloudless sky.

And the moment grew...

3 Ian Blake was bored and this in a way was surprising. Ian 'Blokey' Blake: the bloke who could spend entire weeks reading and re-reading the same book, the well-thumbed copy of Luke Reinhart's 'The Dice Man' that lay beside his bed being the case in point.

This tattered paperback book had changed Ian's life. It was in fact 'Blokey's bible' and indicated as much on the cover. Ian had taped the maroon sleeve of an Old Testament over 'The Dice Man' so that the cover now read 'The Holy Bible' by Luke Reinhart.

Next to the holy bible lay god. God was small, white, plastic, cuboid and covered in black spots, one spot on one side, two on another and so on until six.

Blokey's boredom was interrupted by a loud knock on the door. Shit, he thought. He crept to the window and peered cautiously out from behind the puce-coloured rag that hung from a nail and professed curtain-like properties. The image that imposed itself upon his eyeballs sent a shiver of relief quickly followed by a wave of disappointment through his taut wiry body. The figure that stood gazing towards the window belonged to Frank and not the bailiffs. Frank, but Frank minus Suzie, which was the reason for his disappointment. Blokey was in love with Suzie, or more precisely, in lust.

He wasn't quick to answer the door of the ground-floor flat he'd squatted in Springdale Road on the west side of the London borough of Hackney. Frank was one of the few friends that Blokey still had; but not for long if his planned seduction of Suzie went ahead. A week ago he'd snogged Suzie on the sofa whilst Frank had slumbered in a drug and drink-induced stupor; Blokey had kept the image and feeling in his head to aid his hand relief and vice versa.

"Alright Bloke."

"Alright Frank."

Frank stepped over the threshold. "Not been evicted yet then?"

"What's it look like?" replied Blokey, feeling slightly irritated by Frank's statement of the obvious.

"Any day now though eh?"

"Yeah right, want a coffee?"

Blokey made the coffee and they sat in silence, alternately sipping the hot black liquid and puffing on their fags.

Frank bored Blokey. In fact, most people bored Blokey; all Blokey could think about was the dice. He knew that his obsession had driven away most of his friends, but then why have friends? Blokey only had friends so that he could lose them. Blokey had always enjoyed role-playing games: Dungeons and Dragons and that sort of thing, but he tended to suppress this interest in order to avoid ridicule by his peers. But now he had the dice, and the dice was everything.

Blokey wished Frank would disappear. "My sword has pierced your armour and broken two of your ribs, lose four stamina points. If you are still alive, you decide that discretion is the better part of valour and leave the vicinity of this abode," he incanted under his breath as he stared thoughtfully at the white plastic cube in front of him.

"What was that?" enquired Frank.

"I need a shit, and I've got no bog roll," replied Blokey.

"Oh I see," said Frank as Blokey walked out of the room and into the bog. Locking the door behind him, he sunk his arse onto the cold, cracked seat and produced a sheet of paper, a stump of a pencil and the dice from his trouser pocket. The dice would advise him whether to kick Frank out of the house. Letting off a fart, he proceeded to commune with god.

Frank could stay for the time being.

4 The basement of Seaton Point was smouldering. It was full of smoke; thick and black at the top, thinning to grey and petering out into white wisps at the floor. The mice leapt and squeaked over its dizzy aroma.

It was not ordinary smoke. At certain times of day it became stale, coarse and angry, but mostly it adorned itself with coloured plumes and giddy perfumes. It was smoke conjured by an alchemist from an enormous cast-iron cauldron that hung in the centre of the basement and swung like a pendulum above a hungry fire. The fire oozed from a hole smashed out of the concrete foundation and glowed an incandescent red that burned straight from hell.

Shelves sagged on the walls, crippled by the excess weight of bulky shapes wrapped in neatly labelled plastic bags. Condensation made the bags shiny and slinky and dripped onto the books that littered the floor. They were all spell books with broken spines and bruised pages, bleeding inky gore as their secrets died. The fire licked at their corpses and the mice crawled over their backs and shat between their lines. The alchemist had patiently attempted to pry at their secrets and they had failed him. In a rage he had maimed them and left them for dead.

He was tall, hunched-over and skinny. His clothes were black and manky and stuck to him like a second skin. Most of them had been stolen from victims of the night. The shoes had belonged to a pimp, though their snakeskin coating had long faded and the alchemist's big toes had gnawed through the uppers. As a sarong, he wore a long, velvet curtain that had once hung in his favourite brothel. His leather jacket had belonged to a drunken punk who had been killed in a fight. The graffiti on its back had sweated away. The alchemist had long, bony fingers; his nails were broken and black. His face was hollow, his eyes sunken, his mouth a withered crack. Sometimes, when he was excited, his black tongue would flicker in the crack like that of a poisonous snake.

The basement was his lair and although the claustrophobic heat and stench often made him paranoid, it also comforted him. He believed himself to be an important man, one who could tolerate hardship for his cause, and his cause kept his fire burning. The brew in the cauldron bubbled and burped all day and all night as he added to his concoction. He believed in himself. He believed in success.

Success was not a subject that the alchemist had hitherto been familiar with. Indeed, it was his lack of success, his abundance of failure, that had led him here. He was unemployable and had forfeited any entitlement to welfare benefits when he'd confided to the DSS that he actively sought employment by beating up the managers that would not give him work. This culminated with a stint in jail where he tripped upon the idea of revenge. Year in, year out he mulled over the endless possibilities of repaying the wicked world that had cast him out. Inspired, he studied science with an urgency that earned him some praise and an early release. After which, the wicked world had lost sight of him as he disappeared into the basement to set up his laboratory and wreak revenge.

The alchemist sought the recipe for gold, but not ordinary gold. He wanted to make a gold that brought nothing but trouble. He wanted to infest the wicked world with this grubby wealth and watch it throttle the goodness of mankind. He wanted the devil to inherit the earth.

In the evenings, the alchemist skulked in the dark streets, leered from the shadows and observed his prey. He sought seedy personalities, followed them to their dingy homes and took samples from their lives: skin, hair, blood, nails, excrement, eyelashes, snot, saliva, the air that they breathed. He gathered up their ingredients and he moved on.

When he had gone, his prey would shudder, unable to get warm. They sought him in cupboards, closets, in the creases of their curtains, the fuzz of their TV sets. He was like a clammy virus, settling like a film over their lives. They became empty.

The alchemist would mash their pulp together into bars of soap which he wrapped carefully to protect it from the heat and smoke of his lair. Then he labelled the parcels: sloth, insanity, sin.

His experiments with the cauldron were not as encouraging as he might have hoped. No matter how much waste or gunge or seediness he added, the foul concoction bubbled and churned into yoghurt, which was expelled via a tube leading away from the cauldron. He did not actually know where the tube deposited the yoghurt. He fancied that it was solidifying around him, making his home more secure. Or perhaps it was being sucked up by the clouds and made into acid rain. Sometimes he imagined it diluting the mud, and that one day the surface of the earth would collapse in a swamp of yoghurt. He did not care where it went. All he cared about was the creation of his destructive gold. The scraps of his seedy citizens were not enough to pollute the world; he needed something else. Some other secret ingredient evaded him: but one day, maybe he would find it.

5 Stan Bates lifted the sledgehammer high above his head, steadied himself, then bashed it with all his strength against the basin of the toilet. The doomed bowl shattered into thousands of tiny pieces, sending shards and splinters of shattered ceramics cascading from the point of impact like sparks of fire from a roman candle.

He stood back to admire his work. He was pleased. The loo had been utterly devastated by that one skilful blow, leaving the bathroom floor strewn with small, sharp bits. He grinned smugly. He was doing his duty as an upstanding citizen.

The bath was next. It took Stan not one; not two; but a total of three blows to trash it to a satisfactory standard. A great surge of adrenalin accompanied each swing of the sledgehammer as he battered the living daylights out of the tub. He stood back again and lit a fag. No two ways about it, nobody would ever lie in that bath again, or piss in that toilet. Dead toilet, dead bath.

After doing the sink, Stan left the bathroom and joined his two assistants. They were busy slicing away with chainsaws at the floor in one of the bedrooms. It was the top floor of a two storey house. Already you could see right down to the storey beneath through the holes in the floor where the boards had been chopped out. Stan grabbed his chainsaw and made himself useful. The buzzing of saws and the crashing of dead boards as they fell down to the ground gave him an electric sense of excitement as the three bailiffs systematically disembowelled the house. Soon the building would be rendered uninhabitable for ever: an empty shell of a house, derelict and deceased. It was all in a day's work.

Squatters had previously occupied the place. They'd left peacefully a couple of hours earlier when the bailiffs had enforced a court eviction order. The house, in Homerton, would eventually be demolished to make way for a motorway. At least, that was the idea.

In any case, the faceless bureaucrats of Hackney Council meant business when they insisted that the borough would no longer be the squatting capital of Great Britain. Hackney was going up in the world: it was going to become a posh place. And if trashing a few perfectly decent houses was what it took to get rid of the cheap scumbags who threatened the councillors' aspirations, then that was what had to be done. Hackney was upwardly mobile. It stood to reason. At least, that was the idea.

The bureaucrats didn't anticipate the sequence of events shortly to follow which would explode from the rotting heart of the Nightingale estate in Lower Clapton, and in particular, from one of its six 22-floor high tower blocks – Seaton Point.

Stan and his crew had fulfilled their contractual obligation to leave the premises unfit for habitation. It was the least they could do. Stan liked his job. He enjoyed the pain in people's faces as he made them homeless; he loved watching them suffer. That was what the bastard was like.

Finally, all the doors had been pulled off their hinges, sawn in half and thrown into the garden to rot. After the removal of the upper floor's boards, the staircase had been hacked into sawdust. The boards of the lower floor had also been destroyed, so that entry through the front door would result in an immediate ten-foot drop straight down to the cellar. The interior walls had been hammered down leaving ugly piles of bricks and plaster everywhere. The windows had all been smashed joyously by the exhilirated vandals. They'd performed well, without cutting any corners, leaving a bomb site behind them.

And then off they went to their next assignment.

6 Iolanthe found himself pulling into outer London around an hour after leaving home. The traffic on the M25 had been a tough obstacle course, but he was well used to it by now: it was all part of the rat-race deal. It came with the territory, like those seemingly hard-won compensations: the immaculate abode, the quiet weekends away from the crime-addled estates of the big old metropolis, and the annual two weeks of climbing mountains in South America or cycling in Botswana.

On the tube in the evening he would see the wino-bums, their faces misshapen by all those years of doing nothing; all of those lived-in countenances and deep, sunken eyes that seemed to say to him: "look, look at all of this, just look here at all that there is of me;" and then, "**this is what life does to us**".

But you couldn't look at them really, not really; it was all much too close to the skinniest, boniest bone of possibilities, the possibility of everything, simultaneously of everything and of nothing; and that inevitable final realisation that nothing we do means anything at all. That one day we will all be on that slab, all cold, all used up, all gone, nothing at all left there, nothing nothing nothing at all.

The most irritating and perpetually infuriating thing was that there was just no in-between, neither half-measure nor compromise: it was either get in on the hassle or be a bum. The deal had been signed and sealed long ago.

Having parked his car in the appropriate place, Io showed his travelpass to the armed security man at South Norwood and made his way down onto the platform. It was warm, the smog was up and clinging: a minor cloying foretaste of the stifling, stinking death of the earth, playing any time now on a poisoned and deserted street or a barren plain near you but for a limited period only. A completely separate performance like all of our lives had always been. Io shook his head abruptly, attempting to shake these morbid thoughts loose from himself: but it was of no use, they simply would not budge. Things had been getting that way lately, more and more.

Approximately forty-five minutes later, a tin of sardines pulled into Holborn station. As it slowed to a halt, the side nearest to a boarding and alighting platform split open at regular intervals along its silvery side. Its load of spent fish, now somehow metamorphosing themselves into oleaginous, writhing and mostly besuited worms, spilled out onto the cold damp asphalt of the station platform, making immediate anthropomorphic beelines for the stairs, desperate for daylight: desperate for light and – for some of them – perhaps also truth.

It was, supposedly, a new day. Io climbed the slimy steps with the slimy rest and crossed the slimy street, dodging the motorcycle messengers in their angry full-faced spiked visors, and skipped into the foyer of Ernst & Young, across it and towards the lift; but the daylight hadn't helped, and he felt so empty inside and he felt like a fucking fool.

The lift. He was still in the lift. Ah yes, of course. Iolanthe pulled himself upright by his haunches, balancing on the ball of his right hand, then stretched and rubbed some of the crust of slumber from his eyes with his soft, white knuckles. His skin had been looking very good lately, which was a queer thing considering the absence of natural light here in his cell. The light had just flickered on to summon him from his rest, which could only mean that the yoghurt was due from the tube soon.

Bending forward slightly towards the button-panel and his feeding tube, he put the sticky and dairy-stained tendril into his mouth and pursed his lips. He counted, the fingers of one hand in the air: five, four, three, two, one... BINGO!! Out came the solution, bang on schedule. He pinched his nose with the thumb and forefinger of his other hand. For the last few days it had smelled bad, but felt very good.

Some forty seconds later, the flow subsided as a warm and comforting glow spread uniformly throughout his body. He slumped into one corner of the lift, feeling quite peaceful for now.

Sixteen hours later the effect of the strange, smelly yoghurt had begun to subside from him. He was beginning to recall snatches of the dream from the night before, and as the overhead light flickered out, he rolled over onto his right shoulder and fell back half-asleep, a little uneasy.

7 Lee Christo arrived at Paddington station at 10.35 PM. He had spent the last two hours wondering if he had made the right decision, staring aimlessly out of the train window in the direction of his own non-existent reflection and then gazing at the many others who were located in carriage F. There was one in particular: she caught his imagination and his hawk-like gaze. As she sipped at her British Rail tea whilst desperately trying to prevent it from spilling all over her, she appeared to be lost in her thoughts. She was young; not pretty, but she had a beautiful throat. The jugular seemed to pulsate through the surface of her dark mediterranean skin. He was thirsty: it appealed to him. But now as he left the train

and followed her along the platform, he thought better of his desire.

Two nights previously, Lee had been seen in a dark alley in the Montpelier district of Bristol, feeding off a middle-aged man. A woman had screamed; he'd been disturbed, and fled for fear of consequential retribution. That was it: he'd had enough, he was extremely fucked off now. The emotional turmoil caused by the Poppy episode; his stress, his depression; and now this – he was angry with his own foolishness. Normally he was so careful about conducting his killings in private; about not being visible to those who could destroy him. It was all getting too much. Even though the vampire had always liked living in Bristol, he had no choice now but to leave, even if his departure only turned out to be temporary.

As he left the station, he felt comfortable. London had appealed more than any other city. An overwhelming feeling of belonging filled his cold, lifeless body. This city was big; he could be anonymous, lost, unseen. He already felt calmer than he had in a long while. He'd use this night as a consort with which to partake in a journey of exploration; of alcohol consumption, nicotine addiction, fraught intimate liaisons with worthless bodies of any description, and blood-letting until it filled his veins with a hit more powerful than any heroin.

Mr. Blood-Junky had arrived in the vampire's playground. He was an addict desperate to obtain a fix in whatever form possible. The options were endless; the night was young as he surveyed the virginal expanse. A pure, untouched city to taint and pervert with the fanged kiss of the vampire.

To the centre of the city he flew in the Friday night, which was electric with its pulsating neon, suffocating car fumes, sirens and noise. Music and chaos; splendour and deprivation. Humans wandered in their droves along the frantic, energised streets to each of their awaiting destinations, tiny insignificant cogs in the machine of capitalism. The city was in monetary and bloody motion.

A sense of satisfaction found him as he sat in a busy bar in Soho, devouring the visual feasts that fell upon his ageless eyes. Humans made drunken conversations, unknowing of their role as prey to his as predator. Lee's vision became blurred and his actions became sexual as he interrogated a woman about clubs that Tululah Climax, his drag queen alter-ego, could make money in.

She reciprocated his advances with French kisses, fumbled gropes and confirmation of the existence of two clubs: one in Kings Cross, the other in Soho, both of which would more than adequately suit his needs. He had whetted her appetite; now she was curious. As he dragged heavily on his cigarette, he listened intently to her persistent questions.

"Where are you from? What do you do? Are you gay? Are you bi? How long have you lived in London? Are you single? Do you have any drugs on you? Will you come back with me? Will you fuck me? Buy me a drink? Can I pinch a fag?"

He handed her a lit cigarette, but said nothing in reply. He smiled at her, knocked back his alcohol and put his hand to her throat, stroking it gently as he gazed longingly at the surface of her damp skin.

"Why won't you answer me?"

She spoke with slurred speech as her sweet, pungent, alcoholic breath filled his nostrils. Mixtures of perfume, sweat, sexual hormones, life and blood aroused his senses; it was sexual. He had strong desires – he could fuck her, he could drink her up. He could tantalise her, tease her, suck her, squeeze her – then leave her cold and motionless in some gutter.

She poked him with her finger: "You're doing it again, you're not answering me."

"I'm just thinking." He stared into her eyes and then back at her throat. "I'm thirsty, do you want another drink?" He rose from his seat.

"I've got booze back at mine. Come to my place and I'll quench your thirst!" She laughed loudly as she stumbled out of her seat and fell on top of him.

"That's fine with me" he replied, with excited expectation at the thought of his inevitable sexual and bloody fix.

The city was breathing. It was a sentient concrete jungle. The moon was a crescent but the stars were less visible in the orange and purple sky as lilac fluorescent clouds rushed past into the early morning.

Forty minutes later, he was with her in the front room, on the small sofa which only just accommodated them both. Then onto the floor: onto the Indian rug. There was no music, only the endless drone of cars on the busy road below, constantly rattling the window as they drove past. He fucked her, or maybe she fucked him, there was little in it; she moaned, he came, she laughed and slumped upon his chest. She was hot, he was cold; he held her, desperate for a cigarette. The craving quickly became unbearable as he noticed how close her throat was to his mouth. His heart began to race.

He gripped her tightly, lurched forward and sank his fangs into her neck. She screamed a banshee wail as her body stiffened with adrenalin and pain; she tried to struggle but was unable to move. He placed his hand over her mouth. As he fed in the silence, she heard the window rattle in its frame for the very last time.

8 "You can't leave me, not now. I need you more than she could ever understand. Look at me" – she was shrieking now – "look at me!"

Frank obliged. She was tall and gaunt, and her wrinkled hysteria lines seemed to hold her eyes apart. Her nicotine-coloured skin was matched only be the yellows of her protruding eyes. She had a head the shape of an extra-terrestrial, an impression which was accentuated by her hair – or what there was left of it – which was pulled back into a bun like the grandmother she was soon to become. Her lips were thin and her nose narrow and pointed. Her still pert breasts, small and slightly uneven, were clearly visible through her nightdress. The nightdress itself was ripped and blood-stained but retained a silky quality, and the gently shimmering folds clung to her figure and gave the impression of a far more beautiful form than that which in reality lay underneath. It clung to her tightly in her anger as her body tensed and slackened, tensed and slackened, sending rhythmical waves down to the bottom of her skirt.

Edie's rage aroused Frank. She could excite him in ways her daughter could never conceive. She was his secret – the only thing in the whole world known to him and him alone. Sometimes she seemed less than real – with nobody else to confirm his experiences with her, she could have been a facet of some weird perceptory disease. But Frank knew she was real, and to all intents she was his. But then he was hers too and she knew it. He would oscillate wildly between the depths of disgust and the heights of desire. He reviled, then revelled in her until he could barely distinguish between the two, and he had to go back to her. Whether he was ravishing her or merely restraining a lunatic he was unsure, as he grabbed her by the wrists and pinned her against the wall. Or was he attacking her now? The violent urges so easily flipped into lust.

Edie wrapped Frank tightly with her skinny legs, hitching up the nightgown and easing his still unfastened jeans down to his ankles with her dexterous toes. He was hard before the belt-buckle clanked onto the wooden floor. She gripped his prick as if she were squeezing a nearly empty tube of toothpaste, working her way up from the base to the cap. She made as if to fold it half way up as she guided him inside her, as if he didn't already know the way.

It was fast and it was brutal. He still had her hands manacled to the wall, and he wanted to really chain her there, the bitch. The haggard old cow. SHE needed HIM? Even now he despised her for making him need her so desperately. For keeping him there in her disease-ravaged whore's minge. He came quickly with the word 'whore' foremost in his mind and withdrew immediately. He hated her, hated himself and hated everything in that rat-infested pit with its damp-stained, peeling walls, its rotten floorboards and its harsh solitary bulb for light. Flat number 40 in Seaton Point was a self-contained and self-sustaining parallel universe for Frank. It was constant night yet the sun never set: it was a cold sun, too intense to look at directly yet too feeble to provide for more than the haziest of shadows.

This one room, the only furniture a wormy old wardrobe and the single sheetless mattress where they would lie, shivering, was Edie's room: she had made it like this purposely. She forced Frank to hug her fleshless frame in the vain hope that there may be some warmth left in her fetid corpse. Frank felt that he had experienced necropohilia many times, from both sides of the grave, sometimes simultaneously, for he often felt he was dead too when he was with her, that they were the perfect match, the dead fucking the dead; the living oblivious and probably indifferent to their accursed state.

Frank was finished so he tossed her aside, as discarded and pathetic as a used condom. Edie just laughed: the taunting laugh of one who knows she will win even in crushing defeat. She reached for the Gitanes, took a cigarette for herself, then threw the box to Frank. They would get through ten boxes a day between them. After all, the dead do not have to feel guilty about chain smoking. The dead do not have to feel guilty about anything.

Frank lay down next to his prostrate lover and lit her cigarette. He then stared into the distance and lit his own. They did not talk, there was nothing to say. The physical communication in their relationship spoke in lustful and hateful tones, but they rarely voiced their thoughts; they were unworthy of the air that would be spent in expressing them. They communicated through fucking; through fighting; and, mostly, through silence.

Frank blew out a series of smoke rings: some wide and cumbersome, others smaller and denser. Brave, young and stupid kamikaze rings shot across the bed to be dashed into oblivion on the side of the wardrobe. Edie spitefully swatted all those which lingered within an arm's length. Some she teased for a while, poking her skeletal index finger through the hole and marvelling for a moment, before thrusting the finger in and out, in and out in a grotesque parody of what had gone before, then destroying the image with one dismissive flourish of her hand. She found this inexplicably hilarious, laughing in a manner which Frank found tragic. She was triumphant and he would avert his gaze from her. She did not need to say it, he knew the reasons for her satisfaction well enough: I bet you wish you could destroy me so easily, she was thinking; and of course he did.

He wished he could reach inside his brain and obliterate all memory of their having met. He'd change history, give Suzie a dope-smoking ex-hippie mother who was did pottery and lived far from the city in an old farmhouse in Cornwall, which they would visit together every summer. They'd drive down in their battered old Vauxhall Chevette and their children, one girl and one boy, would compete with each other to be the first to see the sea. Frank and Suzie would share their kids' wonderment, glimpsing the magic of being a child experiencing the world as safe and exciting and new as we all should experience it throughout our lives.

Frank wished he was a child again, anticipating his next birthday with impatient eagerness, always wishing he was that little bit older; to have no regrets. Suzie would drive and their son would be travel sick and have to sit on Frank's lap, and they would gladly break every law in the land to make their children happy. The farmhouse would be full of the fruits of a lifetime's attention, every room crammed with possessions, souvenirs, artwork and love. It would not feel cluttered, however – it would be tidy, but you wouldn't feel afraid to put a cup out of place. It would be a home. The nearby beach would only be accessible to a handful of boats, one of which would belong to Suzie's stepfather, and they would have little contact with other people; but then they would not need any. It would be their own special place and they would all have great times there.

Another favourite ploy of Edie's for murdering Frank's smoke rings was to challenge their integrity by blowing her own smoke into them. The fusion of the two sets of smoke resulted in the instant demise of both, leaving nothing but a stale smoggy stench. The smoke was transformed into nothing, just disappearing for ever and ever and ever.

Edie was never satisfied, but Frank was spent and so had no reason to stay further. Edie had no use for him either in that state: he was now utterly useless to anyone.

9 Malcolm stared at his unshaven reflection in the mirror. What metaphysical revelations would his ablutions conjure up for him today?

Sexual hang-ups with deep roots in childhood experiences were a pre-requisite for being a philosopher. Look at Nietzsche – the bloke never got his oats in his whole life: he'd been saving himself for his sister. Malcolm didn't have a sister, or a brother for that matter. Only Child Syndrome: a classic cause of later-life fuck-ups.

Malcolm's early morning routine was fastidious, and he washed compulsively. Only good could come out of this state of affairs, he deluded himself. It was during the unhappy times in life that you were tested and, if this unhappiness proved not to be terminal, you learnt, and you may have got an exciting anecdote or two out of it if you were lucky.

Malcolm's lifescape was depressingly bleak, a wasteland of banality and boredom. His life would be immeasurably improved by some great calamity, yet it was perverse to wish for such a thing when he was scared shitless at the possibility that he may not pull through alive. It would have to be foisted upon him by fate – his life was in effect controlled by luck. He needed to appear to the outside world to have come through some great trauma whilst having safeguarded his own flesh. Then, he would appear to have grown to all and sundry and he'd have a better life. He was bound to come a cropper pretty quickly given the right circumstances – he was unlucky like that. But misfortune would be miraculously transformed into the greatest thing that had ever happened to him. The excitement of this insight left its mark in the shape of an inch-long cut on his left cheek as he jerked the razor involuntarily.

Redditch was not the place to encounter dramatic catastrophe. In Redditch, calamities tended to ferment like fine wine, sometimes developing over whole lifetimes of slowly attritional routine, brain-numbing conformity and triviality. It was not uncommon for those of the older generation to be carted off to the mortician having finally been pronounced defunct, only for it to be discovered that they were ready-embalmed and pre-packaged for the hereafter, a smile on their faces for the first time in sixty years.

No, Malcolm wasn't going to find excitement in Redditch. He had to head for the city, the deprived inner-city that he had heard so much about on the news. To Malcolm, this was a semi-mythical place inhabited by people who were not quite the same as him. Somehow they had always seemed a little less than human – the single mothers, drug dealers and drunks who didn't live to the same standards as the decent folk of Redditch. It was time for Malcolm to broaden his horizons and associate with the criminal fraternity for a while. Life would be less sterile, more real, closer to the struggle for survival rarely glimpsed by a bank clerk from Redditch.

Malcolm remembered a character he had met on one of his rare excursions to the pub and sociability. "Smeg" or "Dregs" or some such depravity had been taken by this specimen as a name. He'd sported spikey green hair and had 'Meteors' tattooed on his forehead, Malcolm recalled, and the stupid fucker had contrived to draw the 'e's the wrong way round. Malcolm had been out "on the pull" as his mates had always put it – how difficult could it be? – but he had instead wound up in the corner with this gibbering wreck of a youth, skinny, gaunt, and not making a great deal of sense.

Malcolm had felt the utmost disgust for the ambulant abortion who had latched onto him. Wherever this man came from would be a good enough place to start. Amongst the drug casualty's rantings had been the name of the organisation to which he'd professed allegiance, the Hackney Hell Crew. Hackney – wasn't that the place where there had been a black woman MP? To Malcolm's limited reasoning, it had to be the sort of desolate scrapheap he was seeking.

His decision was made. Grabbing together his few meagre belongings and withdrawing the money from his bank account that he had been putting by for a Club 18-30 holiday in Ibiza, Malcolm set off on his journey that very afternoon.

Malcolm found the centre of Hackney disappointingly tidy, nice even, with its old churches and semi-pedestrianised high street, not at all what he was looking for. He noticed a marked difference in the people, however, from those he had observed during his wanderings through various parts of Central London earlier in the day. Quite apart from the different racial mix, there was a conspicuous lack of the well-heeled promenaders of Kensington and the trendy bepierced colour of Camden. The older people looked like they shopped exclusively at Oxfam, while the younger crowd's clothing was largely uniform, the crusties excepted, with baggy jeans and puffy black jackets very much to the fore. The young black women nonetheless possessed a certain style and swagger, and nearly all of them were good looking.

It was time to search out the estates. This didn't take long. Malcolm soon came across an imposing group of six huge, grim, filthy-grey edifices which towered over the park facing them like great ugly monoliths. Malcolm had never seen any less desirable dwellings.

Exactly the right kind of place, he sensed intuitively, from which to embark on the adventures that were beckoning him.

10

Ned and Ted Barber stood outside the flat wondering if they'd be needed, hoping that they would. It was Stan's job to knock at the door and see if the squatter inside would show up and leave sensibly. But if there was any aggro, the twins would be there to back up their boss.

Stan knocked and waited, stroking his cosh. A face peeped from behind the puce rag that was the excuse for a curtain in the front window. Some fucking weirdo, thought the bailiffs. They'd have him, if he gave them half a chance.

Blokey was concerned. In a way, he was glad that he still hadn't managed to get rid of Frank. Even though the bastard was getting on his nerves, and he only put up with him because he wanted to shag the geezer's wife, any ally was welcome at this moment of crisis.

"Fuck me, it's the bailiffs!" he told his mate.

Frank wasn't too bothered. He didn't live there; it wasn't him that was getting evicted.

Another knock. Blokey didn't know what to do. He got his dice. One, two or three, he'd ignore the knock. Four, five or six, he'd answer the door and front it out with the bailiffs. He rolled: six. He walked over to the door and opened it cautiously.

"You must be Mr. Persons Unknown," said Stan. "I'm Stan the bailiff and I've come to repossess this property. You probably haven't got anywhere to go after this, but if you like you can always go to Hackney Homeless Persons Unit and spend all day in a queue before they turn you away."

"You've obviously got the wrong street" said Blokey, pointing at Stan's eviction papers. "This is Burma Road, not Springdale Road, which is the next turning off Green Lanes after this one."

Stan was thrown for a bit. Whilst checking his map and papers, wondering if he'd made a mistake, Blokey slammed the door in his face.

"Right," said the squatter, "we're barricading ourselves in! Pick up everything heavy you can find, and we'll block the doors and windows and keep those bastards out!"

Frank nodded, unconvinced. He watched sceptically as Blokey got a few items of furniture and began wedging them up against the front door.

Just then there was an almighty explosion as a beautiful shower of shimmering shattered glass cascaded into the living room like sparks of fire from a roman candle, leaving the floor strewn with splendid glistening splinters. The bailiffs were smashing at the front windows with their coshes like cops escorting their guests back to Stoke Newington police station. Blokey had been pulling Stan's leg. They weren't standing for the squatter's cheek – he'd picked the wrong bailiffs!

24

In seconds, the glass had been completely and violently removed and Stan and his men piled into the squat like the SAS. Frank got scared and ran out through the back, hopped over a garden fence and disappeared, leaving Blokey alone in the firing line. Blokey locked himself in the bog. Dropping his trousers and shorts in case he shat himself in fright, he sat on the bowl and got out his dice, trying to work out what to do.

One, it was a fair cop, he'd face the bailiffs and do whatever they suggested. Two, he'd argue the point with them on moral and political grounds. Three, he'd take them all on unarmed in a suicidal display of defiance. Four, he'd follow Frank's example and run off out the back. Five, he'd stick his head down the pan, pull the chain on himself a few times and eventually drown. Six, he'd stay locked in the bog and see what happened.

Six. He could hear sounds of demolition coming from the other side of the khazi door as the stormtroopers trashed his flat. Within minutes, Stan, Ned and Ted had scattered all Blokey's possessions over the pavement outside, breaking as many of them as they possibly could in the process. They pulled the doors off their hinges, ripped out the light fittings and electrical sockets, smashed up the fireplaces, destroyed the staircase, pulled down the banisters and knocked holes in the floorboards with sledgehammers. Then they thought about Blokey, locked in the bog.

"We know you're in there, cunt!" shouted Stan. He and his boys were stroking their coshes, hoping that there would be a ruck. "Come out peacefully, and you might get less of a doing over than you're due anyway – if you're lucky!"

Blokey rolled the dice again. He hadn't even decided which number meant what before the door came crashing down, courtesy of Stan's left boot. The Barber twins got him one by each arm, hoisted him up, hauled him out of the bog and slammed him hard up against a wall.

"We've got a few questions for you, scumbag!" Stan bellowed. "You're here illegally – got it? We're taking over – legally. The law's on our side, so you'd better get the answers right!"

Blokey nodded, acquiescent. He didn't have much choice.

"Where's the drugs?"

"You what? I haven't got any fucking drugs!"

Stan grinned and winked at the twins, who in turn leered at the dice man menacingly.

"Come on, you must have some drugs! You're a fucking squatter – all squatters have got drugs! We're here protecting law and order mate, and that includes confiscating the drugs and disposing of them in the appropriate manner, know what I mean? Hand them over, or else you're fucked! As if you're not already! Get my drift?"

"I haven't got any drugs, but I've got a few cans of Tennents and a packet of fags stashed away if that's any use!"

Stan gave the signal. Ned held Blokey down while Ted got a bicycle pump and rammed it as far as it would go up the dice man's arse. Then the twins grabbed a wrist each and squeezed, tight. The pain was excruciating, Blokey's arse hurt like hell and his hands started to go all numb as the circulation was cut off. Simultaneously, Stan started pumping Blokey up, causing unpleasant inflating sensations to erupt deep inside the victim's arse. When Stan got bored of this he began slapping Blokey about the cheeks viciously. The squatter's face stang unbearably.

"You're a fucking joker, son! You're having a laugh! All you have to do is tell us where the drugs are and you can go down to Hackney Homeless Persons Unit a happy man!" Stan kicked the dice man in the side of the head to emphasise his words.

Blokey blacked out. Stan didn't know his own strength; he'd booted the dice man harder than he'd meant to. This displeased the bailiffs somewhat, as an unconscious victim was less fun than a man who knew exactly what was coming to him. Ned and Ted got a bin liner full of old dog food, mouldy potato peelings and other refuse and tipped it over the squatter's face. They bound his wrists and ankles so that he'd have trouble getting up when he came round. They bandaged his face with masking tape so that he couldn't shout. Then they got his bicycle, snapped its frame in two, and put it in front of him so that it would be the first thing he saw when he recovered consciousness. Then they left him there, the bicycle pump still up his rear, and went off in the van to their next assignment.

When Blokey came to, his wrists, ankles, head, cheeks and arse all ached terribly. He couldn't move properly: all he could do was wriggle about a bit in his bondage. The knots were tight: he couldn't shake them loose. His front door didn't exist any more: all that remained was an empty space. He'd been done over, good and proper. And so had his pushbike.

Using superhuman effort, he managed to wriggle to the front door and out onto the pavement outside, like a large earthworm.

A neighbour approached, a young woman of punk persuasion. He'd seen her walking past plenty of times before and liked what he saw. He'd never plucked up the courage to talk to this particular babe: he never managed to formulate the right words. Even if like Blokey you were a gregarious sort of a bloke, it was always difficult to shoot off banter to strangers who had you melting with desire, frustration and silent lust. And yet here he was, bound and gagged, his trousers and underpants round his ankles, a bicycle pump stuck up his arse, covered in stinking garbage, staring up at the chick.

She was horrified; she let out a little gasp. Charitably, she unbound and ungagged the wriggling squatter, then ran away, unwilling to be involved further. Blokey arose, pulled the pump gingerly from his arse, wiped himself down and seethed, furious, surveying his scattered and broken possessions.

Blokey was a proud man. It was one thing having his home broken into and devastated by the bailiffs. It was another, being assaulted and humiliated in the course of the eviction. But being shown up and made to look ridiculous in front of a bird he fancied – that was unforgivable!

Blokey was red in the face with embarrassment, anger and hate. The bailiffs – especially the boss – had to pay. He got a dice and rolled.

One, Stan would hang. Two, he'd be shot. Three, Blokey would get four wild horses, use strong ropes to attach Stan's limbs to a horse each and then get them to bolt in opposite directions. Four, he'd take him to the top of a tall building and throw him off. Five, he'd slowly, over a period of several days and using a variety of sharp instruments, mutilate the bailiff with carefully paced lacerations and amputations, working gradually towards the more major arteries and appendages until he eventually bled to a long and painful death. Six, he'd make him swallow a piranha.

Four.

11

Lee Christo found himself south of the river, and he was still thirsty. He travelled across the city for the rest of the night, making three more kills. As the sun greeted the cool morning, dawn brought light upon a scavenging, sleeping, soulless city. The buildings appeared dull and lifeless as he made his way to Kings Cross. This was a cold moment, expectant and haunted by the grave awareness of his indulgences – two of which had been needless. Alcohol had always brought out the merciless side to his nature.

Lee sat in a cafe, drank some cheap coffee, and waited for a bed and breakfast to open. He suddenly felt drained: he needed to rest and recuperate. The day brought with it a mixture of withdrawal and guilt, and he felt as if he were a different creature. His pallid complexion, his heavy, drugged, cold eyes and his blood-stained shirt attracted too much attention from an undesirable world. It was time for him to cut himself off.

The bed and breakfast was cheap. The room was small and claustrophobic, but at least the bed was adequate. He fell onto it and slept until the evening.

Time flew by in the big city. Three weeks had passed, and Lee had fed his way through a dozen bodies, all of which he had killed. His victims mainly resided in zones four, five and six of the public transport network for he felt it was safer that way. Suburbia was unappealing, save for its distance and its quiet, innocuous energy. The bed and breakfast had become a seedy home where he slept during the day. He was out for most of the night, not always to feed but also to earn money.

Tululah Climax worked for four nights in the club in Soho he had been made aware of by his first London victim, but he was told by the management to leave before the fifth. She didn't protest but left quickly via the fire escape into a back street. There had been a guy who had been paying her much unwanted attention and she was relieved to get out of there. The slaps on the arse had been a nuisance, although he had given her a fifty quid tip one night. The money had been good, but it hadn't been worth all the gropes and fumblings of large, sweaty, uninvited fingers. The bastard was more of an animal than she could ever be. He would have to be killed at a later date.

The club in Kings Cross payed less well, but the people in the audience were more drugged up and subdued, and Tululah worked there three nights a week and received no hassle. This continued for a while but she needed more money. Getting drunk one night at the bar after a performance, she got to hear of a club in the East end that was looking for drag queens in particular. And so she travelled to Hackney.

The venue was more of a dodgy pub than a club, home to fruit machines and strippers. But when a scruffy, unshaven Lee eagerly showed the polaroids of a gorgeous Tululah Climax to the landlord, he looked in dazed bewilderment and decided there and then that he wanted him to start that night.

Six nights later, the members of the audience were particularly rowdy and boisterous, being as it was a Saturday. Lee could hear them while he transformed himself into Tululah in some stinking broom cupboard of a toilet at the back of the pub. He was working in what he considered to be the arsehole of cabaret land.

As he put on his long silken black wig, he realised that he hated Hackney. It was grim. There was nothing that appealed apart from six huge high rises situated nearby. They reached into the sky as if they were great bleak monoliths from some sci-fi film. Powerful and daunting, one in particular filled him with an inexplicable feeling, the explanation to which he was unable to drag from the quagmire-like chasm of his mind. He mused over the co-incidence of the tower block's name as he applied thick, luminous silver shadow to his eyelids. **Seaton Point**, a place lurking familiarly in his past – the rugged cliffs, the wild coves, endless beaches and turbulent, raging sea. He was overwhelmed with fascination whenever he looked towards the tower.

She put on her black high heels and long satin gloves, made her way into the rear of the pub and waited unseen behind a huge, shimmering gold lame curtain. After being introduced, she walked onto the stage to shouts and whistles of appreciation. Lee was no more – the blood junkie, the vampire and the man melted away in a haze of dry ice, smoke and alcohol fumes. Only the woman existed now – sexual; audacious; spell-binding. She was complete, and the audience believed in a fantasy that was in fact reality – for, unbeknown to them, Lee's magic vampiric powers enabled him to alter his genitals at will from male to female and back again whenever he felt like it.

Displayed before the audience eyes was Tululah Climax: untouched, but incredibly tainted in a way that was beyond their comprehension. It was deeper than their wildest imaginings; more bloody than any newly-slaughtered carcass. They were the lambs, and one would be sacrificed. He was unaware of this as he stared across the crowded room at Tululah. He stood in the shadows, captivated and enchanted by the spectacle.

12 *The clank, clank, clanking resounded right to the centre of my being until I felt that it was emanating from someplace within. The boundaries between me and the world became blurred and I felt that I could look upon myself objectively.*

What I saw was absurd; laughable, but utterly unfunny. I was stumbling through dark, damp tunnels, with all the activity of the world above me echoing with an indecipherable drone – and always the unchanging beat, resounding all around me. I was naked; my lumbering, awkward frame was covered in grime and sweat for it was unbearably hot. Although there was nobody else around, I clutched my groin as I ran, as if ashamed to be in the presence of my own self. There was comfort to be gained too from this action, for this was the only part of my body still capable of feeling and it needed to be protected, so that it should not succumb to the same fate as the rest of me.

The tunnels were faintly lit and this provided an enduring hope of escape for, in the absence of artificial lighting, there must have existed an escape route to the outside. This spurred me on, though the end result would, I knew, always be the same. I found the opening, as usual, after several miles' searching, and in the same place as always – I would always recognise the location, but the next time I would never remember the way. Neither would I ever be permitted to poke my head above ground and see for myself the reason for all the noise. This was seemingly to remain forever beyond my grasp: I was destined always to imagine, to fantasise, never to experience.

Frank woke from the dream to find Suzie lying peacefully asleep beside him. What sweet visions of the future was she dreaming of now? He had rehearsed in his mind how the dream would sound to her, but how could she possibly understand? His recurring dream, which had recently returned after a long and welcome absence stretching back to pre-pubescent innocence, was, at the point of waking, far more real and significant than anything experienced during his daytime consciousness. Frank could find a meaning in his dreams which was more profound than anything that could come from being awake. Sometimes, he wished he could disappear into his dreamworld forever – he might suffer greatly there, but at least he knew why he was suffering and could accept that the blame lay entirely within himself.

He lay motionless for what seemed like an age, staring at the impossibly beautiful woman beside him, her distended belly a gift of which he knew he was utterly unworthy. Her breasts were already prepared for the task that lay ahead for them, and Frank envied her intensely for the link with creation and nature which came so easily to her. He could only guess what she was dreaming. She was flying high above the heads of the awake, visiting exotic corners of the world and communing with still undiscovered tribes in the depths of the Amazonian basin where she would divine sublime destinies for their unborn daughter. Unhindered by time or space, she would next take her child to see the pygmies in Africa, the aborigines of Australia, then the eskimos of Canada, accumulating as much ancient knowledge as she could. Their child dreams with her mother and travels, as she will in sixteen years' time, about to embark upon another great phase in her life. She will be born with all of the knowledge needed for adulthood. All that remains is for her to learn how to be a child.

"What a future lies in store for you, my daughter!" exclaimed Frank aloud. "My progeny, my pride."

Suzie awoke with a fulfilled smile on her face. She was, it appeared to Frank, permanently happy. Even when she cried, which was often, the tears were always shed for the future. For Frank, tears were always for the past.

He leaned over and rested his hand upon her belly. The huge rounded form and the thought of the prize curled up inside thrilled him, allowing him to briefly imagine a glorious, concrete future, instead of the wild unrealistic fantasies which consumed him when he was with Suzie's mother. How it would destroy his wife to know his horrifying secret: to know that the woman she had loved, mourned and then finally laid to rest, was at that very moment holed up in some squalid tower block awaiting Frank's certain return.

Where would the chain be broken?, Frank agonised. Three generations of women – one unborn and untouched; the second in the full bloom of young adulthood; the third dead, buried, but not yet gone, stubbornly clinging to the world as if she had been happy when she was there in life. As if she was happy now! Only the pain of others, it seemed to Frank, could satisfy her: even if those others included the child she had carried and nourished inside her, just as Suzie was doing for their child in her turn. The dead must go, so that those not yet born may live. Didn't she understand that?

These thoughts were struggling to get to the surface and show themselves on his face, but he was well-practiced at keeping them deep beneath his skin where they belonged, and he smiled tenderly at his wife as she drifted silently back into her travels.

30

13

It was one of those days. Kelly had smelt it as he'd stepped out of the flat. He'd suffered days like these many times before.

The bus journey to sign on was hell. Everyone in the queue, everyone on the bus, everyone right down to and including the driver seemed retarded, stupid, pathetic. Not worthy of the gift of life. Every conversation he tuned into was full of inane shit. Drivel. Soap-soaked banality. "Ooh Bianca said this." "Did she?" "Oh and then..."

Fuck off! Just shut up and die!

Kelly didn't like people. The world would be a wonderful place if not for humans. Always interfering. Playing God, thinking that the world was just there for their benefit. Kelly prayed for the next plague or global disaster. Every few millenia or so there was one, cutting the humanoids back down to size and saving the planet from ruin.

Despite his distaste for the public at large, Kelly Greaves blended in perfectly. There was nothing eye-catching about his looks. A complexion that bore the scars of volcanic episodes of acne lurked behind large, thick, brown-rimmed specs that were partly hidden by a fringe of lank, slightly greasy brown hair. The green snorkel parka with fur-trimmed hood rounded off an appearance which to most people spelt out the words train and spotter.

He'd been severely bullied at school and had found the usual way to stop the beatings: humour. He'd lost that some years ago as the tedium of life in general and his inability to escape from his mother's apron strings had turned him into a morose, humourless character.

The fortnightly chore over, he decided to wander into town and see if there was any good skirt about. Have a good letch. It was summer and the hot bus ride had assured him of a good gaze at the tits and legs in the high street. He hadn't had sex, let alone a girlfriend for about four years but he loved to look, storing faces and features for wank fantasies late at night when he couldn't sleep. Now and again a girl would catch him staring at her and would return his gaze, usually with a look of annoyance or contemptuous disgust. Kelly would feel for an instant that they had glimpsed into his soul and had seen that there was nothing there but filth, lust and disease. His cheeks would immediately redden and he'd look away quickly. These faces also stuck in his mind, but he could only associate them with images of hate and death.

Basically Kelly Greaves wanted to die, but he didn't have the guts. Yellow through and through, he wanted to kill himself, but it had to be easy.

So engrossed was he in his voyeuristic hobby that he nearly jumped a foot into the air when a hand tightly gripped his shoulder and yanked him back into the real world. Kelly froze for a second, stricken with fear and guilt.

"You old cunt, Kelly, how ya bin?"

Kelly stared into the face of his neighbour Mick the Brick. Mick, as was apparent from his moniker, was a bricklayer. His jumper, a typical Army surplus stores navy with elbow patches, was spattered with pug. His black woolly hat was ever present, and Kelly only had distant schoolday memories of what most of Mick's head looked like. The face gleaming demonically revealed a large mouth with a single tooth hanging like a lone stalactite from the roof of a particularly stinky cave.

"Fucking hell, Mick, you nearly frightened the fucking life out of me."

"Dodgy thoughts son, must be."

"Why aren't you working then?"

"Day off innit. Got the shits," replied Seaton Point's most famous bricklayer, giving an outrageous wink whilst tapping the side of his nose. "Ain't seen you round the estate much," he continued.

"Nah, Mum's ill at the moment. Legs are playing up. Had to look after the old bat."

"You'll have to come round to one of me video evenings" said Mick, "there's one tomorrow night. Our Marty has got hold of a copy of Animal Farm. Quality might be a bit dodgy, but it's fucking hard to get hold of these days."

Kelly was back-pedalling by now, trying to escape the rancid odour of Mick the Brick's gob and the threat of one of his infamous video nights.

"Ned and Ted'll be there" Mick shouted at the receding figure. "Eight o'clock, I'll be expecting you."

Kelly winced. That was all he needed to round off his day. An appointment for a night in with the estate's premier nutters.

Fucking great.

14

By eleven o'clock of a Monday morning, Iolanthe O'Neill felt that a rather stiff mug of strong black coffee was in order. In truth, he felt like this long before then, but there was the ever-omnipresent question of etiquette, office politics and keeping one's nose clean for the boss's arse later. So 11 AM it was and he was damned glad that it was here at last. He exhaled noisily, pushed his chair back, pivoted himself momentarily on the pristine heels of his sensible shoes and then made his way at last to the coffee percolator for a shot of temporary nirvana. He walked across the fitted carpet, which had always seemed to him to be not so much carpet as the missing evolutionary link between carpet and its predecessor in the floor-upholstery chain, linoleum.

It appeared that he was some kind of a junior trainee architect hopelessly stuck in the upper-white-collar equivalent of a dead end job. A waiter for the boss class in the high-class high-rise restaurant of nowhere. He poured the coffee and proceeded to stand around idly for a little while: he couldn't return to his work station until he had dispensed with it in its entirety, because both food and drink represented a clear danger to his word processor. He was 34. He was nowhere. Just a junior trainee architect.

"So how was the weekend then, sweetie?"

Io turned his head slightly and his eyes came to rest upon the attractive form of a young woman, aged about 26 in all probability, who appeared to regard him with a strange degree of fond familiarity that he couldn't fully get his head around.

"Oh you know, Jeannie" he found himself immediately coming back with; "my mother-in-law came around like I was telling you with much dread at the end of last week and, of course, it was just like I said it would be. All she seems to want to do is pour down that gin that she loves so much, and cry, and then after the gin gets a little bit of a hold on her, she manages to control the sobbing thing really quite adequately, but by then she just can't stop drinking it, so a short while after that she just lapses into this sort of catatonic state; you know, staring bolt ahead, glassy-eyed, right into the deepest shallow depths of nowhere, slack jaw agape and dribbly-drooling away."

Jeannie appeared to be gazing over him lovingly now: it seemed that Iolanthe had a peculiar way with the vernacular that some women just loved. Only some, though. He went on:

"But the thing is that the kids just love it all: little bastards. It's like they're thinking, they're willing her, 'drink granny drink' so that they have a new toy to play with. It seems to me that that's all anyone or anything must be to kids, just another toy for their temporary and arbitrary amusement should they happen to feel like it, and the rest of us aren't really any better once we get a little older. Still, she can afford it now, and there doesn't seem to be a whole lot else for her to be getting up to at her time of life. You can't help but feel for her, what with the old man gone and all – she certainly felt for him for long enough: damn near thirty years it must have been. Now there's nothing there for her but the great big yawning chasm of her self and absolutely nothing to fill it with, just the booze to stretch it out and then hermetically seal the crater over for hours at a time with that big old alcoholic clingfilm; and I guess that's what's waiting for **all** of us someday in its infinite variety of infinitely terrifying ways. She can afford it: he certainly left her enough so why the hell not? Damn good luck to her I say! It sure is a pretty sad thing to watch, though, to sit there seeing it happen a stretched-out second at a time. How about you? I'm sorry, I mean, what did you manage to get around to doing? Anything?"

"No, not much at all really Io."

There was that very strange more-than-a-hint of familiarity again; abject familiarity with this woman that he felt he had only just met. And yet at the same time it seemed both very natural and very exciting, like hot spicy food in his stomach that had been damped down with a rich, delicious and cool raspberry jelly. The feeling quivered away in there all by itself, yet somehow it spread osmotically through the remainder of his fibre, nicely clouding his brain and his vision. He began to feel an identical stirring somewhere below his belly. But who the hell **was** Jeannie? She carried on regardless, completely ignorant of his rapid-fire thoughts.

"Saturday night I took a video out and watched it in the evening. Friday I just slept, I was tired after the afternoon!"

She looked up at him and their twin sets of for once crystal-clear eyes momentarily met, as the furious storm waves of the Atlantic Ocean crashed against those oh-so-jagged rocks somewhere along the coastline of South America.

"I slept right through to Saturday lunchtime. But it was just so sad, this film I mean of course."

She put her hand across her mouth and giggled, and a couple of the other people who were by now also standing around and drinking their equally hard-earned caffeine-respite glanced up, but it wasn't for very long, it was only for less than one second, just like so many things are.

"It's a small town in America and there's this man, Martin he's called, and everybody thinks that he's really mean but he's not, he's just not, he's really just like you are Io, soft and sweet." She was talking about the film now.

She put her hand onto his shoulder in a sickly stereotypical gesture and he felt, in a sudden flash, that he hated her at that moment and he really felt like hitting her, but he gagged and gulped and swallowed inside his brain and forced the impulse back on down. He was at work and so it just wasn't done; it wasn't done anywhere but especially not in the office. He didn't know who the fucking hell she was anyway, so why should he want to strike her?

But in a subsequent flash, Io knew that he wanted so much and so badly to misbehave. It was the job – the job was claustrophobia, like being trapped all alone in a very small elevator. Jeannie, meanwhile, was continuing to rattle the bars of her own personal cage in distinct ignorance of it all:

"Are we going to stick around here for lunch again today then, Io?" she went on. He looked up rather impassively. Jeannie had her head lolling suggestivelty onto one shoulder blade, and appeared to be exhibiting a leer about her face. It was somehow very strange and unusual to see a woman leer, particularly slap-bang in the middle of your pristine architect's office, your mundane and sterile job with everything computer-controlled and very much in its place. Lustful animal passion wasn't generally apparent: but there it was, as plain as day. Io wasn't really sure where exactly he fitted into it all.

"Yeah, sure" he told her nonchalantly, and he knocked back the dregs and the grounds of his coffee as he went with it.

15

Malcolm stood dwarfed by the tower blocks, in awe of their skyscraping height and ugly grey grandeur. Kids played football, fought and sniffed solvents on the concrete forecourts which darkened in shadows as the flats took away the sunlight. Malcolm noticed that one of the blocks was casting its shadows in four directions, at right angles to each other. He didn't pause to consider this, but walked towards the block, which on the face of it was no different from the others, but which had some special eerie magnetism to it. Malcolm had always felt a sense of having suffered, something which he could not materially substantiate. This particular tower block – Seaton Point – radiated a grave aura of tragedy that was somehow unworldly, ethereal, mythic; mirroring his own narcissistic angst which had yet to hook itself onto anything solid. He felt a calling: Seaton Point; he didn't know what to expect or what he hoped to find there. Hadn't his hopes and expectations always been passive, awaiting stimulation from external phenomena which rarely materialised? But Malcolm sensed that the tower block might lead him to something, towards events in which he might participate, even if they eluded his control.

The first entrance he came to was locked, guarded by a smashed-up entryphone machine. He pressed a few numbers at random: nothing happened, the machine was useless. He went round the back to find another door. Finding it unlocked he entered, just in time to see a tall, thin, wizard-looking bloke glide from the staircase and disappear into an invisible corner. The strange figure was wrapped in a velvet curtain and emitted somewhat frightening vibes. Freaked out, Malcolm didn't fancy hanging around, so he ran up the stairs away from the weirdo. A few flights up, he paused to recover his breath. He was still carrying his meagre possessions in his rucksack; it had been a long day, and the load seemed to become heavier as the day wore on.

It was on this floor that he noticed the lift. Normally he didn't like lifts, but he needed a rest. He pressed a button and waited for the lift to turn up. Malcolm wanted to get to the top of Seaton Point, to put distance between himself and the velvet-clad apparition. It barely occured to him that he might climb into a trap, his escape routes increasingly scarce and tenuous the further up into the sky he went.

Deep, quick breaths: Malcolm was in a mild state of panic as he struggled to keep up with his accelerating pulse. He clocked some of the graffiti: infantile drawings of sexual organs and suchlike. A sticker said "No muggers, no burglars, this is a working class area. Don't rip off your own. Class War." The stale smell of piss and spilt beer. Old cans, crisp packets, fag boxes, used syringes and condoms, bloodstained bandages and other refuse littered the floor, as well as all the other floors in the tower. The lift finally arrived and the door slid open; he hopped in. A choice of even numbers awaited him, from ground to 22. He pressed the button marked twenty and the door closed. He sat on the floor, knackered. A bit of whirring and creaking and he was on his way up. Shortly, the lift stopped and opened up. He arose and got out.

Malcolm was scared shitless. He'd sought the sordid depths of London lowlife of his own volition, yet now that he was at this strangely inverted threshold he felt disturbed, unsure of how he'd fit in. He'd be taken as an outsider, a fraud, unless he developed a routine that he could spin out to his advantage. For fuck's sake, he panicked blindly, he might never leave Seaton Point alive!

Finding a window at one end of the floor, he looked out. Blimey! It was a hell of a long way down. Malcolm succumbed to a nauseous wave of vertigo, and puked. An old drunk came out of one of the flats and patted Malcolm on the back amiably.

"Fuck off!" said Malcolm. "Leave me alone, I'm being sick!"

"No problem man!" said the drunk, offering the middle-class wanker a swig of his Dragon. "Drink some of this, boy, and you'll feel fine!"

Malcolm did as he was told. He passed the bottle back to his new friend, and threw up again.

"You're taken real bad, man!" said the drunk. "I'll leave you to it! My name's Timmy! Don't forget to drop round next time you're up here! Flat 77! Nice meeting you!"

Still nauseous but touched by the warmth and hospitality that he'd been shown, Malcolm shook Timmy's proffered hand. The pisshead went back into his flat. Malcolm got himself together a bit and staggered about, unsure of what he was supposed to be doing. Dazed, he climbed a flight of stairs. Then he wandered down it again. He stumbled around the floor, exploring his pockets, looking for his fags. It was funny how his fags were always in the last pocket he checked! Finding them, he repeated the ritual for his lighter. Same story: last pocket. He got a snout out of the box and lit up.

An anarchist shot out of one of the flats, grabbed Malcolm by the collar and slammed him against the wall. "What are you doing smoking on my floor?" the activist demanded menacingly. He snatched the fag from Malcolm' mouth, lobbed it to the ground, extinguished it beneath a heavy army boot, and punched the smoker in the stomach. "This is my floor, and nobody **ever** smokes on my floor, get it?"

"S-s-sorry, sir," responded Malcolm, winded. "I'm new to these parts, and haven't learnt the rules yet."

"Well, you'd better learn them pretty quick! What the fuck are you doing in my tower block anyway? Are you here for a revolutionary purpose? You'd fucking better be!"

"Er, er, of course I'm here for a radical reason," Malcolm improvised. "I'm homeless, and I want to open a squat in this block of flats, so that I can turn it into a free-for-all, do-what-thou-wilt commune with my comrades and start subverting the whole of Hackney. Do you know of any empty flats, sir?"

"Well, seeing as you're clearly here for the correct reason, I reckon I can sort you out!" said the helpful anarchist. "My name's Nutter Nigel, and I've changed the locks of all the empties on the top ten floors of the block so that I can allocate them to deserving squatters who have a sound revolutionary perspective, encompassing theory and practice! A dozen flats are already occupied by my men, and their chicks! Let me get the keys and I'll show you around!"

Nutter Nigel got his keys, a large bunch. He jangled them a bit, kind of twirling the ring around his thumb. He led Malcolm down to the fifteenth floor, unlocked an empty, and gave a guided tour of the flat like an estate agent. It was spacious, with plenty of fixtures and fittings. It had electricity, hot running water – everything! Malcolm was well pleased. This was just the sort of place he could imagine himself living in! It was a fine start to his new life!

Having other things to do, Nutter Nigel gave Malcolm the key and departed, leaving the tenant to survey his new pad. After twenty minutes of sussing the place out, Malcolm was getting bored. He decided to step outside and investigate the floor he was on.

The first thing that caught his attention was the lift. He pressed the button and waited. The floor was odd-numbered, he reflected: he'd never been in this lift before. He waited and waited. Fuck all happened. And then something happened, he imagined.

The lift never arrived. But instead, it left an imprint on Malcolm's consciousness, telling him that he could do whatever he wanted, be a leader of people and take charge of his situation for once. There was something magical about this lift; it was communicating with him, offering transport of a far more valuable kind than the vertical ferrying he'd expected. It was taking him to terrains that he'd never previously explored: the mysterious expanses of his hidden self. Potential futures opened up like flowers blossoming in front of him. Fate, wonderment and apocalypse radiated silently from the forbidden interior of the lift shaft. The newest inhabitant of Seaton Point was overwhelmed by psychic messages and revelations; confidences leading him to territories from which, he knew, there could be no turning back.

Malcolm realised that he was Buddha, Jesus Christ and Genesis P. Orridge all rolled into one.

16 The next day and eight o'clock had arrived all too early for Kelly. All day long his stomach had been turning cartwheels. Mick wasn't someone you turned down an invitation from. He tended to take everything personally. A bit too personally.

He'd got his mother's tea ready and settled her down in front of the TV for her usual evening's entertainment, watching shit. Nelly Greaves had sensed her son's irritability and snappiness. He needed more company really. She'd have liked him to get a girlfriend in some ways, but that might mean he'd put her in a home and she couldn't have that.

Kelly stood at the end of the corridor until the minute hand clicked to the twelve. Eight o'clock, bang on. He knocked at the door to number 37. An animalistic coughing fit made its way along the hall to the front door which then creaked open a couple of inches. Mick's bleary right eye stared menacingly through the crack, then relaxed a bit when the brickie clocked Kelly's unshaven face.

"Alright" Mick sang cheerily as he removed the latch chain. He was dressed exactly as he had been yesterday, including the trademark woolly hat. Kelly thought that he probably still kept it on in bed or in the bath. Mick bade Kelly enter with an extravagant sweep of his right arm.

The flat was a shit pit. Pure and simple. Empty beer cans, dog ends, dog shit and half-empty cartons of take-away food spread themselves around the hall and kitchen. Kelly just stopped himself from retching at the rank odour.

They entered the sitting room. The once white walls, lit by a single bare bulb, were now nicotine yellow. No pictures of any kind adorned them. Debris littered this room as well. The Barber twins were seated on the sofa, and one of them rose to meet Kelly as he entered.

Ned Barber approached him and gripped his hand. Ned stood at six foot four: 18 stones of pure muscle. His balding head was cropped close and he took great delight in watching Kelly's eyes bulge in pain as the bones in his hand started grinding under the vice-like grip. "Long time no see" Ned boomed, releasing the mangled hand.

Kelly sucked in air quickly, trying to ignore the throbbing pain. As Ned sat down, his brother stood up.

If Ned was a terrible sight, there was something worse about his twin, Ted. He stood only five foot six, and his haircut was the only feature he had in common with his brother. Behind his pale grey eyes was a brooding menace. You could tell that Ted took a great pleasure in other people's pain.

Kelly, still in agony, had the same damaged hand clasped by brother number two and another fearful squeeze began. Competition between each other was what ruled the brothers' lives. Ted had to hurt Kelly more.

"Aaagh!!," Kelly screamed as the pain became too intense and his knees started to buckle.

"Fucking leave him alone, Ted" came the other Barber's voice from the fetid sofa.

"Fucking loser": Ted spat out the reply. He released Kelly's hand and span sharply around to face his brother. Kelly moaned in relief and slid onto one of the piles of rubbish.

Ted's facial expression had turned from one of pleasure at inflicting pain to one of maniacal rage. Ned started to rise, his right fist cocking back as if in slow motion as Ted approached.

38

"Woah, woah, steady on lads;" Mick's oval frame got between the sibling rivals. "No fighting eh? Let's just watch the film."

Mumbling obscenities under their breaths, the brothers sat, as if in one motion, onto the sofa. Ted was lifted slightly in his seat as Ned's superior weight caused the dirty furniture to lean. Kelly, his worst fears being realised, staggered onto a camp chair that had been placed amid the litter. From his uncomfortable position, he surveyed the rest of the flat cum skip. Mick's wife had left him ten years ago and household hygiene obviously wasn't top of his agenda.

There, cowering in the corner, he spotted Mick's put-upon pit-bull – Fang. The poor dog was completely neurotic, one of the reasons being Mick's tendency to punch it in the face as hard as he could to encourage it to bite. A torn left ear and plenty of scar tissue bore testimony to the dog-fights that Mick and the twins organised in the tower block basement.

There was another knock at the door.

"That'll be Marty" said Mick, rising from his seat. Satisfied that the twins weren't going to kick off again, he turned and left the room. There were muffled voices, and then a wheelchair appeared through the door, bearing a rather manic occupant. Behind that was Mick's daughter Martina.

"Hello everyone" shouted Gerry Tucker excitedly, for it was he in the wheelchair. His thinning blonde hair hadn't been combed for months, and as he spoke his brown and yellow teeth flashed like a wasp near a streetlamp. On his lap were eight cans of Tennents Super. He wheeled himself into pole position for the video as Martina sat herself down next to her father.

Marty was a typical Seaton Point girl. At the age of 13 she exuded an earthy sensuality irresistible to her father's sitemates. On the pill at 14, but casual with its intake and her charms, she was pregnant by 15, married by 16 and divorced by 19. She shared many things in common with Mick and her weight had piled on with her love of lager and takeaway curries. Her favourite things in life were porn movies and crimpelene tracksuits.

"Got the vid girl?" Mick asked her.

Martina nodded, pulling the unmarked cassette from the bag that lay at her feet and passing it over. Mick inserted it into the video-machine and they all settled back in their respective vantage points to watch the show. Mick and Martina expectant, excited; the twins, arms folded, waiting to be impressed; Gerry slurping noisily from his second tin of Tennents; and Kelly, just trying to blend and disappear into the surroundings.

Half an hour later, Kelly felt even worse. His choice of munchies – pork scratchings – rose uneasily in his gullet as he viewed a raven-haired teenage girl furiously masturbating a pig. The pig was obviously enjoying it but Kelly, and in his opinion the teenage girl, weren't. The hour and a half dragged on, with the twins trying to outdo each other with tasteless jokes.

Gerry became more and more excited. He guzzled his beer at an incredible rate, his character turning with every sip. Shy and gentle when sober, the chips on his shoulder piled on top of each other as he drank. He had been a brickie with Mick but a loose scaffolding board had sent him tumbling to the ground three floors below. Whether it was an accident or the fact that Gerry owed around five hundred quid to the scaffolder, no-one could say. Gerry hadn't walked since. He became louder and more incoherent as the film ground on. Everybody ignored his babbling and screeching.

Through all of this Mick and Martina sat staring silently at the screen, their faces showing no sign of emotion except once. During one of Kelly's many expansive glances around the room he noticed a single line of drool run down from Mick's mouth. It was quickly absorbed by his shirt sleeve.

17

Blokey was sore, and not only in his anal region. He couldn't quite believe what had happened – and in front of that bird he fancied! The bastard bailiff would pay. No one messed with Blokey; at least, that was what he liked to believe. The bailiff from hell would pay all right, and it would cost him his life!

Two hours had passed since Blokey's eviction, and his seething anger had died down somewhat into a dull thud, like a rubber mallet bouncing repetitively on his brain. He fingered the plastic dice in his pocket: four, four, four bounced the mallet. Blokey shut his eyes, pulling the puce curtain he had salvaged from his scattered belongings around his shoulders in a futile attempt to keep warm. The street was empty except for the sound of the tin can tumbleweeds rolling and rattling in the wind; the rhythm of the rubbish interspersed with the wail of the serenading sirens, punctuated on occasion by shouts that jolted the night air like the crack of a gun. This was the symphony of the street, lulling Blokey's bruised and battered body further towards sleep.

Dark shadows danced on the inside of Blokey's eyelids, his brain manipulating them into a grim dance of death. Now he could make out the distorted figures of the bailiff's lackeys as the images gained clarity, their faces leering towards him from out of the darkness. Blokey wasn't concerned with them: they were only carrying out orders, it was their boss that he wanted. Still, he thought, you had to be a spineless fuckwit to follow orders; but no, Blokey was scared of them. He'd met their type before: psychos, you could see it in their eyes. It was the boss he was after; Blokey wasn't scared of him, oh no. The boss would pay for sure, oh yes, he had rolled a four, four, four...

The leering faces melted back into the blackness. Another image came forward to replace them, a figure, small at first but getting bigger and bigger fast, a falling figure whose terrified scream got louder and louder. Blokey looked up into the fat face of the bastard bailiff, the screaming mouth filling the whole of his vision, plaguing his eyes. The image passed, and then there was a sickening crunch, squelch and the tinkling of teeth on concrete as the body came to rest. Blokey was asleep now, and for the first time that day he felt happy, a feeling confirmed by the wry smile that cracked his serene, sleeping face.

Blokey settled back in the chair, took a drag on his fag and surveyed the smoke-filled scene that opened up in front of him. The punters in the club were few and Blokey had chosen a seat near the back so as to hide amongst the shadows.

The last two days had been pretty positive for Blokey. He had secured himself a new abode, an old church on the Nightingale Estate. The church had been squatted a few years back but had lain dormant ever since. However, the corrugated metal deterrent was no match for Blokey's ingenuity and he was in and had the place secured within half an hour. Blokey was now the rector of St. Terry's pentecostal church of the seventh apocalypse, and that made him feel divine – that and the fact that his pocket was full of a cashed giro, money that he now spent, and in his opinion spent well.

From his vantage point, Blokey was a voyeur of the movie of life, but there was no script to this movie – or was there? The actors seemed to accept the roles that had been dished out to them; roles which, however, they didn't seem happy to be playing. Blokey couldn't understand why they didn't do anything to change their lot: their passivity angered him. Their lack of control over their lives and their meek acceptance filled Blokey with contempt for his fellow humans.

His misanthropic musings were cut short by the arrival on stage of a vision from heaven! Blokey didn't believe in that sort of shit of course, but there was something different about this act: he or she was gorgeous. Tululah Climax was her name, and she or he was the reason for Blokey's presence at the Candy Club. He'd seen her the week before and vowed to come back every week.

Blokey believed Tululah to be the ultimate in role-playing. Unlike the other drag acts, she had a strange, alluring air about her; an unearthly quality that Blokey couldn't quite put his finger on. Maybe he fancied her, or him come to that. Whatever the reasoning, Blokey had to meet her; he wanted desperately to talk to her. But that wasn't for him to decide, and he retrieved his plastic god from his inside pocket.

Out it came: the cube. One, he'd go up to the performer and say "'ere, darlin', fancy a shag?" Two, he'd try a more subtle approach and offer to buy her a drink. Three, he'd follow her about all night until she eventually took notice of him. Four, he'd run over to her and rip off all her clothes. Five, he'd go up to her, go down on bended knee, and propose marriage. Six, he'd go home and forget all about it.

He rolled the dice. Two.

"'Ere love, fancy a pint?" said the dice man, having approached the transsexual vampire who by this time was propping up the bar and smoking a fag.

"I don't drink," lied Tululah. She just wanted to get rid of the bastard.

"Gosh, how rude it is of me – of course, ladies don't drink beer," said Blokey. "Would you care to join me for an orange squash?"

Just then there was an almighty shattering of glass, followed by a pair of armed bandits with stockings over their heads who came bouncing in through the window, waving guns about. "The first person who moves is dogmeat!" one of them shouted. Everyone froze.

"OK!" hollered a bandit. "I want to see all of you up against the wall, with your hands up! Get it?"

The assembled punters did as they were told.

"Alright you lot" shouted the other bandit, "let's be having your wallets! And you people behind the bar – we want your night's takings!"

The punters dared not move, because if they did they'd be shot. One of the bandits frisked them, removing any valuables he could find while the other one remained handy with a gun. The staff at the strip joint bundled the takings together for the bandits. They weren't bothered about the takings; they just wanted to get home in one piece. The boss wouldn't like it, but he could go to hell!

One of the felons counted the money. Fives, tens, twenties... even a couple of fifties. He was rich! The other one stood there, his gun pointing at the hostages. Then he lit a fag. His concentration had faltered!

In a flash, Blokey went into action. Normally he wouldn't have bothered, but he wanted urgently to impress Tululah. He attacked bandit one, punching the bastard on the nose; the criminal dropped his gun. The dice man headbutted his opponent vigorously and down the geezer went. Blokey kicked him a few times whilst simultaneously picking up the gun. Then he swivelled around to face the slow-witted other bandit who was still counting the money.

"Alright you rotter – drop the gun!" Blokey had his own shooter aimed straight at bandit two. The miscreant did as he was told.

"Both of you – get lost! I ain't into calling the police or nothing 'cause the police are cunts, but I do want to have a nice quiet evening – so fuck off, and we'll call it quits, yeah?"

The prostrate bandit picked himself up off the floor, his hands held to his face trying to stem the tide of blood that flowed profusely from his severe facial injuries. The other bandit helped him to his feet. Tails between their legs, the two would-be armed robbers made themselves scarce, leaving the valuables behind.

"MY HERO!!!" slurred a very drunk Tululah, staggering across towards Blokey. The transsexual had taken advantage of the confusion to drink half a bottle of whisky stolen from behind the bar in one go while everyone else was distracted. She wasn't in complete control of her actions right now, but she was certainly in a female heterosexual mode. She'd revised her opinion of Blokey. He wasn't so bad after all.

The dice man couldn't believe his luck as the vampire draped her arms around his neck. He gave her a bit of a feel and a bit of the old chat: "come here often, like?"

"Every week, to do my show!" As if Blokey wasn't aware of this already. "But we don't get very many armed robbers round here usually! You were really cool, sorting those bandits out. How do you fancy coming back to my place for a shag?" Tululah was well impressed by Blokey. She couldn't wait to get her fangs into the geezer's neck.

"Alright darlin'," replied the Dice Man. He couldn't wait to shag the vampire!

After a bit, the pair went off together, back to Tululah's room in Kings Cross.

18 Malcolm and Timmy sat in Malcolm's new squat drinking bottles of Dragon. Malcolm had shaved off all his hair, except for the little ponytail that he was cultivating at the back of his head. He'd got his dick pierced and had persuaded Timmy to do the same. He'd painted the walls of his flat black and daubed the floors and walls with plenty of psychic druidic symbols in red and white. He'd covered the lift servicing the even numbered floors of Seaton Point with a similar variety of cryptic patterns and runes, and had also taken to drinking his own urine.

The flat was attracting whispers from the other residents of the block of flats. The neighbours were generally broad-minded, the tower having always accommodated more than its fair share of nutters. Malcolm, who tended to dress these days in a white loincloth, had received a certain amount of verbal stick from some of the kids on the estate, but generally they were scared of him and left him alone.

Malcolm's messianic tendencies were escalating. It had been a strange couple of weeks since the anarchist had installed him in his new abode. The guru clicked his fingers and vanished in a flash of blinding white light before reappearing seconds later, hovering three feet above the ground in the lotus position. Building a spliff in mid-air, he looked back on the events that had kept the ball rolling since his revelation in front of the lift.

Malcolm went out to get some fags. Returning to Seaton Point with his snouts, he walked inside and lit up beside the stairwell on the ground floor. As he inhaled, a strange thing happened. From nowhere came a wisp of weird pink smoke which stank of yoghurt. Bright spangle shapes and thick red bubbles appeared from the smoke and danced eerily, up and down, rotating, hovering. A sudden flash of lightning shot across the floor, accompanied by a piercing thunderclap which was oddly high-pitched. Amidst ever-increasing clouds of smoke the figure appeared, dressed in the same velvet curtain it had worn when Malcolm had first set foot in the tower. The weirdo stood transparent: an apparition which seemed to sway and distort as if seen through an invisible layer of intense heat. Malcolm froze, afraid, ice-cold.

"You will do my bidding," the alchemist hissed.

Malcolm struggled to get his words out in response. He stammered a bit, uselessly.

"You will do my bidding", the spectre repeated. "The punishment for not doing my bidding is death."

"Yes, s-sir," Malcolm replied, stuttering.

"It is my destiny in this godforsaken tower to conjure up a miraculous apparition! To let loose a supernatural occult being, a god who will make the block somewhat less godforsaken! Know what I mean?"

"Yes, sir."

"You will help me. You will organise a pagan cabal, according to your own instincts, yet ready and dedicated to do my bidding at your command, via my command, as I instruct you. Get my drift?"

"Yes, sir."

"The name of your cabal is the Temple of Psychic Doom. The 'the' is spelt with two 'e's. You will have forgotten about this conversation by the time you reach your flat, but you will carry out my instructions, nevertheless."

"As good as sorted, sir."

The alchemist approached the guru. Malcolm wanted to flee, but he was transfixed; he couldn't move. Thin, curved fingers like supernatural snakes extended and lengthened from the alchemist's outstretched fingertips and reached towards the frozen squatter. They grew ever longer and more spindly, until finally they were touching Malcolm's forehead. The guru screamed as the fingers painted patterns on his face, searing agony throbbing mercilessly through his entire being. He'd never felt such intense pain before in his life. And the fear... What nameless secrets were hidden beneath the darkest depths of Seaton Point? What ancient evil would determine the manner of his doom? He couldn't reflect on these questions for long. Almost immediately, he was fainting, blacking out...

That's funny, thought Malcolm as he chucked the burnt-out fag onto the floor: I only lit this five seconds ago. Deciding not to worry about it, he pulled out another and sparked it up.

When he reached his flat, Malcolm couldn't remember any of his exchange with the alchemist. But he had sussed out the fact that, not only was he Buddha, Jesus Christ and Genesis P.Orridge combined, he also had bits of Mohammed, Satan and Charles Manson thrown in. He was of the opinion that he was engaged in a divine mission of cosmic justice, a good against evil battle between himself and an ancient magician from a subterranean hell which seethed deep beneath the tower block.

Malcolm thought that he probably represented the good side of this battle, but he wasn't sure, and in any case wasn't too bothered. He was blissfully unaware of the possibility that he may have been a puppet, the alchemist secretly and silently pulling his strings.

It wasn't until the next morning, in the mirror, that he saw his new reflection. Across his forehead, indelible in dark red and black: the mystic symbols, weird runes in hieroglyphics of a forgotten language. Bizarrely, Malcolm wasn't freaked out by his revised countenance. He merely took it as proof of his magical powers and godlike tendencies. It confirmed what he already knew.

Timmy was his first recruit. Others would follow.

19

It was close to midnight. A strange wailing sound, neither cats nor police sirens, filled the chill night air. Around the corner staggered Mick the Brick and his hoppo Gerry. Pissed.

The four-pack of take-out lager and the bag containing the foil containers of the takeaway curries were on Gerry's lap. He'd become used to being Mick's after-hours shopping trolley, but it did have its compensations. The builder's reputation meant that despite Gerry's habit of annoying almost everyone, he got left alone.

It had been a good night down at the Crown. Mick had won twenty quid pool-sharking and Gerry had got a good handful of fleshy arse. Mavis hadn't complained when he'd stuck his hand up her dress: she'd been far too gone to feel anything.

They were going through their Derek and Clive repartee, but it was much funnier than that faggot Cook, or at least that's what Mick thought.

"I'm a niggerrr and I fucked a white chick" Gerry bellowed, timeless and tasteless, "and love is colour bliiiiind."

"Oi, I'm a fucking nigger" Mick shouted in his face. Gerry went pale.

"I, I was only joking Mick, honest" he stammered, "Derek and Nutter Nigel?" he added weakly.

"I'm only joking too, cripple" Mick said, releasing a hideous laugh. Gerry breathed in deeply, relief flooding through his system.

They reached the front door of Seaton Point, which on this occasion resembled an opening to some sort of nuclear shelter. The thick corrugated steel had been sprayed incessantly by the local street artists and the bladder contents of resident piss artists. Mick fumbled in his left hand pocket for his key, dropped it, cursed, then retrieved it from the pavement and unlocked the heavy door. Then he dramatically lifted his right leg, pointed his arse at Gerry's face and let rip with a raucous fart. "Wahey" he shouted.

"Dirty cunt."

"Breathe in boy, it's good for you."

Mick backed through the front door pulling Gerry with him. Bang! It swung back, crashing against the wheelchair, pitching its occupant sideways and almost over.

"Watch it" Gerry yelled, clinging desperately to his precious cargo. Mick grunted and heaved the chair inside. He practiced his straight right on the lift button. Gerry tried to resurrect the sing song. "I'm a..."

"Shut up a sec." The lift remained silent. The left hook was applied to the second lift's button. Gerry belched loudly. Nothing else stirred.

"Fucking lifts, for fuck's sake" Mick screamed, "they're never bleeding working."

Gerry glanced up at the stairs. "Six flights of the fuckers" he groaned.

"I'll see you tomorrow" said Mick, starting to ascend the first flight.

"Aw c'mon mate, don't fuck about" Gerry whined.

"I'll bring you a clean pair of trousers in the morning." Mick suppressed a giggle.

"Bastard! Bastard! Bastard!" Gerry had risen to the bait as usual.

"Alright, calm down." Mick relented.

They lightened the load by sharing one of the cans, then started on the expedition. The wheelchair was folded and left by the lifts, a bicycle chain and lock coming in handy to secure it; Gerry kept these strapped to the side of the chair in case of emergencies such as the one that they now faced. One can was balanced precariously in each of the pockets of Mick's checked shirt; the third can he stuffed down his Y-fronts. The chill made him suck his breath in sharply, but the sensation of the cold can made him stiffen slightly as well. His mind instantly registered the sensation for future experiments.

Gerry tied his shirt into a makeshift sling which Mick fastened around his mate's neck, inserting the curries carefully so that it all rested on Gerry's back. Then, with the minimum of effort, Mick hoisted his drinking partner onto his back and began the ascent, whistling 'Two Little Boys' under his breath as he went.

They reached the flight just outside Kelly's flat, no problems, but it was in this vicinity that the twelve pints that Gerry had consumed started to take their toll. Partly through kinship, partly through feelings of guilt over Gerry's accident, Mick was used to helping his associate. "I'll hold yer dick when you piss" he often commented, "but I'm not gonna wipe yer arse." This time though, the brickie had his hands full.

"Mick, Mick, I'm gonna piss meself" Gerry whined.

"You'll have to hold on."

"Don't think I can."

Meanwhile, Kelly was going through one of his insomniac phases. It was during these long, sleepless nights that his psychotic tendencies reared their ugly head. The hairs on the back of his neck bristled as the shouts and screams erupted just outside his flat.

"Help, help, burglars" screamed his mother as she awoke with a start from her slumber.

Kelly snapped, his temper overcoming his habitual cowardice. He steamed down the hall, picking up the heavy chair leg that he kept by the front door for emergencies. "Bastards" he screamed, flinging open the door and jumping out onto the landing, legs splayed, chair leg above his head.

Mick jumped backwards in surprise, instinctively gripping Gerry's legs tight. The combination of the shock attack and Mick's vicelike grip was too much for the jinxed alcoholic whose under-siege bladder gave way, releasing a hot stream of piss through his trousers and onto Mick's back.

Kelly, seeing who he was trying to attack, stopped his swing with such panic that he threw himself backwards into his hallway. Unfortunately, the mixture of gravity and shock had a similar effect on the two-headed curry and beer monster, and backwards they tumbled.

Mick was aware of the screams behind him as Gerry's body acted as a cushion. The sound of fluid gushing and the smell of curry filled his senses, and then his head caught a step with a fearful crack and darkness engulfed him.

20 If the morning's second half hurried on by with greater rapidity than its predecessor, then this might have been down to one of three things: either that was just the way things went in offices and other such drudgerous workplaces – which of course it was; or because Io was more than a little preoccupied with his new friend and was excitedly considering just what exactly her hints the size of planets might mean; or even, in the haphazard snatches of time when he could actually concentrate properly, because of the fascinating nature of his current hypothetical work problem, which assumed the form of a kind of a test that stood between him and his potential for promotion.

It seemed that a lift system had been designed for a new luxury skyscraper hotel building in the city of Chicago. In the United States during the final decade of the twentieth century the prisons had gotten so overcrowded that it had become necessary to instigate a kind of 'care in the community' programme for the more minor offenders such as the serial killers, the rapists and the child-molesters: that is to say, those who hadn't actually stolen any money from the banks. When this way of doing things had too began to backfire, then the obvious next step was for the state to wash its hands of its responsibilities and invite big business to fill the gap. The prison service was floated on Wall Street and tender offers were proffered. New ideas and concepts floated up from the rancid green cesspool of corporate consciousness like an extremely bad smell.

Thus it came to be that crime was sold off to the most efficient operation: the highest bidder with the lowest overheads. The question of quality of service to the clientele was never once broached, as it was naturally assumed that the magic of market forces would quickly sort this out in a fashionably entropic manner. The winners of the enormous multi-million dollar contract, BAUDRILLARD DECONSTRUCTION INC., had the immensely innovative and phenomenally exciting idea of both housing and hiding the long-term prison population, by now more than 65 per cent of the whole of the USA and whom nobody – not even the sadistic guards and wardens – wanted to see anyway, in the lifts of large hotels in cities all across the United States. It was hoped that this idea could eventually be franchised and sold to the gullible remainder of the world too: like Dunkin Donuts, Mickey Mouse, television, cancer and everything else that the USA had ever produced.

The concept was based on the premise that, America constituting such a large land mass, different cities experienced saleable weather at different times of the year. This meant that at any given time a lot of the country's hotels would be largely empty anyway, and so nobody need know. In addition to this, a massive network of underground tunnels was to be surreptitiously built nationwide spanning all 51 states – including the newly-gentrified and thus incorporated Hackney – to facilitate client movement between the new penal-institutions-cum-luxury-penthouse-suite-complexes as the climate switched around during the changing course of the seasons. This would have the joint effect of creating an enormous employment boom in the building trade whilst simultaneously removing almost all independent street crime in one fell swoop. It seemed to be a really good idea and capitalism did love its artificial booms, so everybody who mattered was going to be very happy indeed with the arrangement.

Back in the real dreamworld, Io's immediate task was to devise a method of keeping the ungrateful prison populace alive without ever letting them out of the lifts and at the same time keeping those lifts moving up-and-down, up-and-down for 24 hours every day whatever the weather; the unstated suggestion was that the two things really ought to be very directly linked. He thought back to his engineering training at Poole university in Dorset: fluid-in-motion. Hydraulics. Fuel tanks and siphons. Plumbing and pipes. There appeared to be some connection.

Now what was the easiest and most nutritious foodstuff that you could move through pipes?

Of course – yoghurt!

Io set to work.

Lunchtime came around almost too quickly. Jeannie's leer had certainly stirred the contents of Io's lunchbox and he prayed that, unlike lunchtime, he wouldn't come too soon. He felt a peculiar sense of half-dread and half-exhilaration that he couldn't quite explain. He hated her and he loved her so passionately, and that left him in such a state of total bewilderment that Jeannie had no trouble whatsoever in steering him into the nearest stationery cupboard, pulling the door to and Io's zipper open. They were alone in the dark; everybody else would be munching on their posh sarnies and quaffing cappuccino now, completely oblivious to just what was on offer on the menu in that stationery cupboard back at the office.

Jeannie had pulled Io's semi-erect beef bayonet from its sleeping place and was planting delicate kisses all over the bell-end, pulling away and coaxing the blood forth to fill the spongy tissue that would render his member proud and ready for action. Io gasped loudly, pulling Jeannie's head towards his love-lance which she immersed in the warm, wet cavern of her mouth.

Io fumbled with the top two buttons of her blouse in his eagerness to fill his mitts with her milky mounds. Jeannie's hands simultaneously snaked around to her back to free her breasts from their prisons and thusly into the hands of their liberator. Jeannie had stopped sucking Io's joystick and had moved upwards, enabling Io to kiss and nibble on her over-ripe raspberries. Jeannie then moaned and led Io's hand towards her crotch, thrusting herself forward as his fingers made contact with her sopping wet bits. Io's fingers massaged the engorged labia and throbbing clitoris before sliding a finger into Jeannie's velvet hole, forcing a gasp from between her lips. Jeannie had turned around now and by resting one knee on a shelf had engineered herself into a position whereby she might be able to take Io's pork sword doggy-style: he responded by easing his spam javelin into her.

Jeannie's hands cupped his balls as if trying to force all of him up into her tunnel of love. They were moaning together in time with the thrusts, their grunts becoming louder and more strained as the tempo of their lust intensified. Io's fingers found Jeannie's clitoris and rubbed and pressed to the frantic, frenetic rhythm of their sexual symphony until they could hold themselves back no longer, orgasming miraculously in concert until, with the dying clash of cymbals ringing in their ears, the music was over.

Io was aware of a blissful background droning noise entering his head, a familiar sound in his half-sleep that he couldn't quite place. He was also aware of his sticky hand clasping his shrinking penis like a lost dog obsessively cradling a bone; and that, once again, he was absolutely alone.

21 Tululah was getting pissed off with the bed and breakfast, so when Blokey invited her to move into his place she was delighted to accept. The fact that his abode was at the edge of the Nightingale estate – home to the six tower blocks which had so mysteriously and inexplicably fascinated the vampire – was a bonus too.

Things had gone pretty well between the pair since their initial meeting at the strip joint. After their encounter with the bandits and their subsequent departure to the vampire's room, Blokey had been a little annoyed to discover that Tululah was too drunk to be of much use in the sack department; indeed, she had fallen asleep fully clothed and begun snoring loudly as soon as they'd got through the door.

Blokey was too wired up to sleep and so, acting on the advice of the dice, he spent the next few hours making himself useful around the room for something to do. First he found an old cassette player that didn't work, so he fixed it. Being a typical man, Blokey had always been pretty mendacious but good at DIY. Next he fixed up a chair whose legs had started to go all wonky and wobbly, then he repaired some wiring that was a bit dodgy. He fitted a carpet that needed doing and then he carried out some maintenance plumbing on the hot water tank so that Tululah could have hot running water whenever she wanted. It had been some sort of a minor blockage. Then finally, he put up a few shelves.

When the vampire awoke, Blokey was being industrious with some carpentry, making a nice cupboard out of some old bits of wood. Hey, thought Tululah, this guy's pretty handy. The vampire resolved not to waste the geezer after all but to instead find ways to utilise his talent for DIY to her own advantage.

Tululah was subsequently pleased to discover that Blokey was a pretty good shag too. Despite his love of role-playing, Blokey was deep down a heterosexual kind of bloke, and it was necessary for the vampire to adapt her privates to female mode for the relationship to have any chance of enduring. It had been ages since she'd last met a man who could cut it between the sheets, and Blokey was in turn infatuated with his new lover. She was gorgeous, he decided.

The vampire soon took to hanging around Blokey's place as often as possible. The dark, dingy and somewhat macabre atmosphere of St. Terry's pentecostal church of the seventh apocalypse was the sort of place where a phantom of the night such as herself could relax and feel at home. There were crosses and stained-glass windows everywhere, but Tululah didn't mind that, it would take more than a few crucifixes and bits of garlic to bother a vampire as experienced as she was. There was even an old coffin for her to lay back and meditate in when she was feeling introspective. By the time Blokey had gotten around to asking her to move in permanently, Tululah had already shifted most of her possessions over to the place anyway. And being squatted, the church was free, so she wouldn't have to pay any more rent. The arrangement suited the vampire very nicely.

When they weren't shagging or gazing longingly into each other's eyes, the pair would investigate the locality together. The Nightingale Estate appealed increasingly to the vampire. It had a portentous sense of mystery to it, as if it were inevitable that something of enormous consequence would happen there, sooner rather than later. If Tululah had anything to do with it, she'd make certain that she was right at the heart of the big bang when it came off.

She watched closely the residents passing in and out of the six tower blocks of the estate. Tenants young and old alike; big ones, small ones, white ones, black ones, they all looked disenfranchised, dispossessed and despondent; ripe for subversion. Tululah had always been a bit on the bolshie side, and she could see the potential here for developing the hitherto concealed insurrectionary side to her character.

Then there was the mother of all tower blocks – Seaton Point, which seemed almost to pulsate and radiate all manner of weird and invisible psychic signals. Connected as it was to the church by one of the best ley lines in London, and with its name echoing her past, it was perhaps inevitable that Tululah would develop some strange attachment to this particular block. Seaton Point would become the focal point for the vampire's coup, the exact nature of which she had yet to fathom.

But just for now she was content to bathe in the warm glow of her new love affair. She and Blokey were an item. It was as if they were made for each other.

So there is some romance in the world after all, she thought to herself.

It was love!

22

A bright light. Mick was aware of a bright light somewhere above him. "Left the curtains open" he thought to himself. "Shit I've overslept, it's daylight." Panic set in. Mick tried to raise himself but found he couldn't move his limbs. He stretched his neck upwards and cried out in agony as excruciating pain shot through his head like a knifeblade.

"God what a hangover, I thought I'd grown out of these," he muttered. Confusion surrounded his murky mind and tried to force a surrender. What had he done last night? Where, and who with?

Thinking hurt more than normal. He closed his eyes to shut out the painful white light that seemed to throb above him. Memories started straggling back to him as they invariably do the morning after a session. He'd been down The Crown. That's right. Then what did he do? A vague memory came to him of some games of pool and a number of pints, but not that many pints. Some bastard had either spiked him or jumped him. Nah, the lift. He'd been standing outside the lift with that basketcase Gerry and it hadn't been working.

It's coming back now. A fireman's lift. Up the stairs. A scream; falling backwards, a slow motion freefall.

"Oh shit." The new day dawned on the troubled brickie. "I'm dead."

"YOU ARE NOT DEAD."

If Mick could have jumped, he would have done.

"BUT YOU HAVE BEEN BADLY HURT" the strange voice continued, "AND YOUR COMPANION IS CLOSE TO THE END OF THIS LIFE."

"Gerry, Gerry, what's happened to him? I'm trying to remember but I can only see bits of the past."

"HIS NECK IS BROKEN. HIS BACK IS BROKEN TOO, BUT I SENSE THAT THIS IS THE RESULT OF SOME PREVIOUS ACCIDENT."

"He's an unlucky bastard alright," muttered Mick. "What about me Doc? What's wrong with me? I can't feel me legs. Not me as well?" Mick began to sob. The thought of being like Gerry for the rest of his life was too much for him to take.

"I AM NO DOCTOR, MICHAEL, BUT I CAN TELL YOU THAT MOST OF YOUR BODY HAS BEEN SEVERELY BRUISED AND BOTH YOUR ARMS ARE BROKEN. YOU AND YOUR FRIEND FELL DOWN SEVERAL FLIGHTS OF STAIRS."

Mick emitted an anguished howl. Both arms broken! Bricklaying fucked for a long while and his national insurance was three years out of date! He'd cashed in his personal pension six months ago for a bet on a dog that was a sure-fire winner. Hottest tip he'd ever had. It had come last, the tipster had left town and Mick had been best avoided for a month or two after that.

A question popped up through the curtain of self pity that he had started to draw. "You say you're not a doctor" he asked the mystery figure. "Where am I? Who are you? Is this the ambulance?"

"ALL IN GOOD TIME" came the reply, "NOW YOU MUST REST. YOUR BODY HAS A LOT OF HEALING TO DO."

Mick felt something touch the space between his eyes and sleep drew over him like a warm, comforting blanket.

Mick didn't know how long he'd been out this time, but when he woke things seemed to be a lot better. The throbbing pain in his head had subsided. Gingerly, he tried to move a foot and it reacted favourably. Then he went for the big one and tried some hand movement. His fingers rippled as hoped. Perhaps it was just a dream, he thought.

"NO DREAM, MICHAEL. I HAVE CURED YOU." There was that resonant and reassuring voice once more. "ARISE, FEEL THE NEW YOU."

Mick opened his eyes and winced as the bright light bore down on him. Taking courage, he counted to five and sat up. The light receded slightly. "Where am I?" he asked, still unsure of the location of the person that he was addressing.

"THE HEART."

Mick looked closer at his surroundings. He noticed that he was sitting on something akin to a hospital bed though there were no sheets. The walls seemed to expand outwards, then moments later move inwards again like his bedroom walls had used to when he had a fever or had grown over-tired as a kid. It was almost as if the room were alive, breathing in, out, in, out.

"Fucking hell, I've been abducted by aliens" Mick thought, "I'm in a spaceship."

His lungs seemed in good condition today. Normally on first awakening he would cough a third of a pint of a brown, lumpy substance. He hadn't felt this healthy in years.

He looked to his left. In the bed next to him lay Gerry, No tubes or medical apparatus surrounded him. In fact, the prat had a radiant smile on his face as if he were dreaming of a dirty weekend with Cindy Crawford.

He looked towards the light. It wasn't as painful to behold as before. It hovered in the corner about a foot off the ground, and something appeared to be at its heart. The heart?

"The heart," Mick spoke aloud, "you said something about the heart." He was directing his talk towards the light. Nothing else seemed particularly sentient.

"YES, THE HEART." The reply appeared in Mick's head. It wasn't coming from the light as such but Mick felt that that was the source of communication. "THE HEART OF THIS BUILDING CALLED SEATON POINT" it continued, "I HAVE COME HERE. I SENSE MYRIAD POWERS AT WORK. THERE IS EVIL HERE, EVIL THAT IS TOO ARCANE FOR ME TO DEAL WITH ALONE. I NEED ALLIES, SOLDIERS. THIS IS A BATTLE BETWEEN GOOD AND EVIL. I HAVE CURED YOU AND YOUR FRIEND. A STRANGE MAGIC WILL ABET THESE DARK FORCES. I MUST DO WHAT I CAN."

"Who, who are you?"

"YOU MAY CALL ME GURU. MY NAME CANNOT BE PRONOUNCED IN YOUR TONGUE. I HAVE HEALED YOU."

"Thanks." Mick didn't really know what to say. Surely he'd wake up in a minute. He'd take a sicky off work again. He could get away with one more this month.

Something stirred behind Mick, causing him to jump.

"Christ, what a waste of curry." Gerry sat up. "What am I doing on this bed?"

"I don't quite know what's happening at the moment" Mick replied.

"Well, whatever's happened, someone's cleaned me up. Look, no piss stains, no curry stains."

Mick looked at his mate. Gerry looked a lot better than he had for a long time. It was as if he'd had a month of dry nights.

"Where's me wheelchair?"

"YOU WON'T BE NEEDING THAT ANYMORE."

"Who said that?" Gerry span his head around excitedly. "Did ya hear that, Mick, did ya?"

"Yes. I think it's that light. What do you look like?" the brickie asked it.

"YES I WILL REVEAL MY FORM."

The white light dimmed and a shape began to appear in its midst. Clearer and clearer the shape became. "Man-shaped, it's definitely man-shaped," thought Mick.

The figure was floating cross-legged about a foot off the ground. It was wearing only a white loincloth and its hands and knees stuck out at right angles due to the yoga position their owner had taken. Its head was closely shaven, except for a ponytail at the back. It wasn't clear if the guru was male or female.

"Cor" Gerry gasped. "What are you on about, where's me wheelchair?" he continued tactlessly, ignoring the bizarre situation. Mick winced.

"I AM SAYING THAT YOUR MODE OF TRANSPORT IS NOW DEFUNCT."

Gerry's face was a complete blank.

"YOU CAN WALK" the Guru simplified.

"Hah, you're having a laugh aren't you?" Gerry spat. "I'm fucked from the waist down ain't I Mick?" A high-pitched cackle burst from his lips. "Get it Mick? Fucked from..." His joke was interrupted by a clip round the ear from his mate. "Ow! No need for that!"

"Listen to him. Things like this don't happen every day." Mick was going for the big understatement trip.

"Well I think he's taking the piss."

"Just try will ya." Mick's tone of voice persuaded Gerry to at least make a token effort to please. He sat up and swung his legs over the side of the bed, letting them dangle.

"Look, useless."

"PLEASE TRY."

"Huh, all right." Gerry lifted his feet to ground level. "Nothing, nothing" he whined, "please stop. I want a drink. Please can we go now?"

"Just try Gerry, come on."

Mick had just found an uncomfortable incentive. Reaching down into his now pristine underwear he retrieved the can of lager he had placed there before the accident. It looked as good as new. No dents, no scratches.

"Come on Gerry. My last can of Tennents. You can have it."

"No, no I can't. Please?"

"Come on, give it a try." Mick shook the can invitingly.

Very carefully Gerry lifted himself so that he was almost upright. "I'll catch you, you've nothing to lose" Mick consoled him as he saw the terror in Gerry's eyes. With a defeatist sigh, the alkie let go of his bed and for the first time in two years stood on his own two feet. He wobbled slightly and Mick moved, ready to catch him.

"I, I, I can do it. Look Mick I'm standing. Look."

Tears streamed down his face and snot dribbled into his mouth as he stood there sobbing like a baby. "Look, look."

"I can see" replied his friend, tears welling up in his own eyes. Moving to a corner of the room, Mick fought to control his emotions: bricklayers didn't cry. "Come on, stop crying you fanny and try and walk over here."

Gerry gazed down at his two limbs as if seeing them for the first time in his life. Then, after taking a deep breath, he tottered like a two year old across the short space and into Mick's arms. More tears flowed onto the brickie's jumper.

"A miracle!" shouted Mick, looking across at the impassive guru, "a miracle!"

54

"A MIRACLE WITH A PRICE, MICHAEL. I NEED YOU BOTH TO HELP ME. YOU AND ANYONE ELSE IN SEATON POINT WHO IS BRAVE ENOUGH TO FACE THE EVIL THAT LURKS HERE."

"We're with ya" Mick replied, clutching Gerry to his chest. "We're with ya. Just one thing..."

"YES?"

"Please call me Mick?"

23 Seaton Point. Seaton stinking Point. The Nightingale Estate, eighth wonder of the world – six misshapen pyramids decayed in a few short decades into a state of ancient ruin. The central mausoleum: the final place of unrest for Edith Crawley, housewife (deceased). She was trapped inside this place, aware of its external appearance solely through Frank. And now she knew too much. This was all there was for her now and she preferred not to be informed of the other: her life, her daughter, her granddaughter soon to come. Edie talked to Frank on a need to know basis. Death, or rather her own perverted version of it, had stripped her of all feeling and emotion except for lust, and cool calculation was the way she wished to run her un-life from now on.

Sleep, she had found, was unnecessary and to be avoided. When she had tried it out of the habit formed by her lifetime, it had displeased her, for it reminded her of how she had been before the unmentionable END which she had to keep from her mind at all costs: that one final desperate act, irrational and emotional and weak, which had brought her to this current and seemingly final position.

She had stripped herself of her former weaknesses, made herself strong by developing an invisible armour. She was dead and no longer stifled by the fear that had been the main component of her life – the fear of other people, of her husband's rages, of her own ineptitude. Fear of life and fear of death, which had combined to make her little more than a bundle of ineffectual angst, were gone and gone for good.

Edie lay motionless on the bed, as was her habit when Frank, her only visitor, was not around. She stared up at the nicotine-blotched ceiling and fell into a kind of meditative reverie. Already empty, her mind had reached enlightenment and found nothing there except for her insatiable libido, which was making her agitated. Frank had not turned up, and the need for him was swelling within her. In fact, he hadn't turned up for two or three days, but Edie had little sense of time.

She was mostly disinterested now. She was neither bored nor stimulated. She was merely there, and although the room – always the room – remained constant, her lust did not. In fact, she was beginning to feel gloomy. For the first waking time since THE END, she could hear the distant thunder of her emotions. What would she do if Frank never came back?

Her meditation was broken and she reached for a cigarette, the last one of the four packs which Frank had left her. The lack of carnal gratification was making her tired, and the storm was still brewing.

She needed a release. She began to listlessly finger herself, but her bony arthritic digits weren't up to the task and she soon gave it up. The faintest doubt had polluted the vacuum and it wasn't about to up and go, for that wasn't in the nature of doubts.

Her brain scanned its memory centres. This was a regular, almost mechanical occupation which it carried out for no apparent reason other than that there wasn't much else it could do and total inactivity seemed inappropriate for such a complex structure. It expected to find the usual: nothing, in none of its varieties. Circling nothings with swirling nothings shooting through the nothing, orbiting nothings, huge nothings surrounding smaller nothings, hollow nothings, dead nothings with nothing in between, and nothings which it had as yet failed to discover weren't there. Instead, it found a sensation, and a memory. It found, hidden and cowering from the scrutiny, the final legacy of Edie's final act. It found pain, a small infinitesimal point of pure undiluted intense pain, so absolute as to defy quantification or comparison.

Edie's brain needed to rationalise, to fit this into its all-encompassing scheme of nothing. It could not pass this sensation by, though it knew, somewhere, that this was precisely what it ought to do. It probed and prodded tentatively at first, then tenaciously with its telescopic curiosity. The end. THE END.

Edie Crawley had buried her husband the year before; her daughter had long since jumped ship and moved to London. So there she was, adrift and abandoned in the village of Seaton Point in darkest Somerset, alone in the family home without a family to justify this moniker, and friendless. When her husband had been alive, he had forbidden her from having friends of her own. All friends were their friends jointly, according to him; all friends were his friends only, according to her. Not one had called since the funeral. Not one. Even their daughter Suzie who'd moved to London hardly ever bothered to make contact.

Edie had rearranged the furniture, redesigned the garden, cried herself to sleep at night over her wasted life and tried desperately to recapture those dreams of independence and freedom which had been in her head a thousand times on a thousand tediously housewifely nights. And the whole time she was hating herself for the lack of courage to do something about her situation. Then, a year or so into widowhood, Edith Crawley nee Walker made a decision, the first and last she was to make.

Life had always been decided for her, by her parents, by her husband, by whatever the social conventions of the time dictated. But what were the conventions governing a lonely widow with no friends? Edie could find none. So she decided to make them up. She decided autonomously that it was time to go out, time to face the world and experience life for the first time. Real life. Her life.

She instinctively selected her husband's favourite of her clothes before she realised what she was doing, cursed herself out loud and flung them in a pile on the sitting room floor. Next, she calmly fetched the biggest and sharpest knife she could find and knelt serenely by the pile. A smile swept across her face as she dived into it, picking the clothes up in handfuls and laying into them with the knife. She was not satisfied until the rags were so small and jumbled that it was impossible to tell their previous form. Exhausted, she fell back onto the floor and laughed and laughed until the last grain of her energy was consumed.

After a short rest, it was time for phase two. She gathered together the tatters and proceeded to arrange them by colour – ensuring that the separate piles were made of the most outlandish colour schemes imaginable. Her husband had liked her to look oh-so-respectable; he had liked pastels over all else. But it was incredible how these sober, sombre shades, when arranged correctly, combined into luminous, vibrant rainbows of colour. This task achieved to her satisfaction, she started stitching. The wasted years had involved plenty of dressmaking, and she had always been expert and quick. But now, she was working at triple speed, and her hands were a frenzied blur of activity.

Within two hours she was done, and she held up the finished product next to herself in front of the mirror. She was delighted with what she saw. Dropping her creation to the floor, she quickly ripped off her dowdy house clothes and inspected her naked self. She squealed with delight at the sight of her unadorned form and danced around the room, singing a song she had never sung before. Still naked, she took the mirror, laid it to the floor and squatted over it.

For the first time in her life, Edith masturbated. For the first time in her life, she came. And came and came and came. Then she showered, undid her hair so that it was big and wild, and went out wearing nothing but her new dress and a pair of sandals. She was smiling, and her whole body was tall and proud. At last, Edie knew who she was and she liked it. She liked it a lot.

As she strode into the centre of town, Edie realised that she had no idea where exactly she wanted to go except out, and out was a big place. The pubs looked so mundane, not at all exotic enough for her tonight: for her night.

She noticed a poster outside a particularly dull looking pub. It said 'VARIETY NIGHT, THE FOLLIES COMES TO SEATON.' She checked the time and place – the church hall, tonight! It had already started but she would catch the second half. Perfect.

The hall was heaving with people when Edie walked in. It was a rare piece of excitement for these sheltered Somerset folk – a real event.

Edie found a seat near the back and settled back to survey the surroundings. No-one had recognised her, but she was receiving much attention. And she loved it. She was dynamic, unusual and sexy, not at all like Edith at all; Edith was a different woman. She was Poppy, she decided: a new name for a new life. She was a drug anyone could become addicted to. The allusion made her laugh aloud shamelessly. Husbands were turning their heads and wives were berating them only to be entranced themselves upon setting eyes upon this strange temptress. Poppy made eye contact with them all, smiling warmly, utterly self-assured.

The act on stage, a group of local singers doing a Broadway medley, finished and a solitary figure replaced them. Tall, slim and elegant, balanced on outrageous heels, the figure could have been nearly seven feet tall and seemed far too grand for the humble church hall; it would not have been out of place, in fact, in the real Follies to which the event had rather fancifully compared itself. It was obvious from their initial reaction that the townfolk didn't know what to make of this exotic apparition. She was a drag queen, Poppy knew instinctively, but judging from the wide-open jaws, most of the men had not yet realised. Dressed from head to toe in luxurious shimmering purple satin, her slim adrogenous form was clearly defined. Poppy was entranced.

The drag queen had a deep but feminine singing voice: sultry, if that was possible in darkest Somerset. She sang like she looked, and the whole audience was spellbound. She sang drag queen standards from Marilyn to Marlene, but imbued each number with such an individuality and depth that they all sounded as though they had been written for her and her alone.

They were performed with a tragic undertone of honesty which attracted Poppy immensely. The singer was not merely performing, she was laying bare her life right there on stage: every emotion, every facet of a flawed but brilliant personality. This was what she did because she could, and because she had to; she needed the audience as much as, probably more than the audience needed her. With the one exception: Poppy. This was the reason she had come tonight and she knew it instantly. This was to be the beginning of not a new chapter in her life but a whole new volume.

When the drag queen finished her act and took her bows, amazingly the reception was muted. Poppy could not understand why her high opinion of the performer had not been shared; maybe those narrow-minded, bigoted farming folk had finally realised the performer's real gender, as if that made any difference. Poppy rose from her seat and left the hall, unable to stomach any more second-rate acts after the masterpiece that she had just witnessed.

She took out the pack of cigarettes she had bought earlier. Edie had never smoked a cigarette in her life, but for Poppy they were an essential accessory and she smoked with a casual, practiced ease. She was well into her third when a tall, slim figure approached her from out of the shadows as she knew it surely would.

"I've been waiting for you," she said with a demure smile.

"I know," was the enigmatic reply. No explanation was necessary and this struck neither of them as anything other than natural. "I'm travelling back to Bristol now. Let's get out of this place, I know you hate it as much as I do. My van's over there."

Poppy realised that she really did hate, had always hated the small town of Seaton Point, and she nodded her assent. The mysterious figure, no less exotic for his plain black jeans and T-shirt, took Poppy's hand gently and wrapped his fingers around hers. Furtively at first and then with more assurance, they caressed the backs of each other's hands with the most tinglingly sensitive tips of their fingers. They both knew that not a single inch of flesh was to remain a mystery as they headed off, hand in hand, heart already in heart, in the direction that he had indicated. They were to share everything that night, Poppy and Lee Christo, for that was his name. They were to share every secret; he was to show her how he was, what he was, and what she could become.

Lee was one of a select elite of vampires who had the ability to mutate from male to female and back at will. The ambiguity of his drag queen performances whilst in male mode therefore appealed in a humorous manner to his deep-rooted sense of transgression. Being of both genders, he could give his partners what they wanted whether they were man, woman, gay or straight. Poppy was pleased to find a partner who could satisfy both sides of her newly-discovered bisexuality.

Lee had immediately recognised Poppy for what she was: someone who had a fire within her which only he, separated from the world by what he was and thus so free of the its constraints, would appreciate. He knew he could trust her completely. He would show her everything, take her with him everywhere, kill with her. But he would never be able to feed with her. Unless. Unless he did as she would soon desire and made her into him in body as well as in soul. For he knew that Poppy had the soul of a vampire.

He also knew that this was one wish he could never grant her. She would beg him to do it, lying there in one of his gowns, longing to become him and share in his torture. But Lee knew that his was a fate to which he had no right to ever willingly condemn another. Poppy would believe that Lee was ready to consent to her wish, and yet he would finally betray her, and at that last instant she would know that she had been betrayed, and her last feeling on this earth would be one of pain.

But what other choice would he have? To condemn her instead to a continued existence which he knew would come torment her as his tormented him? This way, she would be able to escape it all for good, or so he thought. Lee Christo was cursed always to betray those he loved. But his curse was far greater than he could ever imagine.

After Lee had hammered a stake through Poppy's heart and set light to her aged, crumbling remains in the immaculate oaken casket atop the downs, he had thought that this must surely be the end of his one true love: that he'd sent her to a final and restful peace, fluttering around the numb dustbowl of insentient eternity until its infinite end. But unknown to him, following a lengthy campaign of mindless vandalism and cold premeditated arson by juvenile delinquents of the area, the local council had discreetly installed smoke alarms and 24-hour closed circuit TV cameras amid the tree-tops of a nearby copse. So after Lee's departure, but before the furnace had had any time to take a proper and visible hold on the slumbering corpse of Edie, the other sort of cops had turned up in riot vans, and had instructed the accompanying fire brigade to put the fucker out.

The police had kicked their way into the coffin and, upon finding the still-intact cadaver that lay within, they'd immediately summoned an air-ambulance. Half an hour later Edie was being rushed through the corridors of the emergency ward of Frenchay hospital.

Edie had always known that she was a little bit different from other people, only she'd never been quite sure as to why this might be. Maybe, she'd speculated, she was a latent alcoholic or the reincarnation of Genghis Khan, or perhaps even the second coming of the magic Lord Jesus; but the truth of the matter was that Edie was actually from Mars.

She'd been brought to Britain by her parents who had settled in Devonshire quite amicably, but both of them had been tragically killed by a gang of skinheads in a knife-fight outside the local launderette. Orphaned, Edie was never informed of her intergalactic origins, and all the paperwork had been lost when the orphanage had burnt down in mysterious circumstances barely a year later.

Now, everybody knew that Martians have two hearts, or at least everybody on Mars did. But that ruled out Lee Christo, and Dr. Jones of Frenchay hospital also.

"My word!" he'd said upon discovering the unbelievable truth that sat there on the scanning machine.

"Ooh!!" the nurse at his left side had exclaimed.

So in spite of Lee's efforts with the stake, Edie was to live on in vampire form. And after a mere three days later she'd discharged herself from Frenchay and headed for London to make a new life for herself. Heading for a new Seaton Point. But the trauma that the betrayal by Lee Christo had caused her would manifest itself in anorexic behaviour, and the lack of blood in her diet would make turn her into a living corpse, unable to leave her flat:

Edie was doubled over in agony when Frank opened the door. He paused at the doorway, unsure how to react. When Edie saw him, she suddenly uncurled herself and flung herself at him in a show of real emotion. Real emotion? From Edie? Frank's uncertainty increased.

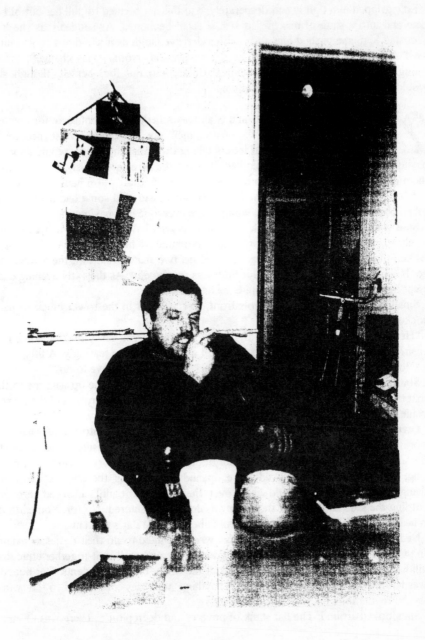

Edie gripped him tightly and desperately, and this act seemed to pull her out of her pain and into a state of mischief as sexual relief beckoned. As suddenly as she had accosted him, she pushed him away with a derisive laugh as if she'd just fooled him, as if she'd been playing with him as she always did. Nothing has changed, Frank thought. But for all her acting abilities, Edie could not fool herself, though she would expend much energy in the attempt.

24 It was Christmas eve, and Stan was scheduled to confiscate for auction the possessions of various council tax defaulters. Most people in Hackney had received letters telling them that the bailiffs would soon be paying them a visit, but the public hadn't taken the threats seriously, realising that there couldn't possibly be enough bailiffs to go round. Stan's firm had been hired by a debt-collecting agency to which Hackney Council had sold some bad debts. Some token confiscations, it was hoped, would scare everyone into paying up.

Stan wasn't having a lot of luck. He might as well have had bailiff written on his forehead, such was the aura he radiated. Potential victims at the flats he visited looked through their letterboxes at him and his two mates, and told them where to go. Nobody opened their doors. But Stan was resourceful. As the early evening dark crept in around the Nightingale estate, he had an idea.

Small children were singing carols from door to door in the tower block to earn pocket money.

"Hey kids" he shouted at them, all friendly. "How do you fancy making some real dosh?" He fished a note from his pocket and waved it at them teasingly. A fifty.

"Not half, mister!" one of the kids shot back. "What do we have to do?"

Stan consulted his list of addresses. "All you have to do is come up with me to the sixteenth floor of Seaton Point and stand outside a flat singing carols until the person inside comes out. Then I'll do the rest, and you can have your fifty."

Greedy for cash, the minors accompanied the three bailiffs into the lift that was working. When they reached the flat, the kids broke into a rousing rendition of 'O Come All Ye Faithful' as they rang the doorbell over and over insistently. Before long, the old granny who lived there opened up, offering the choir some spare change. But before she could hand over the coins the bailiffs charged through, skittling the kids and pushing the granny aside as they entered. No force on earth or in heaven was going to prevent them from liberating the flat's contents.

Ned and Ted always felt a little strange when assigned to do their duties as bailiffs on their own estate. It went against the grain of the we're-all-in-it-together ethic that still had currency amongst some sections of the tower blocks' residents. But nobody ever had the guts to challenge them. If anything, their day-jobs added to the twins' psycho reputations.

Stan looked around. The flat stank of poverty and decrepitude. There wasn't much there. An old telly, a few items of furniture and some ragged clothes. Ornaments, keepsakes, small bits of jewellery. Barely enough to cover the cost of the outstanding debt. He didn't give a fuck. If he had to, he'd take the old lady's entire worldly possessions: the pathetic and meagre assortment of odds and ends that she'd spent her whole lifetime accumulating. It would serve her right for not paying her council tax.

Stan's assistants worked conscientiously, carrying the TV and furniture out of the flat and taking it down in the lift to the van parked outside. The pensioner wasn't saying a lot. She was in a severe state of shock.

"That's fucked you up, hasn't it!" said Stan to the old lady. "I bet you won't be answering the door to carol singers again this Christmas!"

"You'll rot in hell for this, you bad, bad man," she hissed through her dentures, walking into her bathroom. She extracted an old bible from the medicine cabinet, opened the holy book at a random page, and quoted arbitrary passages of the lord's text at the bailiff piously.

"Put a sock in it Doris," said Stan as he snatched the bible from the biddy's hands. "We can auction this book – if we're lucky we'll get all of ten pence from it to deduct from your bill! Fifty pence for the telly! A pound apiece for the chairs and wardrobes! If you're lucky, you might be left with only half the bill still to pay!"

He stalked the flat, putting the jewellery and ornaments into a bag. He noticed an old, faded, black and white photograph of a young couple in wedding gear, getting married. The picture was in a nice wooden frame. "What's this?" he asked.

"It's me and my dear, late husband on our wedding day fifty years ago," came the reply.

"I'll have this as well," said the bailiff, popping it into the bag. "You'd be surprised at how much people fork out for old wedding photos at auctions these days."

"But you can't take that picture, it's – it's special!" gasped the old lady before fainting. She was out cold.

Stan unbuttoned his fly, whipped out his cock and urinated over the prostrate form of the old bag. This had the effect of reviving her. Laughing loudly, he put it away. He reached into a pocket in his overalls and extracted a printed business card which he lobbed at the soaked pensioner who lay wiping her eyes, hair, and upper garments, which were dripping with piss.

"If you ever need anyone evicted, I'm your man," he informed her. "Merry Christmas."

Carrying a sack full of goods, Stan imagined he was Santa as he left the now virtually empty flat. In the ill-lit corridor outside, the kids clamoured around him, tugging at his trousers.

"Where's our money, mister?" asked one. "You promised! Give us our fifty!"

Stan produced the note and held it high above his head, his arm outstretched so that none of the kids could reach, no matter how furiously they jumped up and down. After letting them leap for a while, he put the fifty back into his pocket.

"I've decided that you can't have it after all" he told them, kicking them aside to clear his path. "Beat it, brats!"

The children weren't too pleased. They followed him towards the lift, jostling him aggressively.

"You're a fucking shitbag! You're a fucking shitbag!" ventured one of them, a foul-mouthed four year old who was bravely attempting to trip Stan up and make him fall over.

The bailiff decided that enough was enough. He knelt down, grabbed the kid by the lapels, took the struggling infant into the granny's flat, turned him upside down and held him by the ankles as he carried him to the balcony. Stan observed that the old dear had passed out again. He swung the child over the railings and suspended him invertedly above the long drop to the cold, hard tarmac sixteen floors below.

"I reckon it's about time you learnt some manners," said the bailiff. "Didn't your parents teach you any?"

"Don't drop me, don't drop me" whimpered the toddler. Afraid, the other kids had disappeared.

"What have you got to say then?" asked Stan, swinging the upside-down toddler from side to side in the chilly air way, high above the ground.

"I'm sorry, I'm sorry, I'm sorry," bawled the shit-scared infant tearfully between fits of vomiting.

"You're sorry what?"

"I'm sorry sir, I'm sorry sir."

"Good, you're learning manners" said Stan as he lifted the child back to safety. "And I hope you're really and truly sorry, otherwise you won't get any Christmas presents."

He left the puking minor in the flat with the unconscious pensioner, got into the lift and pushed the button to send it down. He was good with children, he reflected. He had what it took to be a schoolteacher.

Outside Seaton Point, he took the wedding photo from his bag and looked at it casually. This isn't worth much, he thought, snapping the frame in half, we won't get much for this. He tore the picture up and tossed the shreds carelessly into a wheelie-bin before getting into the van and driving off with his colleagues.

25 The flat resembled any other in Seaton Point, though the ten foot by six foot room was clear of any furniture. Peeling wallpaper of dubious taste and cleanliness was adorned sporadically with A3 posters with large simple slogans. Mick took some of them in as he scanned the room – "ONWARD BEERCAN SOLDIERS," "TOGETHER WE'LL CRACK 'EM,"

"SCUM ARMY."

Gerry fidgeted in his wheelchair and picked his nose. The guru had told him to be patient about the miracle that had occurred and to pretend that he was still disabled until the time was right, but he was itching to show off his refound skills. Still, Guru was the boss, that was for sure. After the healing, anything that he wanted doing, Gerry would do it.

Mick and Gerry were not alone. Shuffling uneasily were a handful of other residents. All of them were Crown regulars who had lost the fight against alcoholism some time ago. Most of them glanced uneasily at their timepieces at regular intervals, their throats dry for the opening time of the local corner shop. Only Mick and Gerry knew that the flat was in fact the guru's inner sanctum.

"'Ere, this geezer's five minutes late Mick," a scruffy youth moaned. He was known as White Magic, due to his choice of brew. "Shops open soon."

"Keep your shirt on. He'll be here."

The five others mumbled conspiratorially. There was Aggy, an ageing punk rocker with so much facial jewellery that Mick was surprised that her entire face didn't fall off with the strain of keeping it in place. Mick couldn't understand this fashion. Metalmouths made him feel uneasy, although the thought entered his sordid mind: I wonder if her fanny's pierced?

Muttering in her ear was her mate Joolz. She wore the traveller uniform of old green parka, black combat trousers torn liberally, and boots bereft of laces. Both ears were covered with a multitude of silver rings like a metallic caterpillar snaking up her earlobes. Despite all the lovely English countryside there was to travel in, Mick reflected, Joolz and her kind seemed only to go from London car park to London car park, not too far from the dole office. Occasionally they'd go on holiday to a Brighton car park, but currently she was squatting a flat in the tower block.

The three others in attendance at the first Seaton Point guru session were Arthur the geriatric hooligan, his wife Maude who was every bit as much a hooligan as her husband, and Kelly who had managed to sneak out while his mother was asleep, more out of fear of refusing Mick than any interest in what was going on.

Mick shook his head wearily. Some army. Even Timmy, the guru's first recruit, would have raised the tone of the meeting somewhat if he'd been present. Unfortunately the old soak had recently been picked up in the street by the old bill for shouting aggressively to passers by that he was the first of the new eleven apostles, and from there carted off to a mental institution.

Just then, the air in the flat started to vibrate. All muttering stopped. From a far corner a bright white light started to throb, hum and expand. The visitors shielded their eyes from the blinding brilliance.

"WELCOME, MY PEOPLE."

"Ay?" said Arthur.

"He said welcome," Maude shouted in his better ear.

"Who did?"

"Well I don't know" she replied.

"He did" Mick shouted, pointing towards the centre of the light.

There, the cross-legged figure of the guru became clearer and clearer as the brightness receded. General "oohs" and "aahs" burst from the lips of the congregation and an "oo's ee?" from Arthur elicited a fearsome whack in the kidneys from Maude.

The guru was now fully visible, a shaven-headed figure floating about three feet off the ground. His eyes shone as intensely as the blinding light that had been in the room earlier. The voice had an eerie quality that felt as if it wasn't crossing the airspace, but was coming from inside your own head.

"WELCOME."

The guru's light-filled eyes scanned the room, his features betraying no emotion. Nods and scared grunts were emitted by the surveyed.

"We have brought you some followers, great guru," said Mick rather melodramatically and nudging Gerry as he did so.

"THANK YOU BROTHER MICHAEL. PLEASE ALL BE SEATED."

The scum descended to floor level, all except Arthur who remained standing. "I can't bend down young fella" he sneered, "It's me artheritis."

"EASILY CURABLE. BUT FOR NOW HAVE A SEAT." The guru clicked his fingers in Arthur's direction and the old geezer found himself being lowered by invisible forces into a wooden chair.

"I couldn't have an armchair could I?" said Arthur with a cheeky grin that vanished in double-quick time as he caught a glance of Maude's reddening features. He lowered his head and muttered an apology. Guru looked on impassively.

"THERE IS EVIL IN THIS TOWER. EVIL ABOVE US. EVIL BELOW US. EVIL TO THE SIDES. I HAVE BEEN SUMMONED HERE TO RAISE AN ARMY AGAINST THIS EVIL."

"Why us?" whined White Magic. "Look at us. Why don't you get in some ringers? Some outside help? Mercenaries?"

"BECAUSE THE FIGHT MUST BE WON BY THE PEOPLE OF SEATON POINT. YOU RESIDENTS ARE ALL I HAVE GOT." There was no sign of irony in the guru's voice. "TOGETHER NOW, WITH ME GUIDING YOU, WE CAN DEFEAT THIS EVIL. I CAN MAKE YOU STRONG."

"Fight, you say," Aggy shouted. "But what's in it for us?"

The scum army nodded and murmured in agreement. Arthur raised his walking stick in the air and waggled it about a bit.

"BECAUSE IF YOU DON'T DO IT, WHO ELSE WILL?"

"I for one ain't bothered about good and evil" Aggy replied.

"I should be going, mother will wake up soon" added Kelly.

"They need incentives, boss" Mick interrupted. "Us scum have no conscience." The scum inference met with no argument, rather a mass swelling of pride.

The guru scratched his chin. "INCENTIVES," he whispered to himself, a look of confusion on his face.

"Can I have a word in your ear" said the bricklayer.

The guru nodded. Mick approached him very cautiously and, getting as near as he dared to the strange figure, hissed a short phrase in the direction of his shell-like. Gerry leaned forward in his chair trying to cop a word or two, almost overbalancing himself and thus giving away his secret mobility. Guru nodded again.

"BEHOLD INCENTIVES."

Guru made a sweeping motion with his left hand and to the right of him appeared the scum's nirvana. Stack upon stack of delights. Cans of Brew, Tennents Super, Skol Super Strength, Strongbow Super and myriad two litre bottles of white cider.

A mass gasp shot around the room. For a couple of seconds everyone froze, then with a collective shout of "it's a miracle!" they stampeded as one towards the corner of the room. The bizarreness of the situation was forgotten immediately.

Gerry tried to rise and stampede with the rest but White Magic roughly pushed him back into his wheelchair sending him spinning away from the treasure. Everyone was greedily opening their favourite poison. Arthur, all arthritis magically cured, pulled desperately on a can of Brew. Maude, Aggy and Kelly were all necking Strongbow Super, Joolz favoured Tennents which was also Mick's number one, and White Magic was living up to his moniker and was already a quarter of the way through a large bottle of his namesake. The Skol remained untouched.

Gerry, missing out on beer heaven, gave out an anguished cry and flew towards White Magic. Pulling the shocked youth round he administered the first kick in the bollocks he could remember dishing out in a long time. The stunned White Magic crumpled to a heap on the floor, a mixture of pain and surprise flooding his features. Gerry grabbed a can of Tennents. Opening it, he took a large swig and then proceeded to dance around the room, kicking his legs in the air, and shouting "it's a miracle, it's a miracle" at the top of his voice. Not one of his companions took their eyes off the mountain of alcohol, except Mick, who looked up at the guru, shrugged and then opened his second can.

26

At first it had all been lovey-dovey between the dice man and the vampire. They'd settled in nicely together at St. Terry's pentecostal church of the seventh apocalypse, and they'd been behaving like a newly-wed couple.

Tululah spent most of the time completely female so that she could fit in with Blokey's rampant heterosexual tendencies, and Blokey had even managed to moderate his macho instincts so as not to unduly offend the vampire. However, Tululah's not infrequent indulgences in cross-dressing and gender-altering didn't alienate her partner. The dice man had always been fond of role-playing games such as Dungeons and Dragons, and he was surprised but excited to discover that the pleasure to be gained from role-playing extended to his love life. He could be dominant or submissive, male or mock-female. He'd hit upon a hitherto undiscovered perversity which had enriched his life and heightened his love-feelings towards Tululah.

But then, there had been moments of tension. Tululah wasn't completely faithful as far as Blokey was concerned. She kept having to go off and waste strangers, getting off with them, sinking her fangs into their necks, drinking their blood and leaving them abandoned in lifeless heaps in dark, deserted alleyways. Although this wasn't the kind of behaviour that Blokey really understood, it still made him jealous. He wanted to join in.

"Hey, why can't I be a vampire?" he'd implore her.

"Because it wouldn't suit you, darling!" she'd reply. "In any case, faithfulness has nothing to do with everyday life practice but is in fact a state of mind!"

"But that's not fair! I want to be a vampire! If you can go around snogging all sorts of people and then killing them, why shouldn't I? Seems to me that our relationship's kind of unequal, know what I mean?"

"Well dearest, imagine what it's like to be alive forever, having to kill people all the time – including people you like – to stay sorted and sound? It's no fun, believe me. I reckon you're better off as you are."

As Tululah offered her explanation, she was overwhelmed by an intense feeling of regret as she remembered what she'd done to Poppy, a woman she'd loved deeply. The vampire was cursed always to betray those she loved, but this was simply being cruel to be kind. It was only fair to save her lovers from her own plight, which was a fate worse than death. Tululah choked back a sob. She realised that Blokey might have to go the same way as Poppy if he carried on forcing the issue.

"Being alive forever?" the dice man barked. "Wasting a few folks? I could handle that! What d'you think I am – a wimp or something?"

The vampire shook her head, exasperated. The dice man just didn't have a clue. Blokey was getting more and more pissed off.

He got out his dice and rolled it across the floorboards surreptitiously. One, he'd run up to one of the crosses in the church and crucify himself; he didn't stop to consider how he'd get the last nail in. Two, he'd do a jigsaw. Three, he'd go all homicidal and attack Tululah so that the only chance she'd have of avoiding serious injury would be to use her magical powers and turn him into a vampire, or else kill him in order to defend herself. Four, he'd fit a carpet. Five, he'd put up a shelf. Six, he'd run out of the church screaming, howl like a maniac all the way to Lower

Clapton Road and then chuck himself suicidally into the path of an approaching N253 bus.

Three!

The dice man went crazy!

"Waaaaarrgghhh!" he screamed, launching himself at his girlfriend. He took off like a rocket into the air, landed in his bird's lap, pounded her with his fists and bit her with his teeth. The vampire didn't know what had hit her – he was normally such a mild-mannered guy!

Tululah fought back; she was quite hard and knew how to handle herself. She tossed the dice man away and punched him a few times until he went down. He was lying there on the floor, quivering and vulnerable. The vampire positioned the pointed heel of her stiletto sharp above the prostrate dice man's neck.

"Okay honey, what's the game?" she asked him.

"I wanna be a fuckin' vampire!" Blokey shot back. "You reckon you're saving me from myself by not giving it to me – but it's like this. Either you turn me into a vampire, or else you're gonna have to kill me – otherwise I won't give up until you're seriously damaged. Got it?"

Tululah thought about it, her stiletto still at the dice man's neck. She thought about it for quite a while. Being a vampire, her wounds always healed quickly and unnaturally, but what Blokey was proposing was still an unfortunate dilemma.

Anguish consumed the vampire. Normally in a situation like this she'd have killed her lover automatically. But she couldn't stop thinking about Poppy. Even though Tululah had fallen head over heels in love with Blokey, she'd never completely gotten over her previous lover and the memory still grated a bit. The need to waste Blokey was inevitable, but it had come too soon. Turning him into a vampire would be a terrible act, but she wasn't sure if she could handle killing her loved one so shortly after his predecessor: the grief would surely be too much for her to bear. Tululah was losing it. She couldn't think straight.

Finally, she relented and did the business, sinking her fangs deep into the dice man's neck but refraining from sucking all the life out of him.

Blokey was a vampire!

27

Alone. Alone. Aloooooone. What did that mean?

Back in the **real** lift, Io rolled back over onto his left side and opened his eyes. Strange; it was still dark. He rarely woke before the flickering artificial strip woke **him**, and to the best of his sparse recollections never. Maybe something was afoot; and yes, there was a low and distant rumble that seemed to be emanating from somewhere beneath his grey-steel piss-stenched mattress.

Beneath? Below? Io strained at his temples with the still-limited force of his mind, pushing away at the psychological constipation there, a blocked drain of myriad possibilities; of everything and nothing and all of the unimagined maybes, and then it was gone, the rumbling from below subsided and there was silent peace and dark sleep, and he settled for that.

Ian the wino stumbled along Kingsland High Street. He had wandered around Dalston since dawn, and now he needed a place to lie down and await another ounce of strength to beg up a little wine money.

It was all very clear to him. As opposed to his alter-ego Io, Ian knew exactly who he was. He was 21 and a young wino. He was especially proud of the fact that, unlike a great many of his contemporary artists, he was a genuine wino, one of the old school: that is to say, he only drank red wine, thick and heavy and very very nasty. No dogs, no Special Brew. Sometimes the desperate red resembled Sarson's pickling vinegar, but Ian was preserving a dying culture here and so, sometimes, sacrifices had to be made. Some things are greater than any of us, he often thought to himself after a bottle of Hungarian or two. Not that he had surrendered himself up to any kind of a 'higher power' or any of that hogwash, mind you. Nope. He was simply resigned to his fate and yet inimitably in control of its downwardly spiralling style. Perhaps in later years he might possibly make it onto the surgical spirits but, just for now at least, he would keep the faith. Mostly, however, he never even thought of this for it had become second-nature and automatic for him and he was by now fast becoming a semi-philosophising drinking machine.

The space inside his skull didn't so much ache as pulse with a vague, insistent numbness desperately fighting to be heard above all else – until the end of eternity, as time seemed to stand still, rooted in its own vile and unnamed stink as he negotiated the steps of the 'RIO' cinema to peer through the window at the clock behind the pay desk.

On weekdays you could see a film for under three pounds or, if films didn't interest you, you could instead merely sit in the warm and the dark where mostly there was nobody to much bother you: unless there was the first showing of a popular cult classic, something that was obviously to be avoided. It was of course begging and drinking time gone forever, but it became necessary to take five occasionally, to put a little back into your rusted old batteries and frame in foolhardy part-preparation for that final fall. A bit of a break: the easy life, a temporary thing but sometimes unavoidably necessary. And so here he was. At the 'RIO' cinema they were not usually too choosy over who they let in. It was January and two degrees above zero.

"Four rooms, please."

It was the name of the film. The cinema was not really a hotel, only a kind of day centre. The young woman who worked the first shift there three days a week pushed the ticket across at him, trying desperately to smile a little for the sake of her lowly-paid job as he deposited the vile, filthy, stinking loose change into her neatly manicured and comfortably piggy-small left hand.

"Filthy lucre: yeah, right," she thought. And then, "Pooh!"

Ian had noticed her working there some time ago and had been in love with her ever since then, or at least when he could consciously remember to be. He had once, probably last February he thought, penned a love poem which he had never sent to her. He was too scared. He was terrified of everything so he just drank and drank and drank. The poem had gone something like:

"I HAVE ADMIRED YOU FROM AFAR
I HOPE YOU DO NOT DRIVE A CAR..."

And then it had pretty much just petered out. What there was of the remainder of the poem was **truly** unmentionable. It was just as well really that he had been too afraid to send it, but either way it was all quite meaningless and hardly even worth considering for very long. Ian put the ticket into his mouth and made his way down the stairs to the cinema proper.

Before going into the auditorium Ian made for the gents. It was just to his right at the bottom of the staircase: he thought that he ought to take this opportunity to have his daily crap. It was bad being a professional drunk and having nowhere of your own to defecate into; it was one of the more major drawbacks. He got into the pristine cubicle, pulled down his half-soggy jogging bottoms then his tights and underpants, and finally he relaxed. That always seemed to last forever, that one final moment before you made it down onto the seat. He reached around behind his arse and pulled the seat down, dropping it halfway with an almighty clatter. Ian winced. Other than the obviously precarious state of his head and nerves, he was concerned that the men pissing just a few feet away might think that he was some sort of fumbling, moribund and incompetent junkie: and he did not want that.

He felt around the tops of his thighs, checking for signs of thrush or crabs: but no, there was nothing there, he was having a very good month on the diseases front it seemed.

With those things settled, he finally let the awful stink go with a resounding **SPLASH! CLUNKER! SPLATTER! SPLOOSHIEOOSHIEOOSHIE!!** kind of a sound. All done, he felt a lot better. It took some time and likewise bogroll to clean up the mess that was left between his buttocks but this was nothing out of the ordinary, and by the time that he had made it out of the cubicle and to the sink fully-armoured again, Ian had managed to work up quite a shaky little sweat. Nice.

He splashed cold water liberally over his face, screwed it up into a ball, shook his head like some manic mongrel dog that had just narrowly escaped death by drowning and then cautiously peered into the mirror. There it was: death and hope. It was the little things, the little things that mattered because at the end of the big, bad, pointless day the whole big, bad, pointless picture would mean nothing: nothing at all. He wiped his face with ingrained-oily hands, and exited the bathroom.

It was show-time!

28 The Booth boys felt good. Harry, Larry and Barry Booth were off dog-fighting. It was only a small sideline to them. They had their fingers in all the dirty pies. Harry did a bit of pimping. He ran two prostitutes from a squalid flat he rented dirt cheap below his own in Rathbone Point, the block of flats opposite Seaton. All it took was a couple of quid a week to some schoolkid to put the numbers up round the local pubs and phoneboxes and it was easy money. He saw that the girls were all right for smack and condoms and some occasional food; then he just had to sit back and take the money. Easy money, like the drug dealing Larry did for the saps who wanted their addictions seeing to.

When the spiders started crawling in their stomachs as withdrawal set in, it was Larry they came to see. Their first fixes had been cheap, dirt cheap, but now they were hooked and they had to pay full price. Larry didn't give a fuck how much they squealed. If they wanted their sweeties they had to give him the full whack. Sometimes he'd accept goods, obviously ripped off and red hot instead of cash. Occasionally he'd take a fancy to one of the female addicts and get rid of his dirty water in their mouth as part-exchange.

Barry's bag was purely violence. Dog-fighting was enjoyable but bare knuckle boxing was his favourite. His face was an advert for the 'ban boxing and you'll drive it underground' argument. The top of his left earlobe was missing, bitten off; his nose was splayed across his face; his front teeth were missing and the skin around his eyes a bundle of scar tissue. Barry wasn't the world's best boxer which was why the sport had never beckoned professionally, but he was a dirty fighter and much feared.

The boys were from the Orange Lodge streets of Glasgow, but they had got too cocky many years ago and had fled the swords and malkies of the real Glasgow hardmen, the gangsters who insisted on running everything profitable in that city. The Hackney estate had proved easier meat for the brothers, but they were far from running the show. Seaton Point's psychopathic Barber brothers had given them a run for their money. Seaton Point was where the Booths were headed for now.

An uneasy truce had been agreed between the two tower blocks, and so a bit of inter-house recreation was in order. Jaws trotted beside his owners. The Rottweiler was overweight and a bit too soft for Harry Booth's liking but it was going to fight the Barbers' dog, no question about it. There was a ton riding on this, as well as some pride.

Seaton Point loomed above them. A strange cloud seemed to hang over the block in the otherwise clear night sky.

Larry, the youngest, shuddered. "Gettin' cold" he muttered.

"Ponce" Harry spat.

They went in and made their way down the concrete steps that led down to the basement. The Booths were nearly an hour early. Harry didn't trust the Barbers. Truce or no truce they were fucking nutters and an ambush on foreign soil could be very nasty. Harry felt his back pocket to reassure himself that the cutthroat was still there; instinctively Barry sought solace in the brass knuckleduster in the front pocket of his jeans. Vicious rings adorned his fingers, Ronnie the Rhino being his favourite instrument of malicious wounding.

They reached the entrance to the basement. Jaws yawned and cocked his leg up Harry's trousers. "Dirty bastud" the pimp yelled, giving the dog a swift boot to the ribs. Jaws yelped.

"Leave it oot" hissed Barry, "don't do him befair the contest."

"Contest my airse, it'll be a fucken walkover."

They entered the basement, ignoring the strange smells which wafted around them. What the Barbers got up to down here on their own was their business.

Larry tried the light switch. Nothing. Again. Nothing.

"What a wind up" he muttered. Once more, and a bulb came on in the far corner of the room: a dull red bulb. "How are we supposed to see in this light?"

"A couple of torches or summat, it'll be alright, stop blathering." Barry was impatient for the show.

"Hee, hee, hee," a voice cackled

"What's so fucken funny then Larry?"

"Ay?"

"I said what are ye fucken laughing aboot?"

"I'm no laughing."

"Hee, hee, hee."

A shape whizzed past them and sped back again at the same velocity.

"What the fuck?"

SMASH.

"What was that?" Barry shouted at his brethren.

Harry picked it up. "It's a light bulb."

"Hee, hee, hee."

They looked over to the red light. It was getting more intense, pulsing like a dwarf star that Larry had once seen on The Sky At Night. He wished he was back at home now, tucking into some of the new batch of stash.

"That's no you is it Barber?" queried Harry to the now spinning light.

"Hee, hee, hee."

The smell in the room, not particularly pleasant to begin with, had become almost choking in its density: it smelt like some dairy product about a hundred years out of date.

"L-L-Let's go" Larry stammered.

"I'm no fucken runnin from these bastuds" shouted Barry, "it's a wind-up." He grabbed his younger brother's arm. They'd stand and fight together.

"Hee, hee, hee."

The light began to spin faster and faster. Now sparks were flying off it.

"I've had enough" shouted Harry, reaching into his pocket for his trusty weapon. He opened up the blade and held it aloft so that the red light flashed and danced from the steel.

"Malkie time!" he screamed. Kicking Jaws ahead of him, he ran forwards.

Silence. Darkness. The light had cut out as Harry had leapt forward swinging his blade.

"Hah, ye've done the fucker" laughed Larry in relief. "C'mere Jaws. Good boy. Jaws?"

"WAAAGHH." Thump.

Larry and Barry stared in amazement as their big brother rose out of the darkness. He was wrapped in a glue-like substance which trailed down to the basement floor. It held him like a cat holding a mouse in its jaws. His whole body swayed violently through the air and Larry and Barry ducked as the mass shot past their heads. Harry's mouth was covered and the air erupted in screams of panic from his brothers.

"What the fuck's going on?" Barry screamed. Harry's body shot back past them again and slammed with a sickening thud against the brick wall near the door.

"Hee, hee, hee."

The red light flared again revealing the dying form of Jaws, his mouth stuffed full of the mysterious substance, blood oozing from his twitching body.

The laughing turned into a hideous wailing, painful to the ears. Harry's brothers put thoughts of pride and brotherly bonding out of their minds and turned to flee. The semi-conscious body of Harry peeled itself away from the wall and was lifted airborne again by the ooze. Swinging in a blindingly fast arc his bound and gagged head connected with the head of Barry causing a domino effect on the youngest. CRACK. CRACK.

"Hee, hee, hee."

29

Blokey had assumed the vampire's nervous yet fearless gait. He edged his way along the street, carefully avoiding the inquisitive orange glare of the lamps, the minefield of a thousand imagined judges of the light, avengers of the night; he needed the clear vision of the shadows.

The mortal's fear of death had evaporated: an hour could now be wasted in the sure knowledge that another would always be there to take its place. The rhythms of life, or at least of existence, a term more appropriate to his new condition, had been inverted. Autumn, not spring, was the season of rebirth, and winter the time of plenty; dawn would bring sleep to his eyes and dusk rekindled his energies.

His thirst and the imperative to quench it were the only reminders of his past. Thirst-drive had replaced his libido, and had lazily eased itself into the behaviour patterns of his past life. He was impatient to make his first kill, to lose his nosferatian virginity and taste for the first time the sweet elixir of warm human blood.

He reached Frank's flat at half past nine, a time when he knew that the geezer would be out at work – he'd taken a second job for extra cash for the new baby, though his day job didn't pay badly. Blokey had suspected an affair, a thought which had previously assuaged any guilt about his lust for Suzie. But now, he cared no further than the practical advantages of Frank's absence. In any case, he would ensure that the bastard would have one less, not more, mouth to feed after tonight.

He stood at the door in the self-conscious manner of an adolescent on his first date, nervously toying with the dice in his jacket pocket, but it could not help him now – roll one, two, three, four, five or six, kill Suzie and drink her blood; end of game.

He had an almost irresistible urge to run and to give up on the undead life before it had begun, but he willed his hand to the bell and touched the button, gradually increasing the pressure until finally it was activated and Blokey heard a fast, dull vibration from the buzzer inside the flat and also from an unreachable place deep within his being, an echo from a lost world. A part of him, the nervous part, hoped that she would not be at home and he would be able to abort his mission due to circumstances beyond his control.

It was a vain hope. Suzie opened the door and stood at the threshold, wearing a multi-coloured dressing gown and daffy duck slippers, smiling warmly.

"Hello, Ian."

"Hello, Suzie."

Blokey could scarcely bring himself to utter her name and it emerged from his mouth reluctantly in a barely audible throaty growl. Suzie's massive belly was barely contained by her dressing gown. It was as if the new life within it was about to burst out and jump straight into the dice man's arms right there. Leaning back on her haunches to support the load, her hair tied back to reveal glowing cheeks, Suzie was resplendent: Blokey's magnificent prey.

"Can I come in?"

"Sure." Suzie moved aside to let him pass. "Frank's not here at the moment."

"I know."

Blokey made straight for the living room and sat down in the armchair in front of the television, trying to compose himself. Suzie followed and positioned herself on the sofa.

Only now, in the light, did she notice the change in Blokey. He was thinner, and the colour in his usually swarthy complexion had drained away so completely that he looked as if he had powdered his face like some eighties-throwback goth. His lips were narrower, and so were his eyebrows and the bridge of his nose. In fact, every feature was perceptibly altered, though when combined their totality was still definitively Ian. He looked somehow desperate, even more than normal, as though he had lost his way and stumbled upon Suzie's abode merely by chance. Whether it was due to the hormones surging around her pregnant arteries she did not know, but she felt drawn to him, pre-maternally attracted to those sad, lonely, crazy eyes.

"Would you like anything to drink? Tea, coffee?" The conversation was sustained by platitudes; much had been understood and misunderstood in the silence. "I think Frank's got some beer in the fridge."

"No thanks," Blokey lied. He had a thirst which encompassed all the anguish of a mortal's thirst, hunger and lust combined. "How's the baby?"

"Fine, it's due in a couple of weeks now."

"That's good then."

Suzie looked at Blokey pitifully. "Ian, I hope you don't mind me saying this, but you look very ill, run down. You're deathly white. When was the last time you ate?"

"It's not food that I need, Suzie, but you're right, I am in need of sustenance," replied Blokey cryptically. For the first time, he made eye contact: his eyes were jet black holes set into the pasty relief of his face.

Suzie interpreted Blokey's words as sexual advances.

"Ian, I'm eight and a half months pregnant and Frank and I haven't made love for over a month now," she said. "Don't read anything into our kiss the other week, it was a moment and a moment only."

Unsettled by the atmosphere, she stood up and walked over to the window, turning her back on her visitor.

"You misunderstand me, Suzie."

Blokey followed and stood behind her, reaching around to hug her waist. He sank his head into her neck as if to kiss her and initiate a sexual encounter. He smelt her perfume and felt her smooth skin with his lips. Courage was welling within him, but he knew that he would have to act quickly or he would certainly lose his nerve. He felt little empathy for mortals now, but he could sense that Suzie's untouchable beauty would soon get the better of him. Suzie squirmed a little but did not pull herself away. She was staring impassively into the darkness outside.

Blokey bared his lethal incisors for the first time and gently sucked at Suzie's neck as if he were going to give her a love bite. Suzie gave off a little moan and then suddenly attempted to escape his hold. "No, Ian, stop please, stop."

Blokey had thought that she was about to acquiesce and his pride was damaged – he still liked to consider that he was attractive to the opposite sex, perhaps even more so with the added ingredient of mystery that was now in his make-up. This enraged him: fucking women!

He squeezed her tightly and snapped his jaw, jagging his teeth deep into her flesh. Suzie let out a piercing scream as if in one last ecstatic orgasm, or so Blokey fancied, and this only encouraged him to bite even deeper and harder. He could feel a tingling sensation spreading from the roots of his teeth right down his spine and into his prick which was now erect. The tingling gave way to an all-enveloping pleasure as the blood gushed forth and he tasted death for the first time. He released and bit in again, clumsily like the virgin he was, but his inexperience did not matter: life was draining out of the now unconscious Suzie as quickly as her blood was draining down Blokey's throat.

Within a few minutes, Suzie was dead and Blokey was sated. He withdrew his fangs and let the corpse fall to the floor. Wiping the blood from his cheeks with his sleeve, he fell back onto the sofa, exhausted. He stared down at Suzie's body and at her bloody slippers which lay beside her, their cartoon beaks still grinning inanely. Blood was trickling slowly from her vagina, leaving a damp patch around the crotch of her dressing gown.

Blokey's elation was short-lived. As he surveyed his first prey, he found that he could feel nothing, absolutely nothing in a way that he had never before thought possible. He would have been saddened by this were he still capable of true sadness.

At that moment, something of the tragedy of the vampire's lonely existence was revealed to him. He thought of Tululah and her yearning for mortality. He thought of Frank, his so-called friend, and the despair that awaited him. He thought all the thoughts of a compassionate being, and yet the feelings to accompany these thoughts were absent. What had he become? What had been the true price of his becoming undead? How had he thrown his life away so cheaply, on a whim?

Eventually he roused himself from his introspection and looked up at the clock. Shit, he thought, it was nearly eleven already: Frank would be back any minute.

He decided to slip out of the living room window to avoid the danger of bumping into Frank on the road. As he made his way through the undergrowth of the small back garden, he cut himself on the thorns. Was it his blood or Suzie's that leaked through the wound? Would Blokey be any more than a pitiful amalgam of his dead victims' deadness from now on? He heard a key being inserted into the front door lock: he had made his escape in the nick of time.

He heard Frank's voice. "Suzie, I'm home, I've got a present for you, Suzie!"

Blokey didn't hang around. He ran to the back wall and clambered over into the adjoining garden. He was already a few hundred yards away from the house when he heard the deep roar of a man's voice behind him.

Blokey's thirst was beginning to return. He would soon have to start searching out another victim.

30 Stan Bates lifted his wife's skirt from the back, slipped a hand into her panties and pulled them down to her ankles. He'd already removed his trousers and shorts, and he was looking forward to shagging his spouse. He'd had an exhausting day evicting council tenants who'd fallen behind on their rent, and he had a further engagement later that evening at the Nightingale Estate, where he was due to evict a squatter from the top floor of a tower block. Shagging his wife would be the appropriate energising activity to prepare him for his next appointment.

One squat wasn't enough for Blokey. Although the church was an ideal haunt for him and Tululah, a further residence was required so that he could put his plan into action.

Dark, gloomy and candlelit, the walls painted black, St. Terry's pentecostal church of the seventh apocalypse was perfect for Blokey and his newly acquired vampire status which had already resulted in numerous fatalities. Tululah too appreciated the environment, especially the decor, which seemed to mirror the unnatural half-life she now had in common with her feller. Bats, cobwebs, strange things screeching in the dark, weird things hovering in corners, nameless phantoms haunting the deep thick shadow – it was top stuff! The dice man and his lover were settling in nicely.

The roll of the dice had determined the method by which the bailiff would be taken out. All that remained was to lure him into a trap and to waste the bastard, making him see the error of his ways. In the brief moment between dropping from the balcony and landing – thump! – on the cold, hard tarmac 22 floors beneath, the bailiff would regret making Blokey look foolish in front of a bird he fancied. The force of the impact would leave Bates flat as a pancake, a grotesque pizza of obsolete bones, blood, flesh and fibre splattered under the mysterious grey shadow cast by the block of flats.

"Open them, wider, you slut!" barked the bailiff, slapping his wife's thighs. He yanked at his cock a few times until it went as hard as it could get. "And keep your fucking balance, bitch! Keep your fucking back straight while you're opening your legs apart!"

Bates wanted his old lady to keep her balance. If she moved too much, rose from her bent over position or tilted a bit to one side, then the wank mag spread open across her back would surely fall off, and the bailiff's arousal would be diminished.

The magazine, open at the centre pages, was Stan's favourite out of his collection. He stared at the picture, continued to manipulate his shaft, picked up his beer can, took a swig from it and replaced it in its correct position, balanced on the back of his wife's head as she faced down. Then he proceeded to massage his wife's cunt so that it would get moist enough for him to shove his huge cock up her dark hole.

Blokey easily forced his way into flat 67 of Seaton Point; it didn't even have a steel door. He quickly changed the lock of the empty, and installed himself. It was a bit of a tip, but nevertheless an appropriate venue for his revenge on the bailiff from hell.

It wasn't long before the residents of Seaton Point, usually so broad-minded, became disturbed by the goings on in flat 67. The neighbours were accustomed to weird gurus, anarchists and druggies; to representatives of a whole range of sad subcultures; to shadowy figures who never came out of their flats; to a variety of psychopaths and nutcases. But flat 67 was truly something else. Blokey had installed a collection of huge speakers connected to turntables which blasted out non-stop electronic industrial noise at hundreds of decibels. Avant-garde rubbish by the likes of Whitehouse and Throbbing Gristle assaulted the eardrums of the tenants of Seaton Point and the surrounding tower blocks day and night. Blokey had cleverly fixed a number of security devices and booby traps to the door of the flat, making it impossible for anyone other than himself to get in and switch the racket off.

Driven berserk by the horrible loud wailing and whistling, local residents complained to the council estate office in their dozens. Blokey himself called the police on various occasions, asking them to investigate the prostitution and drug-dealing racket which he claimed was taking place from the flat. To complete the effect, the dice man contacted the Hackney Gazette and got them to run a front-page feature on the satanic child sex ring ostensibly being organised from the flat. Within a fortnight, the bureaucrats from Hackney Borough Council had been reported to the public environmental health department for their failure to respond speedily enough to the nuisance from the flat, and were under pressure from all sides to organise an immediate eviction. Their jobs under threat, the pen-pushers were forced to get their acts together for a change.

As Blokey had expected, the bureaucrats decided that they needed a heavy hammer to crack the tough nut that was his new flat. They resolved to bring onto the case the heaviest hammer of the lot – Stan Bates and his mates. And so the notorious bailiffs were assigned to evict Blokey from his industrial electronic haven at the given time, as the eviction letter posted through the letterbox made clear. The dice man was given less than 24 hours' notice. He didn't give a fuck. He was ready.

The bailiff stuck two fingers up his wife's cunt and waggled them about a bit. If he shoved hard enough, there would be enough room up there for his enormous love truncheon.

Bates took his lady from behind roughly, banging his muscle deep into her tunnel of love. He proceeded to thrust up and down, working his member back and forth so that it penetrated deeper, deeper into his wife's mystery with each successive stroke.

Suddenly the bailiff's beer can fell off of his old lady's head and crashed to the floor, spilling brown liquid which oozed in a puddle across the carpet. He slapped her about a bit, just to show her, the fucking bitch, and then he continued to whack his swollen tool in and out of her cunt as his gaze greedily devoured the centrefold still resting across her back. Getting on with his shag diligently, the bailiff flicked through the pages of the wank mag.

Nutter Nigel was well fucked off. Having just returned from an anarchist seminar weekend out in the sticks, he'd discovered that some bastard had squatted one of his flats without permission. Nutter Nigel reflected that only his men, or their chicks, were allowed to occupy an empty on one of his floors.

If this intrusion wasn't enough to make the anarchist's blood boil, the squatter was playing non-stop heavy industrial shite at full volume, day and night! Nutter Nigel was losing his mind as the Nocturnal Emissions and Death In June blared out at such a volume that he couldn't hear himself think. By themselves, these transgressions could have been excused. But worse, and unforgivably, there was evidence that the scumbag had been smoking and drinking on the activist's territory. Fag ends and empty cans had accumulated up the stairwell and outside the flats during Nutter Nigel's absence, and he believed the new squatter to be responsible. No one offended the anarchist's puritanical instincts and got away with it. Nutter Nigel resolved to teach the bastard a lesson.

Bates was racing, racing! He was banging it in hard and fast, slamming his gigantic stick right up inside his wife's deep hole with a steady and pulsating rhythm. Back and forth he pounded, his love lance a giant battering ram beating its way towards a satisfactory outcome.

And then it was all over: a volcano erupted, squirting hot, thick, sticky lava far, far into inner space. After withdrawing from his spouse's love tunnel, the bailiff paused to get his breath back, then he looked at his watch. He was running a little behind time.

Bates pulled up his workman's trousers, rolled up the wank mag and put it in his pocket for later on. Adjusting his still swollen rod into a comfortable position inside his shorts, he rushed out of the flat, got into his van and switched on the ignition. His destination was Seaton Point, and he was meeting his two assistants Ned and Ted outside.

Blokey sat in flat 67, his earplugs partly protecting him from the onslaught of industrial electronic bollocks about fascist barbarian armies rolling across the icy wastes of Northern Europe. As one million decibels of tripe by Coil vomited mercilessly from the speakers, the dice man stroked the sawn-off shotgun lying across his lap as if it were a furry animal.

He was waiting for the bailiffs to show up. He planned to use the shotgun to threaten the boss man and usher him towards the windows which were wide open in readiness. Then he'd disable the bastard by shooting him in the elbows and kneecaps, before hoisting him over the balcony towards his doom. As he waited patiently, Blokey rolled his dice a few times, to decide what he was going to have for breakfast on each of the next seven days.

Stan pulled up outside the block of flats. His men were ready, brandishing their hammers. Bundling together the eviction papers, Stan chuckled as he recalled confiscating the possessions of some old wrinkly who hadn't paid her council tax during a previous job at the tower. He'd fucked the old biddy over good and proper!

The even numbered lift, unlike its odd numbered counterpart, was working. Inside, the three bailiffs waited as they rose towards the uppermost storey of Seaton Point.

Nutter Nigel was firm-handed and ready to ruck. He'd collected together a small gang of comrades from some of his squats, and together they intended to evict the recalcitrant newcomer – by all and any means necessary!

Up the stairs climbed the anarchists. They were tooled up and weren't afraid to use their weapons. They ascended silently, their quietness lending an air of grandiosity to their mission. The hour of revolution had arrived!

The bailiffs shot out of the lift at the same time as Nutter Nigel and his crew arrived on the same floor. Blokey was prepared for his assailants, alone in the flat with his sawn-off and with the horrendous atonal dirge which had been recorded by various maladjusted delinquents to whom nobody in their right mind would listen. The dice man was ready to take them all on.

The two firms, both tooled up, met outside flat 67. In unison, the bailiffs and anarchists bashed at Blokey's door, their purpose in common.

"Are you taking the piss or what?" Bates shouted at Nutter Nigel and his mates. "You're copying us!"

"Never mind that," the activist snapped back. "Who are you and what the fuck are you doing on one of my floors?"

Blokey was staying put. He'd wait until they bashed the door down, then he'd start blasting. They wouldn't know what had hit them!

As Nutter Nigel and Stan argued, the twin psychos booted the door off its hinges with a volley of well-aimed kicks. The dice man had removed the booby traps: he wanted his prey inside the flat so that he could deal with them on his own soil. As the door buckled and gave way, the bailiffs charged in.

Blokey was hidden in the kitchen. He waited until all three bailiffs were inside his flat before he emerged.

"Freeze!" he bawled, pointing his sawn-off towards the head of the chief bailiff. "One move out of you cunts and the bastard here gets it! And drop those hammers!"

The bailiffs froze and dropped their hammers.

"You two – out of the flat!" the dice man hissed at the twins.

"Do as he says" ordered Bates. He was scared. He didn't like people pointing shotguns at him. The twins left the flat, somewhat taken aback. The anarchists outside watched, baffled.

"Over there!" Blokey ordered, motioning the bailiff towards the window. Bates did as he was told.

Blokey had a new idea for disabling Stan Bates prior to his fatal descent. Keeping his shooter aimed at the target with his right hand, he bent down and picked up a hammer with his left. Then he walked across the room and smashed the bailiff with it in the jaw, knocking out several teeth. Blood flowed; the dice man started bashing at the bailiff's kneecaps with the hammer and the bastard went down. Bates couldn't retaliate: not with his opponent waving a shotgun at him. He was locked into a no-win situation.

Suddenly, Nutter Nigel crept across the room and came to the bailiff's rescue. Blokey was about to break Stan's elbows when he felt a sharp crack at his gun-toting wrist from behind, courtesy of the anarchist's hammer. Taken by surprise, the dice man accidentally dropped his gun and Nutter Nigel kicked it into touch before grabbing the vampire by the collar and flinging him up against a wall. The other anarchists charged into the flat waving their hammers and their little black flags. The bleeding bailiff, his kneecaps badly damaged, couldn't walk to save his life, but nevertheless took the opportunity to haul himself away on his elbows and slither out of the flat. His assistants, waiting outside, followed his orders to carry him into the lift and get him out of Seaton Point with the most urgent haste, so that he could seek the medical attention that he clearly required.

One of the anarchists did the sensible thing and found the off switch of the record player. The awful noise ceased, giving the neighbours a long overdue spot of peace and quiet.

"What the fuck do you think you're doing, lowering the tone of my neighbourhood with this racket?" Nutter Nigel remonstrated with the startled squatter. "Ain't you got any fucking punk records? And what's all this about letting people drink and smoke on my floors?"

"Those cunts who just left were bailiffs, dickhead!" the diceman spat. He knew all about the anarchists of Seaton Point, and knew that they didn't generally take too kindly to bailiffs. "I was going to waste one of them by chucking him over the balcony, and you've gone and ruined it, you spoilsport! This flat had just been a ploy all along, so that I could take out the meanest bailiff in the whole of the borough!"

The squatting chief thought about it, assessing the situation. He concluded that he'd made a big mistake. Blokey's plan had been noble and courageous, he realised. Swallowing his pride, Nutter Nigel apologised. It was the first and last time that Blokey and the anarchist would meet.

A contraption made of wires and metal plates held together the bailiff's jaw as he reclined in the luxury of his bed at Homerton Hospital Intensive Care Unit being fed baby food through a straw. His knees were encased in plaster, and it would be a while before he'd get back on his feet. The nurses had told him that he could have a limp for life, and that he might well have to accustom himself to using a walking stick. He'd been done over – badly.

Although Stan Bates couldn't open his mouth to communicate his thoughts, the contents of his head were quite clear. Retribution. Bloody retribution.

Blokey had it coming. Death, slow and painful.

31

Clack, clack, clack went the baseball bat as it rattled along the bars of the metal staircase. Down, down, deeper and down moved the two psychos. Clack, clack, clack.

Ned and Ted Barber didn't like being beaten. Only once or twice had they tasted defeat, and that had taken a dozen coppers and very strong handcuffs. Even then the fuckers had rued the day, but their experience in the Seaton Point basement a week previously had seen the twins running away like a couple of two year olds. Mick the Brick had accompanied them that time, with that stupid fucking dog of his. The other three men and a dog that had met them there that night had never been seen again, and the word was that the twins had murdered them and dumped the bodies.

The Booth boys had lived in the flats opposite Seaton Point – Rathbone Point. Feelings had always ran high between the two tower blocks, and rumour had it that Ned and Ted were marked men. They didn't really give a fuck; in fact, they enjoyed yet more notoriety being heaped upon them. But they ruled this block, and whatever was going on in the basement had to be sorted.

There had been no reply from Mick's flat. Fucking chicken. They didn't need him though. Clack, clack.

As Ted remembered the past events, his rage started to increase.

It was midnight when the trio approached the basement with Fang in tow. The dog stiffened two flights before the bottom and refused to budge. Sniffing the air, he began to whine and attempted to back away past his master's legs. Fang yelped as Mick the Brick's para boot punted him up the arse. "Get in there you yeller bastard" Mick hollered.

Another flight down and Ned noticed a strange smell. "What's that whiff?"

"Nuffing" replied his brother.

"Like yoghurt."

It had been three months since the last dog-fight. Fang had won them both a nice bit of money that night. It may usually have seemed like the dog was shot away, but when he had to fight he was like a demon. The local RSPCA had gotten wind that something was going on so the brothers had been obliged to lay low for a while, but now they were back in action. Fang whined again, pure terror in his eyes. Mick cursed and dragged him down the last few steps to the basement. Wisps of smoke curled around the door frame. The Booth boys had arrived there early.

Ned, Ted, Mick and Fang entered the dank basement. Something was different. A weird smell emanated from the room, and an unnatural blackness covered everything. Someone had been down here. This was their patch, their manor, and no one else used this basement without their permission. Even the skagheads knew they had to keep away from the place.

Mick reached for the light switch. Click. Nothing. "The bulb's gone," he muttered.

"Booth, is that you?" shouted Ted.

A whimpering noise.

"Shut up Fang."

"Wasn't the dog" murmured Ned, "somewhere over there," he pointed into the darkness.

"Booth, if you boys want trouble you'll get it," Ted screamed.

Whoosh. A searing red light span around in the middle of the room. The trio jumped backwards in surprise, then moved forward again as the light glared like a flare, eerily illuminating the dank room. Nothing appeared to be operating the light; it was certainly no bulb.

The whimpering sound became louder, and some movement caused Mick to glance to his left. There, wearing a look of terror he would never forget, sat the Booth boys. They were propped against the wall, something resembling slime wrapped around their bodies. The thick, sticky goo appeared to be almost alive. It seemed to move around the three brothers, contracting, relaxing. It covered the mouth of each man, and all three had bulging eyes which gave desperate pleading looks to Mick, Ned and Ted. The Booth boys had been tasty fighters, but now they just looked like frightened little kids.

Something had run towards Mick's feet. Looking down he saw a pool of liquid oozing around his boots, more fluid than the slime. He followed the trail with his eyes as best he could in the strange red light. In the middle of the room lay something twitching. "What's that?" Ned asked.

The light flared brighter, revealing the dead body of Jaws, the Booths' Rottweiler. A massive hole in the dog's stomach was pumping a fountain of blood across the floor and a raw white rib showed through the dark flesh.

"What cunt's done this?" Ted screamed. "Come on then you wankers, where are you?"

A high-pitched whine came from the far side of the room, the part still engulfed in the macabre inky blackness. Steadily it got louder. Fang became increasingly frantic as pain buzzed in his ears and the terrible atmosphere freaked him out. He turned his head and sank his teeth into Mick's calf muscle. The brickie yelled in shock, releasing the dog's chain as he did so. The terrified pit bull sensed his chance for freedom and galloped up the stairs.

"Bastard" shouted Mick. He bent down to feel his wounds, and saved his life in the process. Splattt. A jet of slime hit the wall through where his head had been not one second earlier. The substance hissed, smouldered and oozed down towards the floor.

An ear-splitting laugh tore through the room, and a stick-thin figure appeared within the red light. Looking like the shadow of Nosferatu, the shape jigged and hopped its evil dance.

"I can see you now fucker" Ted shouted, but there was something about the figure that made the psycho stop himself from crossing the room further. This was unknown territory, and he had no weapons. His compatriots continued to stare at the slime oozing across the floor. It was as if it was watching them, waiting to make a move.

"LOOK AND BELIEVE." The figure hissed the words. It lifted its right arm and pointed towards the Booths' huddled figures.

"LOOK AND BELIEVE." A hiss that shook the eardrums.

A trail of smoke crept out of the figure's sleeve. The air became dense and it felt like the room was vibrating, humming. The three friends stood completely still, mesmerised by the terrible sound and sight.

"LOOK AND BELIEVE." The figure slowly clenched its outstretched fingers into a fist, and as it did so the slime around the neck of Harry Booth began to visibly tighten. Booth tried to wriggle, but the slime encompassing the rest of his body tightened also, pinning him to the wall. The trio stood transfixed as Henry Booth's right eye popped out of his skull and rolled down his cheek. The slime engulfed the eyeball, pulling it greedily downwards; the stalk snapped with a noise like a rubber band being twanged. The pressure around Booth's head became too much. The life had already left his other eye when his head became detached from his neck and flew upwards to hit the basement ceiling and roll down to the dead body of his dog. Blood spattered the three men at the doorway.

The figure laughed a hideous yelp of delight.

"LOOK AND BELIEVE."

The trio didn't hang around to see the demise of the other Booths. They turned around, and for the first time in many years they fled in complete terror. The cackling behind them gradually diminished as they charged up the stairwell, out of the front door and into the night.

Clack, clack, clack. Nearly there. Ted snapped back into the present. This was something he didn't know anything about. Blacks, whites, asians, coppers, he'd given them all a pasting, but what the fuck was all this about? Still, he couldn't back out; his brother would never let him forget it.

Clack, clack, clack. He had his favourite toy. Brutus was what he called the baseball bat with two nine-inch nails hammered through the head. Just behind him Ned felt the cool grey metal of his sawn-off shotgun in his hands. That was just as likely to do the business.

Clack, clack, clack. Nearly there. The brothers slid around the corner, their backs to the wall.

The basement door had gone, with no visible sign of it ever having existed.

32

Frank wasn't very pleased.

He looked down at the prostrate figure of his wife, blood oozing out of every orifice, natural ones and also the new ones created by the vampire's fangs.

Frank had had better times.

Erupting into a fit of sobbing, he flew at Suzie's carcass, shook it a few times, checked the pulse and felt the flesh as the warmth began to drain out of it. He couldn't believe that his wife was dead, but the evidence was there, incontrovertible and plain to see.

Frank wasn't over the moon with joy.

He looked at the teethmarks: brutal, vicious bites, the blood still weeping from the incisions faster than the tears falling from his eyeballs. What nameless evil had happened? He stared at Susie's heavily pregnant belly, and prodded it a few times for signs of life.

An optimistic thought occurred to him. Maybe... just maybe...

Frank was somewhat cheesed off, but he hadn't lost it completely. Springing into action, he speedily dressed his wife's wounds with strips of rag which he tore from some clothes that were lying about. Although it was hard for him to admit it to himself, deep down he knew that his wife had been wasted: she was finished. But maybe the unborn child could still be saved? Suzie had been ready to give birth virtually at any minute. Perhaps, just perhaps, the baby could survive such an assault intact; could still exist alive inside its dead mother's womb. More in hope than expectation, Frank shot off to the nearest phone box to call an ambulance.

The fucking phone box didn't work!

It just wasn't Frank's day.

Rushing blindly to find another one, he ran across Amhurst Road towards Hackney Downs railway station. In his panic, he failed to notice the vehicle rushing towards him until it swerved, missing him by inches. The shock of the near miss caused Frank to lose his balance and fall over. The vehicle stopped and the driver got out.

"Are you alright, son?" asked the motorist. "You're lucky we didn't run you over there. Still, if you have to be run over by anything, I suppose an ambulance is the best sort of road traffic to do it."

Frank looked up at the vehicle. It was, indeed, an ambulance.

"'Ere mate," said Frank, "my wife's in a critical condition in the flat over there." He pointed in the appropriate direction. "It looks like she's been attacked by a vampire or something. I reckon an ambulance is just what she needs to take her off to a place of safety."

It had sunk in by now that Suzie was done for. Nevertheless he still held in his heart a little spark of hope for the unborn child. He couldn't be bothered to go into these details for the driver's benefit.

"You're in luck, son! As it happens, the assignment I was on my way to has just been cancelled, because another ambulance arrived there first. But getting your wife off to hospital will keep me busy, alright!"

Then, as if by magic, two medics flew out of the back of the ambulance carrying a stretcher between them. Frank led the crew to the flat and ushered them in. He pointed to his wife, lying limp and lifeless on the floor.

"She doesn't look too well to me!" said one of the medics. "I mean, I ain't a doctor or nothing, but I reckon she's dead."

"Well, I suppose we'd better get her carted off anyway" said the other medic, "after all, that's what we're paid for. She looks pretty dead, but you never know, she might in fact be alive!"

The two ambulance men hauled her up onto the stretcher and carried her into the back of the meat-wagon. Frank followed them and got in.

On the way to Homerton Hospital Accident and Emergency unit, Frank held his recently-deceased wife's wrists and caressed them gently. He felt so fucking guilty! He'd spent all afternoon shagging his beloved wife's mum, and now here was Suzie – slaughtered, victim of some horrendous, nameless atrocity! He'd betrayed her, and now he'd never be able to make it up to her.

He wasn't sure that he could live with the guilt. The thought of suicide assailed him briefly, then receded. He'd get religion, he decided. If this experience had taught him anything, it was that he should do something good with his life for a change. He'd start treating Edie okay, and see if he could help get her out of her appalling situation. If the baby survived, he'd treat it well, give it a good Christian upbringing, make sure it said its prayers, and steer it down the good Lord's highway. He'd start going to church at least once a week, and he'd do his best to convert everyone around him to the righteous path.

His musings were cut short as the wagon pulled up outside the hospital. The medics raced out bearing the stretcher and got Suzie inside where she was immediately wired up to an abundance of weird electrical machines, tubes, and gadgets with clock-style faces on them which measured something or other.

Frank waited at the reception, biting his nails nervously. He was preparing himself for the worst.

After a while a nurse came to see him. "What do you want first, the good news, or the bad news?" she asked him.

"The bad first," he replied.

"Okay, the bad news is that you're wife's dead. But the good news is that you're the father of a bouncing baby girl who appears to be in perfect health."

"Wow!" shouted Frank. "Praise the Lord!"

He was pleased. Maybe it wasn't such a bad day after all.

A little while later he met his daughter. He cradled her in his arms and rocked her to sleep. He was proud. He'd never had a baby before. He'd have to think of a name for her, he mused paternally, staring down lovingly at the baby. I know, he thought, I'll ask Edie to name it. The old lady would be sure to think of something decent.

Later on, after Suzie's funeral, Frank went to visit Edie in her flat at Seaton Point. She wasn't receptive to his suggestion that she should start going out occasionally, get some fresh air and go to church regularly. She was even more disgruntled when Frank refused to shag her, explaining that physical lust had to be overcome to make room for a more spiritual state of mind.

Edie didn't follow Frank's reasoning, but she was more than willing to name the baby.

Poppy!

A fitting name for a baby vampire – which was exactly what the infant was.

33 It was three in the morning. If anyone in the tower block had been up they would have heard a distant skittering, sniggering noise echoing up and down the stairwell. If a resident had been climbing the stairs, they may well have sensed the noise getting nearer and then receding. Maybe they may have felt something brush past them on the stairs, caught a glimpse of a shadow in the corner of their eye, and felt the presence of something evil lurking nearby. Perhaps they would have shivered and pulled up their collar hurrying for the relative safety of their abode. But nothing stirred save for the skittering, sniggering noise.

There was, however, action elsewhere in Seaton Point. In a secret room, the majority of its occupants not knowing how they'd got there, the guru session was still going – just. The beer mountain had lessened considerably since its miraculous appearance the previous morning.

The guru had let his prospective new recruits drink their fill during the afternoon and then watched as one by one each person had keeled over to sleep the sleep of the blitzed.

As they had gradually started to come round, Mick, who had an iron constitution, had taken round the cups of black coffee. Each recipient had slugged the cup's contents back in a single gulp, greedy for the liquid to take away their raging thirsts. The majority suffered the double kickback effect of caffeine bouncing on top of the DTs, the shaking of hands and sweating of foreheads visible to the guru.

After about half an hour the guru started his first lessons for his followers. Aggy, Kelly, Joolz, Maude, White Magic, Mick and Gerry all sat on the floor, Arthur and his executive chair excepted. They had watched in rapt attention as the guru traced diagrams, maps, features and runes in the air with his fingers. Like wisps of smoke the features hung in the air until the guru finished that particular subject, and then they disappeared.

Mick had found himself designated as unofficial lieutenant. The guru seemed to look to him to do bits of running around, or if someone started to get out of order, as they invariably did, to keep them in check. Mick still couldn't see what this assembly of reprobates could do about solving anything, let alone evil. And when Mick thought of evil he immediately thought of the basement that he had never returned to since the Booth boys incident. Something evil definitely lurked there. He started to mention it to the guru but the strange figure merely put his hand up and nodded as if knowing exactly what Mick was about to say. "That is something we must deal with" said the holyman.

During the session, people would occasionally nod off. At first Gerry, anxious to show off his new legs, would jump up and give them a sharp kick to wake them up, but as time drifted on Guru would put up his hand to make Gerry behave. He could see his followers were struggling to understand what he was trying to tell them. The gist of which was that they, the whole of Seaton Point, London, maybe England, the whole world even were in grave danger from evil forces.

Could these people ever understand? Could they ever care? One thing he knew was that they were quite happy here at the moment as the alcohol was still a long way from running out.

The shadow stopped briefly. The sniggering ceased. A form started to materialise on the tenth floor.

Orange vapour began to mill and flow around a focal point of red light, swirling faster and faster; the shape of the alchemist appeared. Six foot four and thin as a rake, he clenched and unclenched his long bony fingers and began to sniff the air, as would a dog homing in on a scent. He suppressed another giggle. There was another presence not too far away. He could feel it. An aura of some strength was lurking somewhere, becoming more powerful the further he ascended the tower, and it was definitely a white presence. A goody goody presence.

The alchemist huffed and spat on the floor in disgust. Good? There was no good in this 200 foot-tall pile of shit. Seaton Point was full of the dregs of human existence. That was what had attracted him to the place in the first instance.

"Must seek out," the character giggled to himself.

The alchemist started pacing up and down the corridor, sniffing at each letterbox. At one particular flat, a dog launched itself at the letterbox with a savage snapping of teeth and a thump as it collided with the inside of the locked door. The alchemist emitted a high-pitched squeak of surprise and fell backwards onto the floor as the dog carried on barking and growling. The alchemist picked himself up, and with a look of venom in his eyes lifted the flap of the letterbox and spat a greenish jet through the gap. A squeal could be heard from the other side of the door, together with the sound of Fang's rapid retreat up Mick's hallway, scattering empty beer cans everywhere.

Not realising that he had come across this creature before, the alchemist realised that the white aura was coming from further up the block of flats, and he resumed his climbing of the stairs, muttering to himself. It wasn't long before he reached the fifteenth floor and parked himself outside Malcolm's flat. This was the one, he sensed instinctively.

On the other side of the door, the drink had begun flowing again.

"Of course I blame the darkies meself" shouted Arthur.

"Oi!" Mick shouted back at him, "are you having a pop?"

"Present company excepted" replied Arthur in a massive U-turn.

"You're talking rubbish man" slurred White Magic. "Everyone knows it's aliens running this planet."

"That's plain stupid" Aggy replied through her mouthful of metal. Kelly snoozed on.

Mick and Gerry had reached the point where conversation was meaningless and were engaged in the more useful pastime of Slaps. That is, they took turns slapping each other around the face, each slap gradually getting harder until someone gave in. The pair were too far gone for their own good and the left cheeks of both were glowing red like a traffic light on a foggy night.

"STOP." The guru's shout made everyone jump. "WE ARE UNDER ATTACK."

"This blokes's a nutter ain't ee?" shouted Arthur.

"Yes, I like him" Maude replied.

Guru pointed towards the door which had begun to glow as red as Mick and Gerry's cheeks. He opened his eyes wide and a beam of white light shot from his gaze and onto the door itself. A battle appeared to be going on between red and white, a flashing magical lightshow. The room shuddered and lurched, spilling cans and plastic bottles across the floor and setting off more screams.

Sweat started running down the guru's furrowed brow as his intense gaze remained fixed upon the door. There was another shudder, then a scream, and finally silence. The room settled down and the guru's gaze softened.

"You beat them boss" shouted Mick, running towards the door.

90

"NOT I."

Thuds, thumps and shouts became audible from outside. The door opened to reveal the figure of the alchemist rolled into a ball, squeaking little shrieks of shock whilst being booted rather vigorously by the burly figures of the Barber twins. Ted, the shorter, was laying in hardest while Big Ned stood back a bit, a baseball bat on his shoulder, smiling an evil grin and adding just the occasional kick. Both were too engrossed to notice Guru or that the door had opened.

"I told you we'd have that fucking weirdo" Ted screamed, putting the boot in again. "No one beats Ned and Ted." The alchemist squealed once more.

"I think we've got our stormtroopers, boss" said Mick, smiling a rancid grin at the guru.

"Alright Mick, want a go?" said Ned, looking up from his work. "'Ang on, who's that?" he added, pointing to the floating figure next to the bricklayer.

"PLEASE COME INSIDE."

"Fancy a drink?" said Mick.

At this, Ted paused from administering the vicious kicking. "Well, since your bloody dog woke me up at this time of night, I might as well" he spat. "Still, did me a favour. Caught this bastard sniffing round the door, doing some sort of hocus pocus. He was so into what he was doing, he never noticed us sneak up on him."

The twins glanced down, preparing to have another go at the alchemist, but the bundle had disappeared.

"Am I dreaming or has the world gone mad?" Ned spoke slowly and to no one in particular.

The twins entered the strange room and stared at the drunken, frightened inhabitants and the even stranger robe-clad figure hovering in the corner who smiled at them benignly. The situation was so bizarre that they didn't even notice that Gerry was up and walking towards them with a can in each hand.

Meanwhile the stairwells of Seaton Point returned to the quiet of early morning, except for a whining and whimpering sound echoing down on its way towards the basement.

34 When Lee Christo alighted from the altar on which his immaculate oak-and-brass casket – his resting-place during the long and tedious hours of daylight – itself rested, it was the first thing that caught his bleary eye, sitting there on the doormat, appearing to twinkle or perhaps even glitter a little. Sometime during the day it must have been dropped through the letterbox of St. Terry's church of the seventh apocalypse: a crudely-handprinted leaflet. An invitation. It read:

DEMOLITION BLUES PARTY ON THE NIGHTINGALE ESTATE!
COME ONE, COME ALL!!

SAFE TUNES, SOULFOOD AND DANCING!; NO DOGS.
@ 79 SEATON POINT, SATURDAY.
MIDNITE ONWARDS: BE THERE!!

Well, the desk-top publishing was OK but photocopying was still photocopying, whatever your tawdry pretensions might be. It lacked any vestige of style, Lee thought. Maybe he could go along and teach them a thing or two about panache, about charisma: after all, wasn't that what life was all about? Life and other things, he grinned wickedly and silently to himself, licking his crimson-stained lips as he strained to focus on the handbill through his awakening head and his bloodied, sleep-encrusted eyelashes.

Blokey had gone away for a bit to visit his parents, and Lee had welcomed the opportunity to spend a few days in male mode.

"Midnite onwards." The vampire wiggled his eyebrows, eyebrows that strangely met in the middle. That was certainly his time, his domain. "Midnite onwards." As it happened, he thought that he might even be able to teach them a few tricks when it came to that too, a few stay-up-until-dawn party animal techniques that were all his own. On Saturday night. Yes, yes, he might well be there. In high spirits following his bloodletting binge that had lasted all the way through to the previous dawn, he felt himself to be very much in a party mood. And the notion of 'soulfood' sounded good to him too.

Lee Christo got up early the next day, which was Saturday; early for him that is, having set his alarm to go off and wake him as soon as it were properly dark: he owned a specially-made clock designed for this specific purpose, imported with no expense being spared from Transplant Ltd and acquired through a discreet little novelties-and-curios operation that he knew of all the way over in Cricklewood, West London. The body of the clock housed three separate light sensors which, in their individual turns, had to come into perfect alignment with the disappearance of direct sunlight before the chime would sound out the dulcet tones of the death march, which to Lee was the most beautiful way imaginable to start the night. Start as you mean to go on, he would often think to himself upon waking. The mechanism could distinguish between artificial light and the rays of the sun, and this seemed to be a trick that only the artisan clock manufacturers of Transplant knew.

He spent the next three hours metamorphosing himself from Lee Christo into Miss Tululah Climax, weird nightclub dancer and dusky gothbabe extraordinaire. This necessitated much getting made-up after first selecting the best possible outfit for the best possible night. She chose a glittering and immaculately-sequinned black velvet gown, sparkling black high-heeled shoes and a pair of black satin gloves that reached all the way up to her elbows. Tululah knew that there was something in the air tonight, as Phil Collins had once prophesied: she could literally smell it through her now-flaring nostrils as the transmogrification that was burgeoning within her grew ever-more powerful and complete. Yes, tonight was going to be THE night: HER night.

When Tululah arrived at the Nightingale estate demolition party, the joint was certainly jumping. The party flat was resplendently thick with stripes of blue-purple-red smoke, if this were possible, cut through with a succession of immaculately timed and primed stroboscopic light-projectors to great effect. It was some contrast to the outside world of the nightmare Nightingale estate that she had experienced on her way over from St. Terry's. Riding the piss-stenched elevator up to the twentieth floor with its accompanying ripped plastic sacks leaking rotten eggshells, chinese takeaways and bacon rinds made eerie by the flickering overhead artificial illumination was the least of it. Not that Tululah was particularly averse to artificial lighting: it was far preferable to the other sort, she thought to herself with a wry smirk whilst simultaneously considering what possible joys the next few hours might have in store for her.

Half-way across the podium-cum-square that led up, on and into the beacon that was Seaton Point, her pristine appearance had not gone entirely unnoticed:

"ALRIGHT BLOSSOM, HOW'S IT GOING THEN? COME OVER 'ERE, I THINK I'VE GOT SOMETHING FOR YOU."

With much decorum and sass, Tululah had thrown both her head and her hair back devilishly, and merely continued walking without having missed a beat. And then:

"OKAY BABY, IT'S YOUR LOSS!"

Finally she had reached the door of the block, put her hand through the gap where a panel had been kicked out a few days earlier, and reached for the plate that would allow her to gain access. Squatting on her hairless haunches, she felt a little nervous, or at least self-conscious at this point. It was only in riding the even-numbers lift up to floor twenty that she wondered how it was that she'd somehow known that this had recently become the easiest way to get into Seaton Point.

Tululah rapped at the door with a tribalistic, rapid staccato beat. The knocker was fashioned into the design of a grinning skull-and-crossbones and apparently grafted from solid gold: very fetching. She looked down impatiently at her stilettos as she waited for attention. Then after about three minutes somebody came to the door.

"Hey, I'm Maxwell, come on in and shake it!"

Maxwell was white, about six foot two tall and had two or three of his teeth gold-capped. Tululah had never seen a white man with his teeth capped in gold before. He wore a dirty grey boiler suit, paint-splattered German paratrooper boots with the toes all scuffed, and his hair in braided, beaded dreadlocks that seemed to be held together loosely with random twists of electrical wire. He grinned at Tululah like an idiot for a few moments, then stepped back and waved her past him, on into the flat.

Tululah grabbed an already-opened bottle of chilled white wine as she passed a table that positively bristled and shook uncontrollably with alcohol, and immediately ensconced herself in a dark corner where she stood alone; leaning against the wall seductively in the shadows, taking occasional pulls of ice-cold wine straight from the bottle. She could instinctively feel numerous pairs of eyes upon her, many of them crawling up her hairless inner thighs with much undisguised tactility. Eventually, after about ten minutes had elapsed, the owner of two of the eyes plucked up enough courage to actually approach her and speak:

"Parties," said the mouth that was about two inches below them, "are the final desperate concretization of our alienation under capital!"

'TWAT', Tululah thought to herself, but her speech belied her true and innermost thoughts. She parried his opening lob with:

"There are parties and there are parties, cuntface. And then," she added almost as an afterthought, "then there are parties!"

"I'm Billy" the man told her, "but I'm not childish."

Tululah just yawned.

"You give me life," he continued, "please don't let me go: you crush the lily in my soul!"

Kate Bush. thought Tululah, astounded; now the bastard's quoting Kate Bush at me. Another man came over to where they were standing. It was Maxwell.

"Hi, House" he said to the first man, whose name was apparently House. "Tonight," he whispered into House's left ear in a hushed and conspiratorial tone, "tonight we burn the palace!"

"THE palace?" asked House.

Maxwell nodded, grinning away to the pair of them with a distinct air of smug authority. "Yes," he finally said. "Chat's Palace."

The party wore on as parties invariably do, with people falling into their various states of stupor, unconsciousness and foul sexual depravity in no particular order. Then, at about three in the morning, Maxwell announced that the time for revolution had finally arrived:

"I've got the petrol!" he suddenly screamed. "Let's go! NOW!!"

Immediately House and three other shady-looking characters jumped up from their previous prostrate positions on the flat's rather ropey living-room floor. Then Maxwell made a bolt for the front door – that is to say that he ran towards it, as opposed to his suddenly becoming some kind of a locksmith. He was carrying a large and sturdy-looking plastic carrier bag that evidently contained a can of petrol, and which certainly stank as though it did. House was carrying a length of rope for some sinister reason. The other three shifty individuals just looked like bog-standard bug-eyed junkies to Tululah, and very probably they were. Tululah didn't care. Things were finally beginning to get a little bit interesting on the Nightingale estate. As Maxwell reached the front door he turned to face the vampire.

"Are you in?" he asked her. Tululah just smiled as she walked toward him. She was in.

Thirty minutes later the six of them were walking down Brooksby's Walk, E9. The streets were deserted but the bug-eyed junkies still seemed to be making themselves useful as lookouts, darting their heads this way and that and resembling moderately shifty ferrets. They had cut through the hospital grounds and then, suddenly, like a long-awaited sunrise, they stood facing the front of Chat's Palace, the world-famous arts centre.

"We'd better find a way in around the back" whispered Maxwell to the others. "I don't care much for the front."

"FIND A WAY IN??" said Tululah incredulously. "Didn't you even bother to do any reconnaissance? Any research at all?"

"No," House told her. "The revolution will be an entirely spontaneous event. Now come here and help me get over these railings!"

Tululah frowned, then moved forward and bent her body in such a way that House could climb onto her and then jump safely and even fairly quietly over the railings. After she had performed the same favour for each of the four others she found that she could easily slip between the railings: she was a very lithe person and sideways limbo dancing was only one of her many special skills. Then the six conspirators crept stealthily round to the back of the building.

After about five minutes of shuffling around in the darkness, Maxwell made another one of his announcements.

"I think I've found our way in, comrades!" he told them all. He was fiddling with a tiny, barred toilet window, a large hacksaw and a butter-spreading knife. You know, one of those old ones with the yellow mock-ivory handles that always look somehow nicotine-stained. My granny had some. There was a clack and a clatter and then three of the five bars were out of the way.

"I think I'd better do this bit, eh boys?" Tululah said, raising eyebrows that nobody could see in the pitch-blackness; but she knew they were there. She could feel them, wiggling about. She approached the tiny space and entered it with ease. Only halfway through did she stop to ask the others:

"Pardon me guys, I really don't wish to appear nosey or anything, but why exactly do you want to burn down Chat's Palace?"

"It's quite a complicated story, really" explained House. "I'll tell you all about it later. We'd better get inside now before some square bastard peers over their garden fence or something."

Tululah had little trouble in locating the famous venue's beer cellar and through it, the trap door into the back yard where the others waited for her return; three of them nervously, and the other two apparently not quite so much so. Maxwell and House were obviously battle-hardened revolutionaries. Tululah let them all in anyway, regardless of their political status.

One of the bug-eyed junkies had come along equipped with a torch-cum-rubber-cosh, which he duly used to illuminate their merry way to revolutionary destruction. When they went into the bar, they happened across the comatosed form of Nutter Nigel, the anarchist revolutionary squatting organiser who ran the top floors of Seaton Point with an iron hand. He was sleeping curled up in the foetal position and an emptied three-litre bottle of Jack Daniels lay cradled in his arms, dribbling its last few droplets of amber oblivion onto the fag-burned carpet.

House crouched down close over the prostrate and unfeeling form of Nutter Nigel and proceeded to rifle through the pockets of his imitation leather jacket to see if there was anything worth having inside. After some sifting through credit-card balance statements, he eventually found an enormous bunch of keys hanging from a gigantic iron hook.

"These'll come in handy, I don't doubt!" he beamed.

"Now will somebody please fill me in on exactly what the crack is here?" Tululah demanded, her head cocked demandingly to one side. Even under pressure, she was still the undisputed mistress of innuendo.

"Well," House began, "Nutter Nigel here is Mr. Anarchy in Hackney, and has been for many years. He also claims to be Mr. Straight-Edge around here, but as soon as he thinks nobody's looking he reaches for the bottle like the rest of us, as you can see." House paused to point at Nutter Nigel's somnolent form. "He organises an anarchist bingo evening at Chat's Palace every last Saturday of the month, and appears to take advantage of the bar stocks afterwards."

"No, I don't mean that," Tululah said. "I mean why do you want to burn this place to the ground?"

"Ah! Maxwell chimed in, right on cue. It was as if everything had been scripted, as if the whole of world history had already been written, every little tiny bit; as though they were merely acting out their minuscule predetermined roles. And maybe it was true as well. Tululah went on:

"So. Why, then?"

"Well," Maxwell explained, "in the evil psychic doom-wars of the time before time began, there was this exceedingly fierce battle waged right on the eventual site of the Nightingale estate, betwixt the forces of light and darkness."

"BETWIXT?" Tululah asked.

"Yeah," Maxwell continued. "Anyway, at this time these evil demons were sealed into a vault underneath the inevitable and – of course – predetermined site of Seaton Point because the forces of light were victorious – or at least they thought they were." Maxwell grinned. "Seaton Point is situated on a leyline. So is the church on the estate, St. Terry's church of the seventh apocalypse, as is Chat's Palace here. Now, after the passing of several millenia, the demons are beginning to break free,

free from their imposed darkness and out into the light so that they may spread their evil through the world once more. The essence of the demon travels constantly up and down through the lift-shaft, spreading evil, right? Now, we have reason to believe that one of the demons has reached the disused lift shaft inside Seaton Point, although it's been so long that the entity probably can't even remember who or what it is. So that we can seal the demon in before it is too late, in order to save the earth, we have to burn down the Palace, to redress the psychic balance of the leyline. You see?"

Tululah saw. She saw that there was maybe more than straightforward anarchist-communist-revolutionary politics in action here, straight-edge or otherwise.

"OK," Tululah said. "Where's the fuel?"

"I got it!" Maxwell exclaimed. He pulled a rusty old paraffin tin-can from his carrier bag and began splashing it around on the floor. Then he ran into the other rooms and splashed it all around the floors in those too. He even managed to do the screen-printing workshop. Finally, he led a trail upstairs and into the office and then returned downstairs, grinning.

"Let's go!" he said.

The five of them crept back out into the yard of the community-based entertainments venue, with Maxwell laying a final trail of his volatile fluid out into the alley and all the way round to the railings adjacent to the front of the building. It was 5 AM, and the darkness of the long night of soul was beginning to ebb its way out into a deep blue colour. Up above the stars were twinkling, but some of them were now fading from view in the encroaching light and warmth of the impending new dawn, and Maxwell's eyes were aching from lack of sleep and stinging from the petrol fumes. Tululah noticed the change in tone of the night sky and began to feel a little nervous; she scratched at her forearms and her bollocks impatiently:

"Come ON!" she intoned to the others. "Let's get THE FUCK out of here!!"

And so, one by one, the revolutionary crack unit, arson division, made their way out over the railings in the same way that they had gotten in over them scarcely an hour earlier. Finally Maxwell reached into the top pocket of his combat jacket and found a book of 'AK PRESS REVOLUTIONARY STARTER KIT' matches. He lit one and threw it through the railings at the puddle that was the last of his petrol, and then they all turned on their heels and ran like bloody fuck back towards Homerton Row.

And Nutter Nigel never stirred, nor batted an eyelid as the fierce fires of Chat's Palace ablaze lit up the skyline for some miles around. Two sunrises could now be seen projected against the East London skyline: it was all very pretty and the firemen were just getting out of bed and having their cornflakes and stewed tea. The Palace never stood a chance and neither did Nutter Nigel.

Tululah just made it back to her coffin in St. Terry's church of the seventh apocalypse before the first beams of sunlight could burn the exposed parts of her exhausted body, and then she slept the sleep of the contented and the accomplished, with a new reason to awake the following night. Something interesting had finally happened in Hackney.

35 The alchemist's face still frazzled a crimson red as he leant over the cauldron, stirring feverishly. The embarrassment of it – getting done over in his own tower block!
Sheepishly, he lifted a bony hand to his head and tilted his hat forward. He winced as his nails connected with the large bump on the back of his head. The shame! A pair of brain-dead thugs with heads like baked potatoes had done this to HIM, in Seaton Point of all places. During the couple of days since the incident he had thought long and hard about how this could have happened, and he had come to the conclusion that height had been the major factor in his downfall.

Down here in his basement lair, he could feel the power surging through his system like electricity through the national grid, shooting around his nervestream and crackling at his fingertips. But the further up the monolithic tower he went, the less control of his powers he seemed to possess. Outside of his dungeon domain, he felt less confident about his plans for world domination. In a nutshell, the higher up he went the less power he had.

That ungrateful muppet Malcolm: the bare-faced cheek of it. Some idiot who had wandered like a lost child into Seaton Point, drawn by the psychic probes that the alchemist himself had sent around London's surrounding towns. He'd given the prat all of his pathetic powers in the first place. Okay, so the guru – the alchemist sniggered at the thought of the word – probably couldn't remember that it was he who had told him to recruit followers. But to make a stand against his creator – that was the limit. He would have to pay.

"One problem though. How to get him down here, or me up there" he muttered aloud in his high hysterical voice.

GLOOP. Another large dose of yoghurt was sucked from the cauldron, through the tube and away. Exactly where it was going, the alchemist could still not be sure. It was strange that he felt impelled to produce this stuff, but his magickal senses told him that it was having an effect **somewhere** in Seaton Point; an effect that hopefully would induce fear and dread in the rest of humanity when it was released into the world. The latest portion having been sent off to its unknown destination, the alchemist pushed his cauldron aside and looked down to consider the fire that flickered constantly from the hole beneath it.

It wasn't working. Something was wrong. Sweat poured from the alchemist's brow, stinging his eyes and filling his lower lip with salty moisture. He drew the edge of the velvet curtain across his forehead for the umpteenth time, raised his arms above his head and then plunged them downwards dramatically. Skeletal fingers adorned by vicious, yellowed nails pointed to the hole smashed into the floor of the basement.

"Shadrach icum vastas Belial. Istus darracam daemonicus daeum."

The alchemist hissed the words under his breath. His eyes shone with an unholy phosphorescence, and drool and sweat dribbled from his chin.

"Shadrach icum vastas Belial. Dominus darracam daemonicus daeum. Madariatza Das Perifa Liil Cabisa Micalazoda Saanire Caosago."

The air swirled around his head and the pages of the ancient book that lay at his feet fluttered back and forth, but nothing came through the hole below him save the constant incandescence of the flame.

The alchemist staggered to the left, exhaustion wracking his body. Leaning backwards, the icy sweat on his back touched the lining of the old leather jacket that covered his wiry frame, causing him to breathe in sharply as a cold sensation ran up his spine. It wasn't working.

He knew the stories, legends and myths of this site. He had read the writings of St. Terry himself. Texts that only the highest magickal initiates or most psychically endowed could find, let alone decipher and understand. Those texts told of ancient battles that scarred the landscape of a forgotten land now known as Britain. An age of forests haunted by elves, boggarts and wolf packs. An age when daemons and gods straddled the land and fought battles in the skies. An age where dragons dwelt within mountains sucking energy from the leylines and hiding unbelievable riches mined by dwarven races scared shitless. An age where the hominid primates were no more than downtrodden slaves to the higher creatures that existed all around.

Some of those creatures still existed: this the alchemist knew. But he could not reach them. There was too much shit going down in this tower of power.

"Solutions must be more drastic than dramatic" he told himself. "Wipe out the scummy third-class residents above, and make an edifice, a beacon for the powers that lurk below. Perhaps then the incantations might work."

An idea came to the alchemist.

"Heat. Heat rises. Fire. Fire causes heat, causes light, causes death, causes pain."

It was exactly what the alchemist was into – fire! Heat! Death! Pain! And for no simple gratuitous purpose – for in the course of conjuring these elements, he would summon the daemon! In a flash, he sensed psychically that his conjuring trick would have to go up through the yoghurt tube.

He chuckled insanely and at great length. He kept shouting to himself:

"Fire! Fire! Fire!"

SEATON POINT

36 Ian found his regular space two rows from the front of the cinema, dead centre, and put his feet up over the empty seats in front of him. It was comfortable stuff. The screen was as yet still a dull blank sunset-rose colour and there was mostly a low, easy silence and calm all around him. In the row behind a man and a woman were discussing early-eighties chart pop music.

"Yeah, man, IT'S AN ILLUSION it was called. I can't remember the rest of the words but it was a really sexy number, you know? All smooth and slow and dripping with god-knows-what!"

The man began to cackle maniacally. It was pretty irritating. Why couldn't people just shut up?

"I don't know what it was dripping with, man, you know? But it was certainly dripping with something. What was the guy's name, now? I think it began with an 'L', yeah, I'm sure it did! Can't think of it for the life of me now, though. Damn!"

My god, Ian thought, these people are complete imbeciles! Not only do they remember the title of the song incorrectly, but they can't recall anything further than the geezer's first initial! They ought to be stabbed!! Ian had a touch of the DTs coming on by now. Then the woman spoke:

"It doesn't matter. Hey, did you hear about Jeannie and Io over in design and planning? It's all over the building! Every single lunchtime when the rest of their section are out at the cafes or wherever, they're at it hammer and tongs in that stationery cupboard they've got in there now!"

"What, the new one, you mean?"

"Yeah, you got it." The woman was munching away at a large bag of sugary popcorn. Half-chewed chunks of the popcorn mixed with her saliva fell from her mouth and onto her chin, jumper and overcoat as she talked. She brushed the crumbs from her clothes like a bison attempting to swat the flies on its back with its tail, and continued talking undeterred:

"Yeah man, he's got this wife and kids up there in the country too, innit? Chah! Disgustin'!"

Suddenly a man came charging down the right-hand side of the seats at great speed. He looked as though he might run straight through the wall and out into the street, causing chaos amongst the midday traffic. He wore the uniform sweatshirt of the RIO cinema. Ian sat up and removed his feet from the seats in front of him. Just as he was about to connect with the wall, the man threw his heels forward and skidded to a halt amid a flurry of dust like somebody in a 'Roadrunner' TV cartoon show. He turned to face the theatre-goers and began jumping up and down in the air:

"LADIES AND GENTLEMEN, PLEASE MOVE TOWARDS THE MIDDLE OF THE CINEMA! COULD EVERYBODY PLEASE MOVE INTO THE CENTRE SEATS NOW!!" he screamed.

There were very few people in the cinema. Somebody else, also wearing a uniform

100

sweatshirt, walked up to him and whispered something into his left ear.

"Oh," said the first cinema employee, rather less audibly than before; "sorry!" Then he commenced screaming again:

"LADIES AND GENTLEMEN, WE REGRET TO ANNOUNCE AN UNAVOIDABLE ALTERATION TO TODAY'S VIEWING PROGRAMME! INSTEAD OF 'FOUR ROOMS' WE WILL NOW INSTEAD BE SHOWING THE 1958 CLASSIC, 'THE BRIGHTON BLOODSUCKER'! THANK YOU VERY MUCH!"

He jumped into the air once more, turning to his left as he landed, then put his head down and charged back out of the theatre.

"Chah!" said the woman with the cascading popcorn sitting just behind Ian.

The lights in the cinema dimmed and the film began. Ian slouched back in his seat and draped his legs over the backs of the seats in front of him again, bending at the knees and getting as comfortable as he could.

The opening titles rolled across the screen accompanied by an old car rolling along country lanes, cascading and careering through the Devon countryside. There was sweet, happy music, and from the back seat of the car came the sound of children singing. Then they began to argue: one of the kids claimed to have seen the sea before the other, and vice versa, but there was neither violence nor tears, only a surreal utopian innocence more often imagined and implied than actually experienced.

The titles ebbed into the distant sea, the music faded and the idyllic vista was replaced with the scene of a small, dimly-lit hovel. A man had an old woman pinned against one of the damp and peeling walls by her wrists, and there was much grunting and pushing and an apparent struggle going on. The camera panned in onto their faces but the terror was all his, it all belonged to the apparent aggressor. The woman's countenance was stretched into a grotesque mocking leer; she looked as though she had been dead for some time as she cackled her fetid breath out at him through her toothless gums. Her skull seemed swollen and her skin was a taut, creased and shiny yellow, the yellow of jaundice, and she wore a ragged nightdress. They were fucking, and there was a great and hopeless sadness to their act. Then it was finally over and they parted and collapsed onto a single bare mattress in their parallel heaps. The man seemed to be silently sobbing and the woman's mouth was closed now, but the deathliness was still there. Dry drool was caked onto her rancid chin as she reached for a box of cigarettes that lay next to the mattress. They each lit a cigarette and the room quickly filled with smoke as that scene faded out too.

It had been quite violent and very fast by 1958 standards. Ian scratched the top of his head vigorously, trying to get a grip on the plot.

A new scene came into view: it was a damp alleyway and a man had approached the door to a nightclub, attempting to gain admittance. He was swathed in tight-fitting black rags and a dapper coat-and-tails, and on his feet there was a pair of shoes that had seen much better days. The man's overgrown toenails poked through holes in the shoes and even though it was a dark scene in an old film, Ian knew that they were made of snakeskin. Maybe it was a subconscious recognition of the genre, he thought to himself. The man ran the fingers of one hand through slicked-back hair as he argued with a penguin-suited doorman over the contents of a carrier-bag that he bore. Ian wondered whether they even had carrier-bags in 1958. They probably did, he decided.

"I don't care who you are mate," the doorman was saying, "you can't bring no yoghurts in 'ere!"

"Pah! Beelzebub will curse ye!" the would-be nightclubber replied.

"I tell you what then, give me the bag and I'll put it in the cloakroom and give you a ticket, alright? Okay? You can collect it on the way out like it were yer coat! The boss says that we need all the quality clientele we can get!"

Reluctantly resigned to this compromise, the man in the snakeskin shoes paid his entry fee and edged his way past the surly bouncers. As he did this he looked up, raising his eyebrows.

"Gold's a-coming!", he exclaimed.

"Cunt," muttered the head doorman.

Inside the club there was pounding house music and a live stage show. A woman who somehow did not look quite right but who nevertheless had an intensely charismatic air that was quite beyond description was up there, singing "THERE'LL BE BLUE BIRDS OVER/ THE WHITE CLIFFS OF DOVER/ TOMORROW/ JUST YOU WAIT AND SEE" in perfect time to some banging techno. She was immaculately decked out in a glittering sequinned gown, and perched on her shoulder was a bright yellow rubber duck with eyes that glowed a malevolent crimson colour into the surrounding darkness: the duck was a menacing thing to behold.

This aside, the man in the snakeskin shoes felt that it was his kind of a place. The dancefloor was swamped and heaving with sweaty bodies dancing furiously to the music as if there were no tomorrow, all loved-up and wearing their demob suits and trilby hats. He reached around to the secret back pocket of his coat-and-tails to check for his cake of soap: it was there. He had gotten it in past the stupid penguins with ease. Ian yawned and rubbed his nose as the film went on.

The man in the lift awoke suddenly, rubbing his nose with the palm of his hand and then scratching his scalp furiously. The lights had not as yet come on but he had an excruciatingly painful stomach cramp, which doubled him upright with a force that he had not felt before. He was itching and aching all over his body and he felt, for some reason, that he badly needed some yoghurt.

37 The alchemist had been busy at his work. The cramped dungeon had become crammed with steel drums which all bore the yellow stencilled wording of 'Hackney Borough Council' on their sides. He had spirited them away from a council depot in the dead of night. Most were empty and rusting though some held chemicals of a noxious nature that the alchemist hadn't bothered to decipher. A spell of moderate complexity had caused the required drums to stand to the magician's attention, then the drums clanked and danced in a row behind the skipping madman. The alchemist cast another spell of invisibility and darkness to cloak the bizarre goings on and a stern look of admonishment persuaded the canisters following him to make their movements as quiet as possible.

The strange procession paused just once on Hackney Downs for the drums which contained toxins to pour their contents, on command, into a pond surrounded by deathly looking trees. The next day the local rag ran a front page story on the wanton vandalism that had caused the death of every single fish and duck that had inhabited the pond. By that time the cast-iron conga was back safely beneath Seaton Point.

From that time forth, the alchemist had toiled 24 hours a day in the making of the chemicals that he required, while the yoghurt-like substance continued to emanate from its source and ooze through its tube out of the basement. The steel drums contained cyanide, sulphur, petrol, home-made dynamite, ammonia and chlorine. Seaton Point had to become a beacon for the daemons that would help him to take over the world. They would rise from the flames he stoked and make him one of their own.

The access points for the mayhem were within easy reach. Near to the basement was the bottom of the liftshaft where the council engineers checked occasionally to see that all of the mechanisms were in full working order. It was also an emergency escape route if anyone became trapped in the liftshaft. This thought made the alchemist giggle once more: "Hee, hee, hee."

The bottom of the shaft was strewn with rubbish. The lift engineers only came in once in a blue moon. The council didn't give a fuck about the residents of Seaton Point. Most of them were nutters, and the sane ones didn't pay their rent anyway.

The alchemist got six canisters of petrol and smothered them with the correct quantity of his home made TNT, of which he was very proud. All he had to do when the time was right was to climb unseen to a position above the lift and cut through the cables, sending the lift plummeting to meet the canisters below. BOOM!

Near to his concealed basement there was also the air conditioning room. Air conditioning wasn't quite the right phrase: here, the ducts met the old boilers which used to send heat throughout the building during the seventies, but this system had long since become defunct. The air ducts still led to the heating vents in the flats above, and behind the giant boilers the alchemist had concealed two canisters of

TNT and many more of his concocted cyanide, sulphur, ammonia and chlorine. Together, these would send a deadly cloud of cyanide and mustard gas into every flat in the tower block.

After depositing his canisters, the alchemist tiptoed back to his lair, delighted by the end product of his week's work, sniggering every step of the way. Raising his right arm in front of him, he traced the outline of a door onto the bare concrete wall. Blue hazy light appeared where his index finger nail had scratched into the surface. A door appeared in front of the still giggling figure and through the portal he went, to sleep the well-earned sleep of the wicked, and dream of his plan.

In the flats above, residents stirred in their sleep and reached over to clutch their partners to them, shuddering at the sudden chill that had crept up their bodies and sent shivers through their hearts.

38 Yet another appointment at Seaton Point! The bailiff couldn't believe it! What was it that brought him back time and time again to work at the tower block where his assistants lived?

Not long out of hospital, Stan hadn't yet had his doctor's orders to go back to work. He still needed a crutch to help him to stay upright, and he wouldn't have been surprised if this new assignment – another squat eviction, referred to him by the council – was a further wind-up attempt by the dice man. To be on the safe side, he resolved to carry with him his new acquisition – a shooter, procured specially for the purpose of settling the score with Blokey, the bastard who'd nearly crippled him for life.

Stan limped into the van and drove to the Nightingale Estate. Cautiously, he pulled up outside Seaton Point where he met Ned and Ted.

Ned glanced around excitedly, looking after Stan's shooter while the boss went through the eviction papers. It was only Stan's third job since getting out of hospital. As a self-employed bailiff, he didn't get sick pay and needed regular work so that he could pay his mortgage. Reluctantly, the beleaguered bailiff had to get on with it and resume his duties.

"Right, boys" said Stan. "We're gonna do over flat 60 on the 15th floor! Ready to roll?"

"Flat 60?" replied Ted, a bit nervously. A surprised look appeared on Ned's face.

"You got it!" said Stan, not noticing the hesitancy in his assistants' expressions. "Let's get the tools and get on with it! I'm still a bit shaky after my recent accident, so it would be better if you two got the works from the back of the van while I sit here and conserve my energy. Hop to it, boys!"

The twins did as they were told, but used the time inaudible to their boss to hold an impromptu conversation.

"'Ere, Ted," said Ned, "ain't number 60 where Brother Malcolm hangs out? We can't fuckin' evict 'im!"

"Yeah mate, yer fuckin' right! Malcolm's the guvnor, ain't 'e? "'E's the geezer who says straight up that he's gonna give us supernatural powers kinda fing, to make us even harder than we are already. Ain't that spot on?"

"Too fuckin' right it is. So what are we fuckin' gonna do, then?"

"I spose we'll afta go along with the gaffer and see what 'appens, like, play it by ear, know what I mean? We can't just refuse to do it, like, I don't wanna go back on the fuckin' dole! On the other 'and, like, I don't fink we got the powers to evict the guvnor from his flat anyway, cos he's, like, holy, innee, know what I mean? He'll soon sort aht anyone who tries to knock 'im off 'is fuckin' perch."

"Yeah, Malcolm's an alright sort of a geezer, ain't 'e? "'E'll understand the problem, like, he'll suss out that it's some kind of a fuckin' mistake. 'E'll put Stan straight, like, and it'll all work aht won't it?"

"Spose so," said Ted. "Alright, let's get the gaffer and fuckin' get up there!"

The trio got to it. Stan limped along, walking stick in one hand, shooter in the other, the twins propping him up when necessary.

They reached the ground floor of Seaton Point. And then: an apparition assailed them!

Translucent green and pink bubbles appeared from nowhere, floating in strange spiral patterns, growing by turns larger, then smaller as if they were breathing in and out. Weird wisps of acrid, ancient-smelling yellow and black smoke hissed out of the stairwell like gas from a pipe that had just sprang a leak. Mocking laughter echoed around the hallway, louder and louder and seemingly from several different sources. Large transparent test tubes full of a clear but glutinous liquid grew up from the floor like grotesque glass plants. Small red eggs floated down from the ceiling: each egg found itself a test tube and submerged itself into the sticky liquid. At once, the eggs grew into big red ripe tomatoes, absorbing the fluid, expanding quickly until they were too big for their tubes; the tubes exploded, sending showers of shattered glass cascading through the air. The tomatoes melted; a sea of viscous red goo oozed across the floor and rose until it was up to the transfixed bailiffs' ankles. They couldn't move. And then, amidst the supernatural chaos, a further apparition – the alchemist, floating magically up from the basement through the concrete floor.

"Hee! Hee! Hee!" he cackled.

Although they were rooted to the spot, the bailiffs still had their powers of speech intact. It was Ned Barber who piped up first.

"I thought we'd done you over good and proper last time. Waddya fuckin' want, bastard? Want us to teach you another lesson?" But in spite of his bravado, he wasn't quite as confident as he had been the last time he'd met the mystic figure.

"Teach me a lesson, will you? HEE! HEE! HEE!"

The alchemist got out his magic wand and waved it; horns shot out of the sides of his head and a tail with an arrowhead on the end of it sprouted out of his arse.

Stan was shit scared. "Okay, what do you want us to do?" he whimpered.

"You can assist me. I have magic powers. But my powers have limits. Down here on the ground floor, my powers are endless. If I chose to finish you off here and now, I could do so in a flash. But higher up in the block of flats, my influence wanes. My magic has a down-to-earth quality. So I need you to help me on the uppermost floors of Seaton Point."

"But once we're up, how are you gonna stop us from doing what the fuck we like if your powers are weaker there?" Ted pointed out.

"You fool! I can't force you to obey me further up in the building. But how do you think you're going to get back down again? It's a long way to jump! And as soon as you get down low enough, I'd just kill you if you dared to disobey me!"

The argument made sense. "Alright you bastard, you've got us done up like kippers" Ned spat. "We'll have to do as you say. But at least you ought to let us know what the fuck's goin' on."

"With pleasure," said the alchemist. "It's like this. There's this guru geezer, right, he squatted a flat in this block recently and decided that he was the new Messiah. All well and good – I like people with delusions like that. I encouraged him, and gave him a repertoire of magic tricks hoping he would help me out and follow my magical path. Well, it didn't quite work out like that. I bestowed some minor powers on him, so that he could float about like a prat in a white robe and conjure cans of Tennents Super and Special Brew out of nothing. But he neglected to follow my path. Because he was living in a flat higher than the tenth storey, and because the fool was less psychic than I'd bargained for, my influence disappeared, and he got on with his own thing. I didn't expect that. The bastard has even taken to doing a bit of faith-healing, which I certainly don't approve of. I've tried to settle the score with him since, but he doesn't return my calls. He never seems to come out of his flat when I'm around, and my alchemical powers simply don't go that far up into the air, know what I mean? You twins beat me up. I'd never have let you get away with it at ground level. I could take you all on now, or I could finish you all off on your way back if I felt like it, but I'm giving you a chance. Help me out – or die!!"

"Get yer drift mate" said a scared Stan, "so what do you want me and my boys to do?"

By this point the tomato sauce had risen, gradually, to his and his assistants' knees.

"Listen" said the alchemist, pausing to cackle at the bailiffs who were stuck fast in the nasty, sticky red glue. "I'm gonna give you a secret weapon, and you're gonna use it to take out the guru who lives in flat number 60. Or else – it's death to the lot of you, as soon as you get back downstairs!"

"We were gonna do the scumbag over anyway, so I've no problem with that" Stan explained. "But what's this secret weapon?"

"You'll find out as soon as you get to the 15th floor!" said the alchemist. "Now get on with it!"

The red sea parted, the bailiffs got into the even-numbered lift and the magician evaporated. Actually there wasn't really a secret weapon waiting for them on the 15th floor. This was a bluff tactic from the alchemist, who was trying to intimidate the bailiffs into sorting out the guru – a task he couldn't perform himself, but for which, he thought, muscle rather than magic might suffice. He'd suffered a kicking himself courtesy of the twins, and figured that their brute force would be more than a match for the guru's minor magic tricks.

"What the fuck do we do now?" whispered Ted to Ned as they ascended in the lift with their boss. "That nutter downstairs is serious, and the gaffer wants Malcolm evicted as well, but we can't betray our great guru!"

"Yes we can," replied Ned pragmatically. "We'll just fuckin' aftoo!"

The lift stopped at the sixth floor to allow somebody in. It was Tululah Climax, on her way to meet some of her fellow conspirators on the upper floors in order to turn Seaton Point into a revolutionary anarchist enclave. Tululah was well dolled up in fishnet stockings, stilettos, purple lipstick, black nail-varnish and a see-through black top. She looked like a right tart.

"She looks like a fuckin' weirdo!" whispered Ted.

"Yeah, but I'd give 'er one, wouldn't you!" said Ned, nudging and winking. "Anyway, I know 'er, she's that goth bird who lives over at the church! Seen 'er walkin' abaht, like. I've had my eye on the bitch for weeks!"

"You'd shag anything!" observed Ted.

The vampire stood there, taking it all in. She took a butchers at Ned, who wouldn't normally be her type. But she'd take great pleasure in stringing the bastard along, just to wind him up.

"'ere, darlin'," said Ned, "Come 'ere often? Sure I seen you in this lift before, like."

"Maybe, sweetie," replied Tululah.

"You're well in there!" said Ted, laughing at his brother. The lift stopped again. The 15th floor: time to get out. To Ned's pleasant surprise, the vampire followed. Ted and Stan walked down one flight of stairs and approached flat 60. The boss brandished his shooter cautiously, and kept an eye out for any secret weapons that he could use. Ned hung around outside the lift, eyeing up Tululah Climax.

"Fancy a shag, darlin'" suggested the twin. "You look as if yer fuckin' dyin' for one, the way yer done up an' all."

"Honey, do you think you can satisfy a real woman? Are you a real man – or just a little boy in short trousers?"

Ned was getting excited; his workman's trousers began to bulge a little at the crotch. He'd found himself a real tiger!

"They don't come no tougher than me, babe" he said, "ain't you heard of Ned Barber? I'm the 'ardest geezer on the whole fuckin' estate – in all sortsa ways! Know what I mean darlin'? So where's it to be – your place or mine?"

"Well honey, I think it's to be mine. I live on the top floor. Would you care to follow me?"

The bailiff couldn't believe his luck. The vampire walked towards the stairwell, suggestively wiggling her arse, which Ned patted as he went up the stairs after her. At last – he was going to lose his virginity!

Meanwhile, Stan and Ted rapped at the door of number 60 vigorously; Ted waved the papers, Stan had his gun concealed beneath his overalls, his finger on the trigger and ready to fire if there was a trick. The door opened – by itself; behind it was an empty hallway. Stan was freaked out; he was surprised that his assistant wasn't also.

"What's the fuck's going on here?" cursed Bates. "And where's Ned gone?"

"I fink 'e's gone to shag that bird," observed Ted. "And 'ere, I don't think you'll be needing that shooter."

"All right then!" the chief bailiff shouted into the hallway. "Stop pulling my leg, let's be having you! It's the bailiffs, and we've come to kick you out!"

They entered the flat and went into the living room. In front of the window by the balcony, Malcolm was floating a few feet in the air. He was dressed in a flowing white gown, had a crown of thorns around his forehead, and he'd grown a beard. He had a bottle of Dragon in one hand and a spliff in the other, and transparent, glowing, throbbing, overlapping circles were coming out of the spliff and dancing merrily in the air.

"Welcome," said the guru. "I've been expecting you."

"Sorry abaht this mate, just doin' me job, like," said Ted.

Stan was scared. He hadn't seen a geezer floating in mid-air before. He got out his shooter.

"OK clown, down to the ground, or else you're dogmeat!" he hollered.

The guru obliged, but maintained the serene, knowing smile he'd been wearing.

Ned went up the stairs with the vampire all the way to the top floor. The bailiff couldn't wait to get his hands on her tits, which were tantalisingly semi-visible through the part-transparent dark muslin that swathed the upper part of her torso.

"Alright darlin', where's yer place?" he cooed.

"It's in here, honey," said Tululah, opening a door which led into a boiler room where tubes and cylinders that were supposed to be servicing the central heating in the nearby flats were located. Very few of the flats had working central heating, but the tower came equipped with tubes and cylinders, just in case. The air in the boiler room was dank and stifling, and there was a distinct lack of oxygen. It appeared that the room hadn't been entered by any human being for years. Pigeons, agitated, flapped their wings, and the floor wore a carpet of old feathers and dead birds. The whole room stank of pigeons both dead and alive. Ned felt frightened, and a little sick; his knob began to wilt.

"What kinda place is this?" he asked. "This ain't yer flat! You live in the church across the road!"

"Of course it's my flat, honey" the vampire lied, "this is where I live! Now, it's time for you to show me whether you're a man or a boy! Let's get down to it, sugar!"

The bailiff didn't resist as Tululah took him in her arms, escorted him into the filthy, stinking boiler room, and kissed him on the lips. He found the goth chick well weird, but he was still desperate to lose his virginity. In his mid-twenties – it was about time! He just hoped he could recover his hard-on and perform. The vampire and the bailiff locked themselves into a passionate embrace, their tongues down each other's throats. As the pair fell awkwardly against the boilers in their passion – simulated on Tululah's part, fumbling on Ned's – the bailiff took the opportunity to stick his hand down the vampire's leather mini-skirt. He eased his palm eagerly into her stockings, and was pleased to discover that she wasn't wearing any knickers. He couldn't wait! He'd never got his hands on a real-life woman's snatch before!

The bailiff screamed!!!

"You're not a bird, you're a fuckin' bloke! You've been 'avin' me on! What d'yer fink I am – a fuckin' arse bandit?"

Ned withdrew his hand as quickly as possible, disgusted that he'd touched another man's prick with it. Tululah had caught the bailiff by surprise. Cackling hysterically, she sank her teeth into the other man's throat. Normally, people like Ned wouldn't have been her cup of tea, she could quite happily live without the occasional bit of rough. But Ned was such a twat, he deserved to be wasted – and Tululah couldn't just resist giving him his due.

The guru floated down to the floor and continued to smile knowingly, sitting in the lotus position. He exuded an aura of calm and peace. It was as if the whole world was one big bouncy castle, a gorgeous, fluffy great bubble, lined with teddy-bear fur. It was beautiful. Even Stan couldn't help but be touched by the vibes of tranquillity and love.

"PEACE BE WITH YOU," said the guru, without moving his lips. He hadn't spoken aloud, but the telepathic message came across loud and clear. Stan relaxed his grip on his shooter, but nevertheless kept some composure.

"OK man," he said, "sorry to put a bit of a downer on things, but we've got to clear this place out, catch my meaning baby? We're bailiffs, man, and like, peace and love and all that, but we've got a job to do, and if we don't do it, we could be in deep shit!"

"Hey" said Malcolm, "relax! Everything in its own time! You've got all night to evict me from my flat, but at least let me make you a nice cup of tea first. What's it to be – herbal or straight?"

"Straight," chimed the bailiffs in unison as the guru floated across the room towards the kettle. Malcolm poured the water in, flicked the switch and waited for it to boil.

Upstairs, Ned was breathing his last. Tululah was sucking the life out of him, drinking in his blood through the hole in his neck that had been excavated by her fangs. The bailiff tasted horrible. He wasn't the vampire's kind at all, but she was determined to sort the geezer out. Ned quivered a bit and made a few frantic panting noises, then he went all floppy and limp. Realising that the tosser had expired, Tululah spat the unpleasant, macho-tasting blood out and let the bailiff fall lifeless to the floor. Wiping her mouth, she kicked the carcass a few times to make it roll behind a boiler that nobody would ever inspect. After a few days, the dead body of Ned Barber would be obscured beneath a thick layer of dust, feathers and dead pigeons. Nobody would ever find his decaying corpse. Very few people would miss the bastard.

Tululah closed the boiler room door on her way out. She could still taste Ned's blood in her mouth, and she needed a drink to wash it away.

The kettle was just boiling as Tululah rang the bell; the guru floated over and answered the door. The vampire walked in and sat down next to Stan and Ted.

"'Ere, love, seen my brother?" asked Ted. "I thought you an' 'im was off for a shag, like. You done the business already?"

"A girl's entitled to keep secrets!" said Tululah mysteriously. "Have some decorum!"

Ned's brother got the message and shut up, while Malcolm served the tea. Unknown to the bailiffs and the vampire, the guru had dropped several tabs of acid into it.

Stan, Ted, Malcolm and Tululah sipped tea. It was delicious: Tetleys finest with unsweetened soya milk and plenty of LSD. Stan was still thinking about evicting the squatter, but the atmosphere of religious calm made a nice change to his usual routine of vindictiveness and violence. Given his recent major injury, he felt that he needed the occasional break on the job. He wasn't in a hurry. Unfortunately, his lack of haste would allow just enough time for the acid to hit.

"Nice here, isn't it?" said the vampire. She was starting to get all lovey-dovey as the LSD began to kick in.

"Yes, it's lovely!" said Stan. He was in two minds. He was starting to feel trippy and unusually well-disposed towards life and other people. But on the other hand, he was trying to formulate a plan to do the dice man over. He didn't know that Blokey

110

had been shagging Tululah on a regular basis.

"You what?" said Ted. The hallucinogenics were taking effect, and he'd lost what little meaningful powers of speech he'd had in the first place. He was a gibbering idiot!

The guru smiled serenely. He was on the seventh plane. He'd transcended the physical world and entered the spiritual dimension entirely. He floated about the flat, beaming his holy grin.

Ted lost it! It was too much for him! The mystical revelations imparted onto him by the acid were far too much for his tiny mind to bear and he ran out of the flat screaming. The others were spaced out enough not to notice.

Ted shrieked his head off in the corridor outside. He couldn't take it! He was going mad! He needed somebody to beat up, to release his feelings of horror. He didn't know what to do; he was running round in circles like a headless chicken. He couldn't handle his acid!

During the occasional glimpses of reality which crossed his consciousness for mere split-seconds, he felt concerned that his sanity was taking a nosedive. Him – Ted Barber – the hardest geezer on the estate! Losing it! He wasn't a fucking loony – he couldn't be! What about the damage that insanity would do to his reputation? And yet here he was – floundering! Badly! Like a little fish grounded ashore! Helplessly flapping his fins, gasping for water!

Ted went down a flight of stairs and got into the lift. He pressed the button and descended, but before he got out at the bottom, he remembered that the alchemist would kill him unless he'd taken out the guru, so he pressed the button again and went back up, getting out on the floor where his brother had been wasted. The doors of all the flats were breathing, pulsating, and had goblins coming out of them. The goblins were mocking and taking the piss out of him; they were really nasty!

Ted stumbled towards a window next to a rubbish chute. He looked out: it was a long way down. He felt vertiginous.

And then he realised – he could fly!

Ted got hold of a lump of wood that was conveniently situated nearby and bashed it against the window: once, twice – again and again. He didn't stop until every last bit of glass had been knocked out.

Ted had wings!!!

His wings were ten feet long, he had one on each side, and they were shimmering in an acid haze, puffing up and then deflating again. He was going to fly all around the world... to Australia!

Ted jumped out of the window. Stan, Malcolm and Tululah were drinking tea and chatting. They were getting on with each other very nicely indeed. But Ted was falling... No! He was flying!... Shooting through the air! It was great! He was an aeroplane – flying faster and faster; running a slalom around various mountains and tower blocks; missing police helicopters by inches; migrating with several different flocks and species of birds; finding his vision obscured by the clouds in which he was lost... He was being propelled into space like an Apollo moon rocket! It was amazing!

And then he was dead. Flat as a pancake, at the foot of Seaton Point.

Stan had forgotten why he was supposed to be in guru's flat in the first place. He was watching the colours, and listening to the tambourines. They were perfect! And the guru, floating about aimlessly – he was such a cool guy! Tululah... She was great! She couldn't stop chuckling to herself!

Stan had a vision. He felt that he was trapped in a lift, endlessly travelling up and down and becoming slowly addicted to smack. The vision disturbed him a little, and then he got back in touch with his previous, peaceful state of mind. He'd forgotten all about evicting the squatter.

Stan Bates felt completely wasted when he woke up in the strange flat. He couldn't remember how he'd gotten there, and his colours were all funny. The carpet was littered with fag butts and empty beer cans, and still crashed out and snoring on the other side of the room was a transvestite-looking character in goth clothes. A thought crossed his mind: where am I?

The guru floated in on top of a large silk cushion decorated with strange runes. His head was surrounded by a halo of gentle white light, and he was carrying a teapot and some mugs on a tray.

"Fancy a nice cup of tea?" the guru suggested.

The bailiff's palate was parched and he accepted the offer. A nice cup of tea might help him to piece together just what exactly was going on. Bates couldn't remember much of the previous day, only disjointed snippets which didn't seem to make any sense.

Confused, he sipped at his tea. It was delicious!

Once again, the tea had acid in it.

39 The alchemist was nearly ready for the explosion. The apocalypse was drawing near – and about time too! The weirdo was sewing bits of cloth and string together to make a fuse, to blow Seaton Point sky high and unleash the demons – so that he could take over the world!

"Hee, hee, hee," he giggled.

Seaton Point loomed menacingly over Hackney, casting ever-longer shadows until the whole of the borough was in its eerie shade. The tower block seemed to be breathing through its orifices: the entrance at the ground floor, the door of which had fallen off its hinges a day earlier; the open doors and windows on the balconies all the way up the edifice; all the windows which were broken and the many unrepaired holes in the roof. The tower was alive: pulsating, throbbing, a great big monolithic erection about to shoot right off up into the sky. Weird transparent daemon-shaped figures started to dance around the tower: subliminal representations of the evil forces which were preparing to explode into being. The dark creatures of the thirteenth bunghole, sensing that their release was finally imminent.

Blokey woke up. Where was Tululah? He was pissed off: he hoped she wasn't getting off with somebody because deep down he was quite a monogamous and jealous sort of a guy. Waiting for her to return to the church, he killed time by repairing an old motor-bike that somebody had evidently discarded outside having assumed that it had been written off for good after its most recent accident. Ten minutes later, the bike now being in perfect working order, he proceeded to stick up several shelves. Then, realising that he'd put up dozens of shelves in the church and that he and Tululah had run out of things to put on them, he got out his dice to decide what to do next.

One, he'd mend the broken lift in Seaton Point. Two, he'd go and look for Tululah. Three, he'd repair the faulty street lighting along the length of Downs Park Road. Four, he'd have another stab at getting the bailiff to the top of Seaton Point in order to throw him off. Five, he'd fix the broken boiler whose extinction had left the entire Rathbone Point tower block without any central heating or hot water. Six, he'd have a few cans and spliffs and attempt to go back to sleep. He rolled.

Two! Now he had to try and find Tululah.

Frank was having trouble looking after his new baby. Poppy pissed and shat all the time, and kept crying a lot. He needed a woman to look after the baby for him!

Edie wasn't much use. All she cared about was being shagged. Now that Frank had found religion and taken a vow of celibacy, Edie was refusing to answer the door when he came round. He didn't have a clue what she was up to in there. He'd hoped that she'd take an active involvement in bringing Poppy up – after all, the kid was her granddaughter. But instead Frank was left holding the baby – and he couldn't cope, especially given the kid's eccentric habits.

Only a few weeks old, Poppy had developed some rather morbid facets of behaviour. Frank had once had a cat. A hamster too. And even a little guinea pig. But these no longer existed: not since Poppy had climbed out of her cot and attacked these animals, viciously grabbing the furry creatures viciously and digging her still as yet only partly-formed fangs into their throats, draining the life out of them, sucking on their blood until they were drained and deceased.

Frank was a liberal parent. He knew that kids could be a little difficult at times, but Poppy was over the top: she was a problem child. It wasn't normal for babies of his daughter's age to go around killing animals and drinking their blood. Besides, Frank had been fond of the animals. He was sad. He needed a woman, to help him bring up his baby. Where the hell was Suzie when he needed her?

He wept a bit.

40 The guru got out his magic wand, a new addition to his mystic's armoury. It was bright white in colour and it elongated and shortened according to Malcolm's whim. It was exactly the right kind of magic wand for a top Seaton Point guru to have!

He shook it about. Tululah and Stan started shaking themselves about too, in the rhythm dictated by the wand. The guru was pleased. The pair were in his power!

He thought briefly about what he wanted them to do before realising that a gratuitous sex scene was in order. Malcolm could hardly remember the last time he'd got his end away; it must have been ages ago. Tululah, he decided, was pretty tasty. However, the guru was a man of strict moral principles and he would never consider abusing his magic powers by using them to induce women to sleep with him. As a religious icon, he reflected, he needed to set a good example to his subjects by living a spiritual and ascetic life. In some senses, he realised, the spiritual and the physical were all linked up, and healthy expressions of sexuality could help his subjects to transcend the material dimension and get themselves onto the seventh plane. But he wouldn't use his powers in order to exploit people, oh no, that just wasn't what he was about.

Guru waved his wand again. It had the desired effect and Stan and Tululah began removing all their clothes. The great master watched the pair get naked, got his cock out from beneath his robe and proceeded to masturbate.

Blokey climbed the stairs of Seaton Point, hiding a gun that he'd been given many years ago by his grandfather who'd been a soldier during world war two. Typically, none of the lifts were working. He had a feeling that his dolly-bird would be up there somewhere in the tower block. These days, it seemed that all events of any importance took place in Seaton fucking Point. He was certain that he'd catch up with his chick somewhere within the building.

After going up a few floors he encountered White Magic descending in the opposite direction with a carrier bag full of cans. The local off licence had on this occasion sold out of his usual choice of tipple so he'd made do with the next best thing. Blokey kicked aside some stinging nettles which had mysteriously grown in the stairwell and got out his shooter.

"Give me those cans or you're a dead man, get it?" he hissed, waving the gun at the geezer's face.

The scumbag got the message and handed over the cans without complaining. Blokey carried on up the stairs while the other man ran down, scared. The dice man took a look at the cans: four of them, Tennents Super. He cracked one of them open and began swigging on it as he climbed further, stopping only briefly to mend some electrical wiring that had been pulled loose on the tenth floor.

Mick the Brick and Gerry bounced up the stairs towards Malcolm's place to see how the anti-evil plan was progressing. On the fourth floor up they bumped into Kelly.

"Hey, it's bad what happened to Ted, innit?" Kelly observed. "I reckon somebody must have pushed him out of that window! There's been some strange things going on in this here block lately – it don't seem quite right to me. Something fishy's happening, mark my words. And I wonder what's happened to Ned lately – nobody's seen the bloke."

Kelly had hit a nerve. Mick and Gerry both felt uneasy about the vibes in Seaton Point. Nowadays, the whole block was cloaked in an invisible, macabre and tragic shroud. Everybody knew it, and everybody was scared and apprehensive. Mick and Gerry didn't want to be reminded of the situation; they'd been having enough sleepless nights over it as it was. Something nasty was brewing. They were keeping their fingers crossed more in hope than expectation that the guru knew what he was doing.

"Don't be soft, Kelly" Mick told him, unconvincingly. "We're going up to see the guru. And you're coming with us. Know what I mean?"

His delivery was a little threatening; his words were a command. Kelly did as he was told and followed the pair up the stairs. The trio caught up with Blokey a few flights up.

"Alright Bloke?" said Mick. They'd met each other before a few times at the Crown and they were on speaking terms. "You've lost weight ain't yer. What you up to?"

"Looking for my bird, mate" said Blokey. "Ain't seen her around for a while, don't know where she is. You seen her?"

"Nah," said Mick. "We're off up to Guru's place. You know, that weird geezer that floats about upstairs. You can come with us if you like."

"Okay."

They carried on up, kicking aside the weird brambles and bushes which had inexplicably grown over the stairs and corridors of Seaton Point of late and which, on occasions, hindered their progress.

Seaton Point was glowing! It was a flashing fluorescent light pulsating on and off, sending shadow and brightness alternately across the whole of East London. It was an enormous concrete sentinel, a mystical monolith surrounded by all sorts of transparent nightmare shapes: weird daemons, dragons, unsavoury occult characters of every kind, all waiting to explode into action. The whole tower block was going mad!

The guru continued to work his shaft. He'd cast the appropriate spell, and now Stan Bates the bailiff and Tululah the vampire were complying with his wishes. Guru was too holy a guy to get involved in direct one-to-one sexual situations with his congregation, but he knew that there was nothing amiss with encouraging followers to realise the physical side of their spirituality which would help them to get onto the seventh plane. The bailiff and the vampire had both got their kits off and were getting ready to shag.

Conveniently, Tululah was in her female mode. Her ability to alter her genitals from male to female and back at will had been useful throughout the course of the novel; it had helped the plot to hang together.

It had been twenty years since the bailiff had shagged anybody other than his wife. Strangely, the room was dilating and contracting as if they were all on the inside of a massive lung; Stan didn't know if Tululah really existed or not, he was in a dream, someone else's dream; his actions were being dreamt! It all felt unreal and he wasn't in control of what was happening to him. He didn't mind: he was enjoying getting off with the vampire. He was even getting a buzz out of the accompanying hallucinations.

The guru cackled and jerked away at his love truncheon. He'd already shot off once watching his captive performers get ready, but if their show followed the dance of his magic wand as effectively as he anticipated, he'd explode again pretty quickly. Malcolm carried on massaging his prick as his bailiff puppet stuck his massive tool all the way up inside of the vampire.

The alchemist persisted with his deliberations. He didn't fancy getting trapped in the basement when Seaton Point went up: he needed to survive the explosion, so that he could take over the world afterwards. He needed to make a fuse long enough for him to be well away from the big bang when Seaton Point went up, as it inevitably would. To avoid being blown up or hit by pieces of flying rubble, the fuse would have to stretch to the bushes on the far side of Hackney Downs. It would need to be a pretty good fuse so that it wouldn't fizzle out anywhere along its length. The alchemist worked diligently to create the best fuse ever.

It was important that he soaked the fuse in some good fuel to ensure that it did its job properly and to cast the maximum psychic impact onto the force of the explosion. He remembered the bars of soap that he'd made out of the samples of his victims. Sloth, insanity and sin. Clearly, the fuse had to be scrubbed filthy by these qualities before he could put his plan into action.

"Hee, hee, hee," he chuckled.

41 Frank was worried. He'd gone out to the off licence and come back with several cans of Tennents Super, only to find that Poppy had gone. It wasn't normal, babies suddenly disappearing just like that. It wasn't even as if there was any sign of breaking and entering or anything; the flat hadn't been disturbed in any way. The disturbing notion that the infant had let herself out of her own accord occurred to Frank. It was his fatherly duty to track down the child. But where could Poppy have gone?

Seaton Point. All roads led to Seaton Point. It figured.

Frank cracked open a can and began to make his way over to the tower block.

The guru shot a load over the entwined performers on the floor in his flat, his third eruption of the day. Due to the effects of the acid, the bailiff and the vampire were taking their time over their liaison; they were still at it, banging away.

Suddenly there was a knock at the front door. Malcolm put his rod back under his shroud and adjusted it so that it wouldn't be too apparent that it was still rigid. Then he floated over to the door and opened it whilst Stan and Tululah continued their display.

Mick, Gerry, Kelly and Blokey walked in. "What's the crack?" asked Mick. "Fancy conjuring up a few refreshments for us? Blokey's got a few cans but they ain't gonna last us for long."

Guru beckoned them into the living room.

Blokey went mental!

"You're shagging my fucking bird, you cunt!" he barked as he laid into the bailiff, kicking the bastard in the head repeatedly. Pain registered in Stan Bates' semi-conscious mind as he carried on humping the vampire. Tululah didn't know what was going on at all: the combination of the acid and the guru's magic spells had made her oblivious to everything that was going on. She hardly noticed that she was being shagged by the bailiff.

Blokey continued to kick Bates in the head, the ribs, everywhere really. He got out his gun and was about to pull the trigger when the guru intervened by waving his magic wand in a semicircular motion and turning the shooter into a water pistol. Frustrated that his weapon had become ineffective, Ian 'Blokey' Blake aimed a few extra kicks for good measure at the figure shagging his bird in front of him, until finally the bruised, beaten and battered bailiff blacked out into unconsciousness, his wedding tackle still stuck inside the vampire's love tunnel but slowly getting softer.

"And you – you bitch!" Blokey hissed at Tululah. "Shagging that fucking wanker! What the fuck are you doing, you slut? You tart! You fucking slag! It's the end! We're finished! You're fucking dumped, you got it?"

Having made his point, Blokey turned and walked out of the flat in a huff, his pride damaged. He'd always been a bit of a jealous guy, but seeing the love of his life shagging his worst enemy – it was a nightmare!

In the long run, he thought to himself, he wouldn't have to worry much. He had it all worked out.

The dice man went back to the church, got all of Tululah's possessions, stuffed them angrily into a few bin liners and dumped them onto the pavement outside.

On the advice of the dice, he resolved to take a coach to Manchester. There, he'd rent a room and set up a nocturnal painting and decorating business which would become extremely successful. After all, he was getting too old for the squatting and counter-culture lark, and it was about time that he made a new start and did something respectable with his life. He'd do some carpet fitting and carpentry as well, and eventually his incredible talent for DIY would set him up comfortably. He'd even lose all interest in the dice: he'd throw the fucker away! An accomplished and well-paid handyman, Blokey would never have to want for anything again!

Blokey had had enough of weird chicks. He'd get himself a nice, run-of-the-mill housewife, get married and have several kids, all of which would be delightful. He'd be doing very well for himself and his spouse need never know about his vampire status. He'd go out to work each night, fit a few carpets, put up a few shelves, paint peoples' flats in a very professional manner and mend things that needed repairing, picking on passers-by, sinking his fangs into their necks and draining the blood out of them during his lunch breaks. He'd be Manchester's top DIY expert!

And then he'd go back home, put his feet up in front of the fire, and look forward to the decent meal that would appear as if by magic on the table at 6 o'clock every morning on the dot. After that, he'd crack open a few cans of beer and spend the day indoors watching telly. He'd have a nice cat, a car, a nice garden to potter around in at the weekends, and very comfortable furniture to laze around on top of while his wife did the housework. Blokey and his family would all live happily ever after, but first, he had the bailiff to deal with. The dice man had viciously assaulted Bates for the second time, but the enemy wasn't dead yet, and this was an undesirable state of affairs. After rolling the dice again, he resolved not to move to Manchester and meet his future wife until the score with the bailiff had been settled – for good.

The high-rise dive from the balcony of one of the upper floors of Seaton Point – it had to be Seaton Point – still needed to be sorted out.

Meanwhile, Frank was climbing the stairs of the tower block, looking for Poppy.

"Poppy! Oi, Poppy! Where are you?" he shouted. Instinctively, he made his way up to Edie's flat and rapped on the door.

"Oi, Edie!" he shouted. "You seen Poppy? She's disappeared!"

"Fuck off!" Edie shouted back. "You're not coming in here unless you're prepared to shag me! You know I'm desperate for it!"

She was in a bad mood. One of the consequences of not letting Frank in was that she didn't get her regular supply of cigarettes. The resultant withdrawal symptoms had made her very irritable. There were, however, compensations. Edie's unexpended sexual energy was being converted into a special skill, and she'd discovered that, in the absence of a regular shafting, she could grow plants!

By means of contemplative visualisation, she could make all kinds of different growths sprout out of the ground. Over the last few weeks, her flat had been brightened up by a colourful floral display of cacti, fungi, roses, rhododendrons and sunflowers – and her psychic horticultural powers were getting stronger, too! By beaming her mental images outside of her flat, Edie didn't even need to leave her territory to make shrubbery spring up all over the shop. To begin with, a nice hedgerow took shape in the corridor on her floor, all trimmed and manicured into bird shapes. After a while, creepers grew up and down the stairs, and enormous dandelions shot up along every corridor in the block. Green grass grew in every nook and cranny of Seaton Point; thistles and stinging nettles were appearing wantonly, along with primroses, violets and carnations. It was all rather nice, Edie reflected. Her next project was to make tall trees shoot out of the concrete on the forecourts of the Nightingale estate outside. She'd still have happily foregone this power if she could get her oats, but Frank evidently wasn't prepared to oblige.

"You don't understand what I've found out!" he shouted through the letterbox of the locked door that barred his way into Edie's flat. "The correct and proper path is that of the good lord, and that means celibacy! Confronting and then renouncing all earthly physical desires!" He took a pull on his Tennents and continued. "Save yourself, Edie, before it's too late! Places in heaven are limited, know what I mean? There are only a certain amount of tickets available before the show is sold out! Book your ticket, Edie! You don't want the doors of heaven to shut in your face before you get to the front of the queue!"

"Get lost, you nutcase!" Edie shouted, making a tomato plant shoot out from underneath the doorframe. "If you don't wanna fuck me, fuck off!" An aspidistra sprang up from the floor beneath Frank's feet.

"Alright babe, I've got the message" he whined, "but don't say I didn't warn you. You're going to hell if you're not careful! Anyway, you haven't answered my question. Have you seen Poppy?"

"She's not here, and I haven't seen her!" Edie replied. "Now go away, I'm gonna get some kip!"

Frank gave up on the old lady and carried on up the stairs.

There was another knock on the door of the guru's flat. Malcolm had been trying to calm his congregation a little after the assault on the bailiff by Blokey. Tululah was still too out of it on acid to make any sense of what was taking place. Stan was comatose and bleeding from the multiple injuries he'd just received on top of the effects of his previous beating. Mick and Gerry both thought it was quite funny. Kelly just wanted to get away, back to his mum.

Malcolm floated over to the door and opened it. In front of him appeared the diminutive figure of a little baby girl who had blood dribbling over her chin and all over the bib that attired the upper part of her frame.

"Goo! Goo! Goo!" the baby gurgled, crawling into the flat. She'd just wasted a pigeon, a squirrel and a couple of hedgehogs outside. The tiny vampire toddled precariously into the living room.

"Good god!" cried the bricklayer, "it's a fucking baby!"

"You're right there," agreed Gerry. "What the fuck's she doing here?"

"IT IS AN OMEN," explained the guru. "THIS LITTLE CHILD HERE IS THE LORD BABY JESUS. I HAVE SUMMONED HER. SHE WILL HELP US TO OVERCOME THE EVIL FORCES THAT THREATEN TO OVERWHELM SEATON POINT."

"Burp!" belched the baby.

"Where am I?" asked the vampire. "I'm in paradise, where everything is pink and fluffy and beautiful! Get me some marshmallows, will you?"

The guru tried to contain the situation by magicking up another beer mountain. The assembled punters, including the baby, dived in and helped themselves.

Frank continued his ascent until he noticed blood amongst the brambles and briar that had recently overtaken the block of flats. A trail of fresh red liquid led up the stairwell, and he had a hunch that Poppy had something to do with it. Carefully, Frank followed the line of crimson dots.

Seaton Point was lurching from side to side. The people inside the block didn't realise that this was happening, but indeed it was. The tower block was swaying madly all over the place, the top of it missing Rathbone Point by inches. The entire London Borough of Hackney fell silent. All the cosmic energy in East London seemed to be concentrated into this one strange building. It was against the laws of nature.

The alchemist had nearly finished making his fuse. Soon he would drench it with a wicked mixture of soap, yoghurt and petrol. He hadn't had so much fun in ages. He hadn't realised that he was so good at sewing. After all of this was over, he resolved, he'd patch up those of his clothes that had holes in.

"Hee, hee, hee," he sniggered.

The trail led to the guru's door. Frank knocked and the guru opened it.

"WELCOME TO THE INNER SANCTUM," Malcolm announced.
Frank stepped inside, and gasped at what he saw.

42 Frank was no square. He'd lived a life that could be considered colourful, bizarre maybe, even by Hackney standards. After all, he'd been shagging his mother-in-law who'd been officially dead for over a year, his wife had been viciously murdered by a vampire, and his offspring had vampiric and psychopathic tendencies at the tender age of three weeks. But still his jaw dropped with shock as the sight of the guru's inner sanctum flayed his reeling senses.

To his right lay a large flabby bundle, writhing on the floor and emitting low moans. Stan Bates' body was bruising with nasty rapidity around the rib area and dark blood oozed from his misshapen nose. Despite this, Stan rose and tried to give Frank a cheery smile, revealing that both of his front teeth were now missing. Then the bailiff collapsed backwards onto the floor and resumed his groaning.

The mysterious man who had spoken was floating in the air, bedecked in robes, his face reddened as if from some strenuous physical exercise. He seemed slightly perturbed by the surrounding goings-on, as if he had been caught with his hand in the biscuit tin. A small patch of dampness lay on the floor beneath Malcolm and a familiar dank smell reminded Frank of more intimate times.

The main attention-hugging figure, though, was that of the naked form of the tall, lithe hermaphrodite skipping around the room behind the guru. Tits and tackle bounced in unison as the she-man sang in a bright, pretty voice: "Red and yellow and pink and green. Orange and purple and blue."

A clattering noise from a corner, far to his left, caused Frank to tear his eyes away from the captivating cavorter and look towards the cause of the commotion. His jaw sagged even lower. There in a struggling mess was his beloved baby Poppy, wrestling for control of the rolling cans of Tennents Super with the local Sultans of scum – Mick the Brick, Wheelchair Gerry and Kelly Greaves.

"I'm the daddy, you caant" Mick the Brick hissed, picking Poppy up with his left hand and planting a right-handed smacker on her chin. The baby flew backwards into the cans, scattering them and causing several to roll around the floor in beery orbits. Poppy's face contorted and it seemed for a second that the baby might burst into tears.

"You bastard" screamed Frank, "that's my baby you just chinned."

"Baby be fucked" Mick shouted back, "look what the little bastard's done to my tat."

Mick held his right arm aloft and pointed to his treasured, though thoroughly amateur skin painting of a bull terrier. The tattoo was barely recognisable due to two deep scrape-marks that furrowed their way across the hairy forearm, blood dripping from the two red canals.

Frank looked across at his vampire daughter, but no pain was visible in the little one's face as the child cracked open a beer with its fangs and suckled greedily on the contents letting out a series of contented gurgles and burps. Gerry drained his can, farted, opened another and settled back down into the pile of cans. Kelly looked at Frank with doleful eyes, hoping for some help but seeing that none would be forthcoming.

"COME," said Malcolm the guru in a dramatic and persuasive voice. "I HAVE BEEN EXPECTING YOU."

Frank was still reeling from the madness that had invaded his head via his optic nerves. He remained motionless and continued gazing at the spectacle around him.

"I can sing a rainbow, sing a rainbow."

Tululah danced up to him, delivering the words in a deep sexy voice. Frank looked deep into her limitless eyes. Tululah grabbed him by the balls; he gasped.

"Dancing queen, young and sweet only seventeeen." Tululah had moved up several octaves and further into the room, dragging the whimpering Frank with her. He moved on tiptoes, terrified of losing his spunk sacks.

"Please release me, let me go." The vampire dropped down again a scale or two and let go of her catch. Frank slumped to the floor in relief.

"Dada." Poppy waddled towards the kneeling figure of her father, holding a beer can in her outstretched mitt.

"YOU ARE THE FATHER OF THE CHOSEN ONE" boomed Malcolm. "YOU WILL HAVE PRIDE OF PLACE IN OUR MOVEMENT."

"What's going on?" Frank bleated weakly.

A large daisy curled up from the floor by the skirting board that was close to the prostrate figure of the bailiff. Gerry stumbled over and pissed on it.

43 The weird aura of Seaton Point had come to the attention of Hackney's finest, the cop shop in Lower Clapton Road. Detectives Ron Skiddy and Sharon Smoulder were on the case. They were the heads of the department, but given that they were the only two members of P.I.S.S. – the Psychic Investigations Service Squad – their credentials were constantly questioned by other members of the Met. Months of meetings with local psychics, faith healers, mystics, vicars and fortune tellers had alerted the pair to the fact that something weird was going on in Hackney. A further month of wandering around the borough with dowsing rods had finally led them to the tower block.

Ron Skiddy was a copper of the old-fashioned mode. No short leather jackets for him. A crumpled fawn raincoat covered his blue pinstripe suit, which was so old that it was almost back in fashion. His rapidly receding blonde hairline was slicked back with brylcreem, and a trilby stuck to the gluey mess.

Skiddy wouldn't have got anywhere in the force if it hadn't been for his uncle Gilbert introducing him to the freemasons. That lucky break had got him up the Met ladder, and the rituals had aroused his latent interest in all things supernatural. After several attempts to arrest citizens on archaic charges such as witchcraft and necromancy, his bosses had sought to oust him from the Met, but his fortunate connections had saved him and a nice, harmless little slot – or so his superiors thought – was made especially for him.

He was allowed only one fellow detective in his newly created department, and after putting an ad in 'Pig's Own,' the force magazine, only Sharon Smoulder had applied. Smoulder was half a foot shorter than the six foot Skiddy. She had long red hair coiffured into an interesting Egyptian bob and she wore a dark suit, a pencil skirt slashed halfway to the thigh, and vicious-looking black stilettos. There was something going on between these two, you could tell, but everything was kept discreet.

"Does that tower block appear to you to be moving?" Skiddy asked.

"Affirmative," replied Smoulder. "Shape shifting would appear to be manifest at this structure. I would also hazard a guess that those dark shadows that appear to be flitting around the base of the building are none other than demonic entities attempting, or being summoned by person or persons unknown, to materialise within this vicinity."

Skiddy whipped a strange object out from his right trouser pocket and flicked the on-switch.

"Any read-out on the Spectrebionoscope?" asked Smoulder.

"It's going wild!" shouted Skiddy with ill-concealed glee. "This is the one. This is the case that will finally earn us some respect."

"A pay rise would be nice" replied Smoulder ironically as the pair headed towards the main door.

Meanwhile, up in the guru's inner sanctum, things had calmed down a bit. Guru had another convert. Poor old Frank was so fucked up that he was prepared to look anywhere for a god. Malcolm with his abilities to float in mid-air, order people about and conjure up alcohol from thin air seemed like a good starting point.

Stan Bates had fallen asleep again. Tululah had put on her top and was wondering why her fanny was so sore. She was okay in dick mode, but when she tried to turn female downstairs her bits hurt awfully. She lit a fag and desperately tried to remember what had happened. Vampires weren't used to memory loss: when Tululah shut her eyes during her daytime sleep, she was haunted by the eyes of all her victims. She could tell you the number of each victim by remembering the eyes which had had the light sucked from them with the final vision of Tululah or Lee Christo.

The nicotine began to clear her mind, or so she imagined. She went out onto Guru's balcony and tried to work out what had happened lately. Then the vampire leant over, and accidentally fell. It was a long way down.

"YOU WILL BE A MOST VALUED MEMBER OF OUR CONGREGATION" Guru told the disorientated Frank.

Mick and Gerry carried on drinking as fast as possible. Kelly noticed a window of opportunity and legged it home to his mother. Nobody even noticed the goth chick's absence.

"YOU ARE THE CHRIST CHILD." Malcolm gazed down at the fidgeting Poppy, took a drag on the skunk joint he'd rolled and attempted to pass it to Frank. A tiny hand shot out and grabbed the joint before it could reach its intended recipient. Poppy sucked greedily on the reefer.

"My, she's growing up fast" mused Frank with a proud parental smile on his lips.

"I FEEL I NEED YET MORE FOLLOWERS" Malcolm continued, unflustered. "EVIL IS BEGINNING TO SURROUND THIS BUILDING. TIME IS RUNNING OUT."

"I think I know someone" replied Frank, eager to help. "I can go and try and get them now if you like."

"THERE IS NO TIME LIKE THE PRESENT" boomed Guru bombastically.

Frank sprang up and darted towards the door and out. Eager to impress the guru, he ran downstairs to tell Edie the good news, anticipating that she would be bound to follow him. After all, she was the grandmother of the new Christ.

As the footsteps faded into the distance outside, the guru reached towards the joint in Poppy's hand. Snatching her wee paw away, the vampire baby inhaled enormously on the doobie and sucked in all the goodness from it. A startled Malcolm saw the baby's face grow steadily green in hue, and then the child vomited down the front of her romper suit.

44 Frank reached Edie's flat in no time at all. The door was locked and he hammered impatiently on it. "Edie, Edie, open up" he shouted through the letterbox.

"I told you before" came the reply, all throat cancer and bile, "no fuck, no luck."

"But I've got so much to tell you," Frank whined. "Please. Pretty please with sugar on."

"What the fuck do you want, wanker?"

The door snapped open to reveal the macabre form of Edie the undead. Frank was hopping from one foot to the other with excitement. "Your granddaughter," he gibbered. "Your granddaughter is the new messiah, the guru told me. I know it sounds outlandish, but just trust me."

A look of resignation crossed what remained of Edie's face. "Just let me finish off this Yukka plant a minute, will you?"

When the plant creation was completed, Frank took Edie by her bony hand and prepared to lead her upstairs. It was the first time she'd ever left her flat in Seaton Point since she'd been magically transported there, and this had become possible only through sublimation of the unexpended sexual energy she'd accumulated during the time in which she hadn't been getting her oats.

The sound of coughing and very close footsteps caused Frank to usher Edie back into her flat. An exhausted Skiddy and Smoulder arrived around the corner from the stairwell just as Frank slammed the door shut and stood outside to face the two cops.

"Uh, uh, excuse me sir" croaked Skiddy. The residue of his liquid lunch teetered on the edge of his brow and then started a downward process. "Um, um, shit, cough, puff, pant, wheeze."

"What Detective Skiddy is trying to say," the somewhat fitter Smoulder continued, "is who are you and what are you up to?"

"My name is Frank and I'm taking my mother upstairs to meet a friend" Frank replied.

Smoulder looked suspiciously at the door.

"She's very shy" Frank bullshitted, "heard footsteps."

"There's something terrible going on in this building." Skiddy had recovered some of his breath. "Can't you feel it, man?"

"Well, things have been a bit strange lately, but they're not too bad at the moment" Frank waffled. "I must take my mother upstairs."

"Don't let us keep you" Smoulder shot back with a sly look on her face. "We'll just stay here if you don't mind and recover our breath."

Frank re-entered the flat and tried not to shit himself.

"There's something not right here," Smoulder muttered to her partner.

Skiddy nodded and lit up a fag. Scurrying sounds and muffled voices came from the other side of the flat door. Five minutes passed.

"Are you alright in there?" shouted Skiddy.

"Just a minute."

The door opened.

"My god!" exclaimed Smoulder, "your mother, is she alright?"

Edie stood arm in arm with Frank. Her old nightdress was decorated with a nice arrangement of fuschias and marigolds emanating a wonderful aroma of fresh flora. Gloves adorned her hands, she wore fluffy carpet slippers to hide her missing toenails and an old tea cosy covered her balding head. Getting Edie's make-up together had been the most difficult part of the operation, especially when one of her eyeballs had popped out and rolled down to rest on her left cheek. Frank had manoeuvred it back in again using an old pencil. Felt tips had sufficed as facial

125

cosmetics instead of blusher, lipstick and eyeliner.

"She doesn't look well" continued Smoulder.

"I'm 98 you know" muttered Edie. "Can we go Frankie? Mrs. Greaves will be expecting me."

"Sorry madam." Skiddy doffed his hat and stood aside.

"Come on mother" Frank hissed, and the two of them tottered slowly up the stairs and out of view.

"There's something weird about those two," Smoulder broke the silence. "We should continue upwards."

Out of view, Frank and Edie pegged it towards Malcolm's flat.

Skiddy and Smoulder waited until the sound of shuffling footsteps had receded a bit and then followed Frank and Edie up the stairwell at a discreet distance. Peering around the corner they saw the strange couple stop at a flat and give a coded knock. The door creaked open and a brief muttering took place between Frank and whoever was on the other side. The door opened wider to reveal a battered, toothless figure who beckoned Frank and Edie into the passage. The sound of chattering voices and the punk rock record that Guru had put on drifted into the atmosphere before the door slammed shut blocking out the noise.

"Sounds like there's some sort of gathering going on in there" Smoulder observed.

"Yes, and the spectrebionoscope's going wild!" Skiddy replied, "we need to get into that flat to get to the bottom of whatever's going on around here!"

"Maybe we should call for back-up" Smoulder suggested nervously.

"No one believes anything we say, you know that."

"But there might be quite a lot of them."

"We must get inside to find out what's going on."

For twenty minutes the two coppers bickered over the best method of gaining entrance to the flat. Footsteps behind them suddenly made the pair fall silent. Two drinkers were approaching.

"Ah shadda fadda hoo" came the tuneless song of the anarchist punk pissheads as they stumbled down from the staircase, attracted by the sound of the punk rock record wafting through the floorboards into their flat which was directly above the guru's. The coppers slunk into a space beside the stairwell and hid there.

"Ah shadda fadda WHOOAH."

THUMP CLATTER FUUCK BANG.

"Crash bang wallop, harken, who swears – two complete pissheads have fallen downstairs" whispered Skiddy poetically.

The cops poked their heads around the stairwell to witness the mess. The punk rockers were both out cold, though there was no sign of blood, only a yellowy pool of vomit. Both of the unconscious scumbags had smiles on their faces.

"Now's our chance" Skiddy hissed, "we're bound to be let into that flat if we're in punk costume!"

"I'm not wearing that crap" replied Smoulder, reading her colleague's mind and gazing down at her immaculate dark jacket and skirt. "God knows what we might catch."

"But here's our entrance card." Skiddy gesticulated towards the guru's flat. Smoulder sighed; she'd get even with him on this one.

Skiddy had already peeled the leather jacket from one of the punks and was busy scraping the vomit off the front of the degenerate's greying t-shirt. Smoulder saw the irony of the situation as the puke slopped to the floor to reveal the words 'Icons of Filth' on the horrid garment. "Hurry up!" Skiddy shouted as he threw his raincoat and shirt into the space beside the stairs and started tugging at the boots of the drunk, who was out for the count.

Smoulder shrugged, crossed herself and started to undress.

When Tululah came to, she was well pissed off. Her head felt like it had been used as a trampoline by the combined annual general meeting and christmas party of Fat Cunts Anonymous, and every orifice, limb and pore of her being ached to hell and Trowbridge and back, and then some! Blood was trickling into her distended swollen lips and slightly gaping mouth, and then drip-drip-dripping down to stain her once pristine see-through black top. As Tululah painfully rolled her eyeballs – eyeballs that she thought could really do with a shave – slowly taking in the sight of her shattered body, she noticed as she got to her hairy knees and red raw and blistered ankles that the top was the only item of apparel she wore. She also felt as though someone had punched her repeatedly in the face, but then again, maybe it was all down to a brain haemorrhage. Maybe, she reflected, this had been brought on by the copious amounts of drugs she sensed she'd been plied with in order to keep her going like a steamhammer during the course of the orgy. She was getting at least some of her memory back.

Tululah began to tentatively roll over onto her left shoulder and scabbed-up elbow, trying to upright herself a little. However, after completing an infuriating 80 per cent of this delicate manoeuvre she was thrown immediately onto her back again, where she'd begun, by a lightning-bolt of extreme pain accompanied by a cross between the aurora borealis on a good night, the millennium fireworks display in Central Park, New York, and the famous bombing of Nagasaki way back when. Ouch!

It turned out that Tululah had somehow managed to dislocate her left shoulder almost completely. That would have to be popped back in, in an excruciatingly painful manner no doubt, as soon as possible or at least before the tendons had the chance to get too stretched and baggy and all confused.

"Bugger, what a bummer!" she thought to herself, simultaneously recalling the Tennents and acid-fuelled sex marathon from some hours before. She rolled over onto her other side, and much to her relief found that it was all OK over there. She felt like she had been dropped from a tower-block window and had landed on her left side! POW!! Just like that! Maybe? But no, she didn't want to think about that just yet, she only wanted to get cleaned up and rest for a while, or maybe even for all eternity.

Somehow, Tululah Climax managed to get herself upright and shuffle off towards the church that was in the middle distance of her jarred, blurred and tilted vision. She wished that she owned a solid-silver-tipped walking stick like a proper count – or any fucking stick. Her head throbbed like Hugh Grant's cock on a promise, but it was almost beginning to get light now, the dusk dissipating the darkness with some urgency. Fuck, it's going to be daylight soon, Tululah thought to herself as she shambled off.

Back at the church she found that Blokey had changed the locks and dumped all of her possessions outside. She found a closed-down nursery nearby, prised the boards from a window with a clawhammer that her erstwhile partner had chucked into the bin liners full of her stuff, climbed in and spent the next few hours sheltering from the daylight and getting some kip. When night came she awoke and went to see House and Maxwell, who invited her to move into their new squat high up in Seaton Point.

By this time she felt as fit as a fiddle: the regenerative powers that vampires possessed came in very handy from time to time. After dumping her things at her new place she went out, wasted a few strangers indiscriminately in the course of a nocturnal blood-binge and then returned to the tower to discuss with her new friends some urgent revolutionary business that had been occupying her mind for a short while.

Skiddy and Smoulder had now changed into pretend punks. Smoulder tried desperately not to throw up in protest against the revolting stink. The real punks were somewhat conspicuous as they lay unconscious in their underwear at the foot of a flight of stairs.

"We'd better hide these jokers" Smoulder hissed. The cops looked around for a hiding place.

"It's no good, we're going to have to force entrance into one of the flats" muttered Skiddy.

"We can't do that, surely?"

"Course we can, we're the law. Besides, they're all scum in this tower block anyway."

The pigs carried the unconscious figures one at a time down the stairs to the lift on the fourteenth floor and randomly pressed the button to floor ten. Neither of the sleeping punks stirred. When the lift stopped its descent and the doors opened, the filth carried the punks out. Skiddy wandered along a row of flats and chose one which suited his fancy for no particular reason at all.

CRASH. The wooden frame splintered as the copper's size 12 boot thundered into the flat door causing it to fly inwards and bang loudly against the inner wall. He grinned smugly at Smoulder and they quickly dragged the still-sleeping punks into the waiting flat. Then something caught Skiddy's attention.

"What's that noise?" he whispered.

"Never mind that, what's that smell?" Smoulder was trying to hold her breath.

"No, I heard something move." Skiddy put a finger to his lips and tiptoed through the mounds of garbage towards the source of the sound. Peering around a door he beheld the indoor skip that was Mick the Brick's front room, full of its usual detritus of empty beer cans and curry containers.

"This room's probably alive," he thought out loud. He stepped into the gloom in search of the light switch, then a clatter made him spin around just in time to see a wild animal fly through the air at him. Skiddy emitted a piercing scream as Fang the dog attached itself to the policeman's inner thigh and proceeded to chew. Smoulder rushed into the room and clocked Skiddy's panic-stricken face.

"Get it off me, get it off me" he yelled as he hopped around the infested abode with the dog hanging on as if for dear life. No-one invaded Fang's master's home, especially if they hadn't brought the canine any food. "Help, help" Skiddy whined.

Smoulder searched the rotten kitchen for any implements that might come in useful. After finding a rolling pin she approached the twirling form of one man and a dog and bashed Fang on the top of the head. The dog, used to a bit of punishment, merely lost its temper more and strengthened its grip.

"The arse!" Skiddy groaned, "the arse!"

Smoulder understood what her colleague meant. She'd heard that the best way to get a dog to release its grip was to stick a finger up its anus. Today was getting worse for the policewoman. Skiddy looked at her pleadingly; tears of pain rolled down his cheeks as he tried in vain to prise the gnawing jaws away.

Taking a deep breath, the policewoman grabbed the dog's tail and shoved her middle finger, manicured nail and all, up the dog's back passage. Fang emitted a piercing shriek and let go of Skiddy's leg. Bounding past the startled Smoulder, the hound sensed freedom as he entered the hallway of the flat and spotted the front door ajar. The downtrodden mutt shot out onto the landing and hurtled down the stairs, continuing out through the main door of Seaton Point and off to pastures new.

Meanwhile, Skiddy slumped onto Mick's filthy sofa clutching at his wounds. "Bastard fucking dog," he panted.

Smoulder acted quickly. She dragged the two punks into the room and bound them securely with some old tea towels and t-shirts. Then she gestured towards

Skiddy. "Come on, let's have a look at it" she commanded.

He overcame his natural shyness and slipped out of the commandeered leather trousers. Smoulder fetched a bowl of warm water and found the one towel which didn't have too many brown streaks on it.

"You're lucky you had leather on" she purred, peering at Skiddy's groin. "The skin's not broken, but you'll have a nasty bruise there for some weeks." She dabbed the towel on and around the reddened area causing Skiddy to wince. Warm water trickled down onto his testicles and combined with the sharp pain to slightly arouse him.

Smoulder, in true detective fashion, noticed her colleague's growing excitement and rubbed a little more vigorously at the affected area, her hand tentatively brushing against his cluster. Skiddy stiffened and moaned. Smoulder reached over and started to squeeze his shaft and balls through his pants, noticing a damp patch appear as she did so. Slipping his underwear down, she took hold of his cock and licked around the tip tasting his salty juices. Then she slipped his truncheon into her mouth and started to greedily bite and suck at his manhood.

Skiddy stroked the back of her neck. The thought of two other people being in the same room, unconscious punks though they were, added to his arousal. All thoughts of pain disappeared from his mind as he gently lifted Smoulder's head and stuck his tongue into her ear. He manoeuvred his partner around until she was on her knees and put his arm around her waist in order to unbuckle her combat trousers. After pulling them down as far as he could he massaged his tool until he was ready. Steadying himself, he heard Smoulder gasp as he entered her from behind and started to thrust away at an ever-increasing rate. The pair's moans grew in intensity as Skiddy's pace accelerated further and hammered towards a crescendo as he reached round to rub her clitoris as they rutted faster and faster. Both let out loud moans of pleasure as they came together and Skiddy slumped forward, resting his chin on Smoulder's back.

The serenity was broken by a fart and an outbreak of snoring from one of the prisoners in front of them. Then, exhausted by their strenuous activity, the two cops fell asleep for a bit.

45

The first sign that something major-league serious was about to go off at Seaton Point came in at around 4pm on the Thursday afternoon. Apparently somebody had gotten ajar a manhole cover outside the block. Years before, there had been beneath the estate a large underground car-park that had fallen into disuse through a combination of neglect, vandalism and all imaginable kinds of seedy nocturnal shenanigans. The manhole was by now the only entrance to the parts of the car park that hadn't been filled in with concrete. This space now represented the perfect setting for a bomb plot. People would assume that the initial crackles were just kids fucking about with fireworks, and by the time things really got going it would be way too late to stop it all: the permanent autonomous zone of Seaton Point would be in full and irrevocable force.

And so it was that ordinary constable Dimshit was manning the switchboard alone at Stoke Newington station at 4.02pm exactly. Then the phone rang, as telephones often do:

"'Ullo, this is the fuckin' cop shop!" Dimshit was new on the job and wasn't planning to transfer immediately to the diplomatic protection squad or anything like that.

"You must be a dim shit!" came an old woman's voice from the other end of the connection.

"Yeah, that's right!" Dimshit told her. He was already becoming more than a little confused.

"Listen son," the voice went on. "There are these noises going off all around my flat and I don't like it. I'm an old woman and I don't like no noises, see? So I want you lot to come around here and sort it all out don't I? Bloody kids, I expect. Oh yeah, I live on the Nightingale don't I?"

"I ain't going out there missus, it's too cold," Dimshit told her just before he threw the phone back down onto its cradle. And that was that. The call, naturally, wasn't even logged.

Then, at 4.15pm, the first explosion proper rang out, blowing out the whole of what remained of the podium on top of the disused car park outside Seaton Point, most of it having been demolished during a redevelopment programme. Concrete paving slabs, whole and halved, shattered and otherwise, flew up and outwards but not so high that they might break any of the windows of the revolutionarily-occupied upper floors of the tower. The explosives and incendiaries had been timed and primed just right. Everything was going as planned.

Tululah, Maxwell and House had settled in nicely at 74 Seaton Point. Squatting their new place had been made easily possible by House's recent liberation of the bunch of keys from the now-martyred Nutter Nigel. Inside the flat they'd changed the locks, put up some nice red-and-black curtains and installed a couple of black flags out on the balcony; then they had quickly sussed out the best places to set off dynamite from underneath the podium.

There was also the matter of optimum vantage points for sniper postings and machine gun turrets from the windows that faced the stairwells on every floor. Whilst calculating the best mathematical positions for these, Maxwell more than once had the ridiculous sensation that he was being watched, but each time he swung around to meet his potential assailant there had been nobody there. He also imagined that he heard these skittering, sniggering sounds rushing up and down the stairs from time to time. Of course, such notions were pure poppycock and hogwash to a pragmatic man of science such as Maxwell and he shrugged them off immediately. He was merely tired from the excess of revolutionary responsibility that he had taken upon his back on behalf of the proletariat, that was all. And nothing, he realised, could come between him and the impending underclassless uprising!

A week previously, Tululah had discovered the stash of assault rifles, machine-guns, Semtex, dynamite and accompanying detonator fuses hidden away in old tea crates in the basement of St. Terry's church of the seventh apocalypse, but she had seen no use for the stuff – up until now. Now it all fitted into place and it appeared that it had been a fortuitous piece of luck indeed. Stamped on the tea crates in black ink was an apparent address which read:

F.A.O. Fr. O'GRADY,
ST. TERRY'S CHURCH,
LONDON, 1975.

With all of their defences now up and everything prepared, it was a simple matter of pushing the plunger to set off the first half of the Semtex and dynamite and then waiting for the old bill to arrive. The hour of revolution was at last at hand!

The first cops to cop it, as it were, were Dimshit and his mates who drove their flashing Jammy-Dodger van straight into a wall of burning plastic fences by the entrance to what had once been the estate's underground car park. Their screams as their conveyance finally exploded, however, went unheard as four more vans pulled up, two either side of the Dimshit transit crew, right on top of the other half of the Semtex and dynamite. Tululah screwed up her face into an ear-to-ear grin as she pushed the plunger down on the bastards, and then: BOOM! And they were gone forever.

The vampire dragged her right forearm across her sweaty brow, exhaled, and smiled quite cherubically through the grimy window-pane down at the extreme carnage below. If I am honest, she thought to herself, I have never really liked the police very much.

Next to get it in the neck were two armed response units that had been called in as they did their nightly rounds of the east London sights. House jumped up and down repeatedly, giggling uncontrollably to himself as he discharged 2,000 rounds of leaden class justice into the petrol tanks of the two vehicles, causing them both to explode. The thick cunts had been so obsessed with bullet-proof jackets and the like that they had overlooked this simple but effective tactic completely.

House fancied that he heard somebody sniggering away on the stairwell behind him, but when he turned around whoever it was had gone, if they had ever been there at all in the first place. After the smoke had cleared there were no more cops: cops were over! Now it was to be the turn of the people!!

Tululah, Maxwell and House spent the next hour setting up barricades around Seaton Point, to secure it in its new historic role as a self-sufficient revolutionary commune; a no-go area to outsiders. Working away like determined soldier ants on very good speed, they piled up all of the rubble discharged from the pitched battle that had ended only moments before, interspersing it with old pallets from the various skips that were perenially dotted around the estate and then complementing all of this with a wrapping of barbed and razor wire that had been found at the bottom of the garden of St. Terry's church of the seventh apocalypse. The house of god had turned out to be a veritable cornucopia for insurrectionary hardware. Then finally, the three desperadoes found that they had enough razor wire left to encircle Seaton Point some twenty-five times, thus safeguarding the bottom four floors from attack very nicely. Avoiding the basement for some reason, they knew not why, the trio made their way back into the block via the rope ladder to the tenth floor that they had left hanging there very handily earlier.

"Dib, dib, dib!!" said Tululah.

"Yeah," agreed House.

And back inside they went, to spread the good news to the waiting inhabitants of their radical council-housing block.

46 Again Iain awoke early in the lift and it was still the pitch black of night or day, day or night, he wasn't quite sure as to which. Then the pains began: the awful pains. That certainly brightened the place up. Iain was retching, throwing fits like an epileptic, pissing himself and having stomach cramps that would have driven some of the hardest of men to profound despair. The retching continued; not a great deal came up, his diet of yoghurt didn't amount to much in the stomach contents department but the dry puking persisted regardless. Iain wasn't in the best of moods. He knew that the yoghurt needed to arrive soon to keep his sweating, shaking and uncontrollable agony down to a slightly more manageable level.

Hallucinations beset him in his state of acute opiate withdrawal. The supply of heroin that was innately mixed in with the yoghurt had become erratic of late, and subject to random organic variation; one day he'd get a double dose, the next day and his foodstuff would be bereft of what he needed to sort himself out. It appeared that yesterday's hit had been insufficient to service his needs. Of course he wasn't aware that the yoghurt contained heroin, but he knew all too well the nature of the substance that quelled his illness. It was his friend now. He didn't get to meet too many people in the lift.

No dreams these: Iain was wide and terribly awake, and the visions were as clear as the day that showed no sign of making an appearance in the lift. Iain the captive could see it all unfolding before him, as real as anything else ever that he could remember.

A hazy wizened figure appeared inside a ball of pink smoke; the figure seemed to be dressed in a velvet curtain and was giggling childishly, pointing a bony outstretched finger which directed a stream of light straight at Iain's chest. Iain thought that he could feel an intense heat burning into the point of impact.

The lift accelerated: the up and down motions were becoming faster and faster until Iain believed that they would shake him to death right there and then. Then something very strange happened: just when the elevator was about to self-destruct, shatter his bones irrevocably and send Iain O'Grady or whatever his name was into certain dispassionate oblivion, all of the metallic grey lift walls suddenly turned a virulent tone of purple with bright yellow polka dots all over the fucking place.

Iain felt a great sense of evil overwhelm him. It was there in his chest – the enormous feeling of destructiveness, as if he had the ability to wipe out the whole of the London Borough of Hackney with the one deadly explosion that was burgeoning deep inside of him. He imagined that some kind of a neutron bomb was growing ever larger within his ribcage, from just behind the solar plexus – a bomb that needed to be detonated immediately so that he could obtain the release that he so desperately craved. The polka dots were dilating and contracting now, and their brightness varied in time with this. Iain gasped as he felt the impact of his own intrinsic supernatural power wash over him. He was invulnerable, and ready to face the next apparition without a trace of fear.

"You lookin' at me, mate?" Ned shouted.

"Nah," Iain replied calmly.

"You calling me a liar then?" Ned spat, getting closer to the man in the lift and clenching his fists.

"Fuck you!" Iain screamed defiantly and a goth chick appeared, tall and done up in black leather and equally dark eye make-up. She grinned and bared her fangs, blood streaming from them like water from a spigot, replacing the image of the psycho, who rolled behind what gave the impression of being a metallic cylindrical object. Ned withered and died there, and the scene faded out; but just before it vanished completely the cylinder appeared to develop a ring-pull-like form directly at its apex. Very strange.

Then the overhead light came on. It was flickering a little bit and it was somewhat nicotine-stained as well, presumably from before Iain's tenancy of the lift since he'd had no fags in there, but there the light was nevertheless. A light in our darkness, as they say. The stupid little thing flickered away to itself, up there in the ceiling. Up there in the ceiling.

Then the lift wall that lay to Iain's tremulous left shoulder began to bulge, malform and mutate. It was akin to something out of 'The Terminator' – straight up!! The roughly-hewn aluminium and steel coagulate assumed at its centre the fairly distinct form of a man sitting in a wheelchair and bearing a can of Tennents Super. It was Gerry. Not that Iain recognised Gerry, but it was he nevertheless, only with one crucial difference: the head. The awful fucking head.

Gerry's head appeared to have been completely removed, and replaced instead with a fluorescent yellow skull that grinned away at Iain quite sublimely, and definitely very menacingly. But the very worst things about the skull were its eyes: they glowed away with this luminously threatening green malevolence that put Iain in his place and undermined his sense of explosive power. And worse still was the wailing, mewking laughter.

Gerry laughed more horribly and much more damagingly than the most scientifically-advanced form of armour-piercing bullet and as he did so he rolled his skull from side to side, and the sound that issued forth from between his dead ear sockets was that of walnuts rolling around in a biscuit barrel, walnuts rolling round in a biscuit barrel on a rainy, cold and lonely christmas-day Tuesday afternoon in the very veriest bowels of hell.

The head kept on rolling until both sound and picture faded. Next on the agenda was the rotting female corpse that flashed up on the screen placed by Iain's warped and rampant imagination in front of him. It was unclear just how long the figure had been dead: she was somehow an ageless cadaver sending cruel and mocking signals out over the telepathic terrain. As she stuck her hand down the front of her multi-coloured patchwork leggings and started to rub herself, Iain felt the bomb inside his body tighten and then expand.

Edie was joined on stage by Gerry, Ned, Tululah and – finally – the alchemist. The quintet stood side by side in a row, held hands and then bowed; applause and cheering emanated from an unknown source. Reaching into their pockets, they produced some hand grenades and tossed them into the air where they all flew high and wide and changed themselves into a corrosive substance that looked like tomato ketchup. The sauce oozed onto the floor of the lift, rising and engulfing Iain before it solidified, leaving the lift-dweller trapped in a waxen-type mass that plagued away at his skin and threatened to dissolve him right down to the bone as the five monsters giggled and jeered.

The yoghurt-tube began to pump out its goo. Despite his infirmity, Iain was able to pick out some of its strands with his outstretched tongue. It appeared that the yoghurt was especially strong on the smack front this morning, and he felt better almost immediately. The wax melted around him and sank away to wherever it was also that the piss drained. The apparitions faded out and calm was restored.

Iain O'Grady stretched and bounced up and down on the spot a few times. He felt livelier than he had since the evil psychic doom wars of 6,000 BC. Funny, he'd forgotten all about those magical times when he'd frolicked his way around the occult battlefields, shooting poisoned arrows at St. Terry's mob and generally feeling that he was part of a gang – but now he remembered, and he felt great! With the bomb inside him, he felt as fit as a fiddle and moreover invulnerable once again; he alone was in charge, and the lift could no longer restrain him. It was time to leave.

So it seemed, until the floor of the lift began to get hotter. It was mildly unpleasant at first, then it became steadily more scalding and painful. Iain's feet were burning: he hopped up and down and flung himself about wildly, trying to find solace against the walls and the ceiling, but they were the same. It was getting far too hot in the lift and he still hadn't found the exit that seemed imminent yet so far away. The bomb inside him flew out of the hole in his third eye and hovered in the air for a short while before bursting into disappointingly meagre flames in the midst of which Iain imagined vague, teasing and taunting characters which took the piss out of the captive with the menacing, gesticulating shapes of their fingers and tongues. The captive was anxious that someone may have pissed on his fireworks, and the lift was getting ever hotter. It was like being trapped inside a large microwave.

47 Quite an event was occurring at Malcolm's flat, which was packed out. Everyone who was nobody was there: the scum army was beginning to mobilise. The whole floor was covered with a thick layer of plush grass with a few daisies and dandelions thrown in, whilst the mandatory stack of strong alcohol sat in beer heaven corner. All around the room, drink consumption was taking place at an astonishing rate.

Punk music blasted through the room, which was awash with the flow of conversation. White Magic and Aggie were busy arm-wrestling. Kelly Greaves, his nerves strengthened by half a dozen cans, made a drunken and feeble attempt to chat up Joolz. His patter wasn't too bad, for him. In fact, with his mind and tongue freed by the booze he was quite impressed by himself. His body kept letting him down though, and every now and again he'd fall over nearly taking Joolz with him. She wasn't impressed and was one more can away from dishing out a kick in the bollocks. Arthur spoke loudly to anyone within earshot of his martyrdom to piles, much to Maude's disgust.

The other party members were residents of Seaton Point, mainly squatters, together with a few nutters from outside who had heard all about this guru and his strange powers. They had a good idea that something big was going down, but the drunkenly serene atmosphere inside Malcolm's flat made them strangely oblivious to the slaughter taking place outside. They didn't even know that they were now inside the world's first autonomous tower block.

Some of the affiliates were keeping pretty quiet. Frank bounced Poppy up and down on his knee whilst attempting to avoid the child's mouth, at the same time trying to escape Edie's tongue which she kept sticking into his ear, whispering very non-Christian things. Stan Bates ached all over, inside and out; he wasn't sure what had happened. He leant against a wall and tried to focus on his surroundings but everything was blurred. Tululah was speaking to no-one. After fixing up Seaton

Point as a self-sufficient revolutionary commune she'd returned to the guru's flat with a score to settle. As the memories had gradually flooded back to her, filling in the gaps of time lost on acid, she'd become increasingly angry at him. Her anger was distracted only slightly by the feeling that there was something familiar about the corpse-like figure trying to get off with Frank. Edie, for her part, had impaired visual memory as a result of the lack of blood in her diet, and at that point noticed nothing familiar about Tululah whatsoever.

Beyond the tower block, something was moving in the bushes: the area where condoms seeped, used syringes lurked and spent turds festered. It took a person of a very brave or very desperate constitution to venture in there.

"Hee, hee, hee."

Cloaked in shadows, the alchemist unravelled his giant wick. Soaked in the vices of humankind, the fuse would allow him to get a safe distance from the planned explosion. Here he'd have his vantage point to witness the rise of the demons of the past which he believed would help him rule his new era – and at the same time he'd revel in the fact that the guru and his scummy followers were being reduced to bits of bacon!

The fuse ran from the hiding place in the bushes over to Seaton Point, where it hugged the walls behind the barricades so that you had to look carefully to notice it. From there it disappeared down a drainage cover into the basement where it split into two. Resembling a two-headed snake, a sign of impending apocalypse, it branched one way to the lift shaft and another to the air-conditioning room. Loud music cascaded down from an open window on an upper floor. The alchemist suppressed another giggle, squatted on his haunches and waited for the right moment.

Skiddy and Smoulder sat in silence each smoking a cigarette. Only their captives' snores broke through the emptiness. This had been the first sexual encounter between them and neither wanted to say the dreaded opening line. Finally Skiddy piped up:

"Er, I suppose we ought to go to that flat really, my leg feels much better now."

"I guess so. Don't you think there's a slight problem, though?"

"Like what?"

"How about your hairstyle for a start?" Smoulder pointed at Skiddy's brylcreemed barnet: it wasn't exactly punk rock. The policewoman ruffled her Egyptian bob to make it look as unruly as possible. Smoulder's short back and sides was another matter. Looking down, she spotted a filthy old woollen hat that had emerged from a pile of beer cans during the fight with the dog earlier.

"That'll do." She tossed it at Skiddy who donned the disgusting garment, which at least hid his hair.

"Come on, let's do it!" Smoulder enthused hauling her partner to his feet. After adjusting their costumes they left Mick's flat and headed back upstairs.

Smoulder and Skiddy hesitated by the door and glanced at each other nervously, both decked out in their new gear. Skiddy's senses reeled from the unexpected sex and from smell of vomit on his shirt; he'd fastened the zip on the old leather jacket and tried not to breathe through his nose. The leather trousers and boots fitted quite well despite the swelling around his groin area.

Smoulder fidgeted anxiously. The old black coat she wore was way too long, almost scraping the ground and probably infested with lice. The t-shirt was disgusting, the trousers were rolled up four times at the ankles and fastened round the waist with a thick leather belt to stop them dropping, and the boots for some reason had no laces. Shuffling the short way towards the guru's flat with her newly ruffled hair, she'd felt increasingly uneasy.

Skiddy reached out and grasped Smoulder's hand. Trying not to vomit with nausea and nerves, he plucked up courage and rapped at the flat door with a close approximation of the secret knock they'd heard earlier. No reply. One more go and we'll be off, he thought. Whack, whack...

"Oo's that?" Mick the Brick's face peered round the corner. The two would-be punks reeled from the double assault of halitosis and loud Dead Kennedys music.

"Er, we're er, invited mate" stammered Skiddy unconvincingly.

Mick squinted at the pair and sniffed. "Don't think I recognise yer."

Smoulder stepped forward. "Why, you invited us, don't you remember?" she purred in her best hypnotic voice. "In the Crown, Sat'dy night, remember?"

"Ummm, oh yeah!" Mick couldn't remember, but seeing as this was always happening, his memory like a sieve after a good night's drinking, he ushered the pair in anyway.

What a den of iniquity the two coppers beheld. Half the people here are wanted for something or other, thought Ron Skiddy, and the other half are just out and out bloody weirdos. "Just keep your ears open" he whispered to his colleague, "we won't stay long."

The music thumped as the coppers tried to blend into the gathering and earwig as much as possible.

"'Ere darlin', wahey!"

Smoulder jumped as a gnarled hand gripped her right buttock. She span to confront a leering Gerry.

"Do you mind?"

The request left a confused impression on Gerry's face.

"I mean FUCK OFF!" she shouted in her best cockney accent.

Gerry's face went back to its previous leer. "Have a can" he said, handing her a fresh beer. "I like you" he gibbered.

Skiddy was fascinated by the shaven-headed figure who seemed to be the host of the party. He wore only a dayglo orange wraparound sheet, but he seemed to command the respect of most of the revellers. The policeman resolved to sneak closer to him and try to catch some conversation; he edged towards the guru.

"'Ere." A rough hand gripped his shoulder and pulled him back. "Ain't that my old hat?" Skiddy once again faced the bulky frame of Mick the Brick, who was pointing at the woolly monstrosity on the cop's head.

"Um, no, it's mine" came the reply. Skiddy tried to sound authoritative.

"Nah, I'd recognise those old paint stains anywhere, 'ere, let's 'ave a sniff." Mick reached upwards.

"No, no, I can assure you it's mine, I bought it at Millets." Skiddy backed away. His eyes turned desperately towards his partner, but she seemed to be fending off a drunken admirer.

"Looks just like me favourite I lost a couple of weeks ago. Lemme have a sniff, I'd recognise it." Mick removed his own, new-looking hat to reveal his balding head. He was a man on a mission. Skiddy's back touched the wall.

"Got it!" Mick shouted triumphantly. He lifted the filthy garment to his nose and sniffed deeply. "Yep, that's mine. I can smell my home-made vindaloo on it. You a thief then?" He looked threateningly at the shrinking figure of Skiddy, whose hands were on his head.

A couple of punk rockers hearing the commotion turned to see what the fuss was about. "What sort of a haircut do you call that?" asked one.

Skiddy laughed weakly, doing a very bad impression of someone who didn't give a fuck.

"You look like a pig in fancy dress," the other punk sneered.

More people started to gather round, one of whom was Frank. "He is a pig," he said, "that's the bloke who hassled me and Edie earlier!"

"No, no, you've got it wrong" Skiddy whined, scanning various faces for anyone who might show sympathy. Smoulder looked over in the direction of the raised voices and her stomach knotted itself in horror. Her ashen-faced colleague was surrounded.

"Spy!" someone shouted, and a fist shot out of the crowd and caught the copper full in the eye. He screamed, more with shock and fear than pain. A boot lashed out and caught him on the side of his knee causing his legs to buckle under him, and he slid towards the floor.

"Stop, stop!" screamed Smoulder as she ran towards the sparring group. She grabbed a handy ponytail and pulled as hard as she could; the screaming character dropped floorwards. Blows and boots continued raining down on the huddled figure of Skiddy as Smoulder attempted to reach him. An armlock and throw removed another obstacle, sharp fingernails on the back of the neck removed a further, and then a stray elbow knocked her backwards over a prostrate form behind her.

"California Uber Alles, Uber Alles California" the speakers blasted away.

Smoulder stood up as Gerry rushed towards her, drool running from one side of his mouth. She aimed a kick at a punk who was tugging at her leg, but missed and the laceless boot sailed the short distance into Gerry's advancing overheated groin. He groaned, clutching his testicles and crossing his eyes as he slid to the ground. Kicking off her other boot, Smoulder saw that unless she left now, she too would be in serious trouble. She had to get help. Screaming angrily, she belted the nearest partygoer in the face and elbowed her way out of the room. She tore barefoot down the stairs and out, only to find that a thick blockade of sharp and jagged mesh barred her progress. Finding a door that Maxwell and his mates had hewn into the construction, she opened it and stared, horrified, at the scene of utter devastation that awaited her.

The guru pulled the lynch mob away and stared down at the bloody mess that had been Inspector Ron Skiddy. Sweat glistened on Malcolm's brow.

"WHY HAS THIS HAPPENED? WHY HAS THIS HAPPENED?" he intoned in a high-pitched whine to no-one in particular.

"He was a gatecrasher, boss" Mick replied.

"SO YOU BEAT HIM TO DEATH?" The pitch got higher.

"Yeah," White Magic interrupted. "He was a pig. Sniffing around."

"Here, that's Sav's jacket he's got on" another punk commented, "they must've done 'im."

"BUT WE DON'T WANT THE POLICE AGAINST US" said Guru. "WE NEED TO PERSUADE THEM THAT WE'RE THE ONLY ONES WHO CAN SAVE THEM FROM THE FIRES OF HELL."

"Forget it, comrades" came an ear-splitting shout. Everyone span round to clock the unsteady figure of Maxwell, the notorious local weirdo-anarchist, wobbling on the coffee table. "The police are gonna be against everyone in the whole fucking tower block, like it or not! Ain't you looked out the window lately?"

The guru's congregation parted the black curtains and jostled to peer through the windows down at the view of the estate outside. There was a massed gasp.

"There's no turning back, it's REVOLUTION!!!" Maxwell shouted. A large cheer erupted around the room.

"Man the barricades, everyone up to my flat. I've been waiting for this moment. Come arm yourselves, this is our night!"

Fists punched the air and there was a second cheer. The mob charged out through the flat door and up the stairs towards Maxwell's flat leaving behind a whirlwind of empty cans and fag butts. The guru floated in disbelief at the hi-jacking of his followers, whilst in a corner the oblivious Stan blinked shaking his eyes away from the high-powered light bulb. In another corner Frank and his bizarre family whispered, and opposite them, leaning against a wall, was Tululah, her eyes glinting and fixed on the guru's throat.

48 A human chain was forming outside Maxwell's flat. Unknown to most of the other residents of Seaton Point, Maxwell was harbouring an IRA ammunitions stash donated by Tululah from her findings at the church. For the last year or so there had been a fairly quiet patch in the war for Ireland and no London-based provos had come calling. He'd earnt the right to use the weapons now on behalf of the scum army. First Hackney. Then London. Then the rest of Britain. He'd be a fair ruler, but the army of the bourgeois, the pigs, had to be eliminated first. The great revolutionary leader and his comrades had taken out several dozen already, but now he had the taste of blood, and he wouldn't rest until everyone who'd ever worn a copper's badge was given their proper due.

Maxwell handed the rocket launchers, grenades, M16 rifles, AK47s, pistols and sundry other weapons into the eager hands of his army. Arthur moaned as an AK47 was passed back to him. "Bleedin' Russki weapon" he whinged. Maude tutted and swapped it for an M16. "That's more like it!" he shouted.

The scum army descended to the ground floor of Seaton Point and ventured outside through the door that had been cut into the barricades. The fences hadn't been there the last time most of the insurrectionaries had entered the tower, but somehow it was natural and appropriate that there should be the barbed and razor-wire curtain and the barriers erected from old pallets and from debris left over from the battle.

Further afield, the terrain resembled a wasteland left over from a nuclear disaster. Smashing the windows of the cars parked outside some of the neighbouring tower blocks, the scum hot-wired the motors and drove them to twenty or thirty metres in front of the tower block entrance so as to reinforce the barricades. Then they siphoned the petrol-tanks to fill their milk bottles, Mick stopping Gerry from knocking back one of the bottles.

Meanwhile a dark shadow in the bushes scratched its head with a bony finger.

"I'm starting to remember" cooed Tululah in a voice that would cause a eunuch to attempt to get a stiffy.

"W-what do you mean?" replied Guru, his face flushing slightly. His speech had suddenly lost its authoritative tone and was no longer in capital letters.

"You've been a naughty boy, haven't you."

"No, no, I'm here to save the world."

"Like fuck – you're just on one big ego trip. Got yourself a few powers, make a bit of drink, a bit of drugs, float about a bit, so fucking what. Bet you thought it was funny making me and fat boy over there perform for you. Wanker."

"What's going on?" Frank interjected.

"Get back to your corpse shagging, fucker!" Tululah hissed. Frank ignored the insult and carried on fending off Edie's advances. Besides, Poppy had just shat herself again.

"Alright Blokey" Aggie shouted, "come to join the revolution?"

Blokey snapped out of his seething rage for a moment, long enough to realise that something was going down here. He'd been so engrossed in his mission that he hadn't even noticed the devastation all around. "What's happening now?" he queried, looking around at the bomb-site that he'd walked into on his way from the church to get the bailiff over one of the balconies.

"It's the big one!" Aggie looked as if she'd had a lot to drink. "Us scum done a pig upstairs, Maxwell and his mates have done loads of the bastards outside and now we're waiting for the other fuckers to turn up. It's a fucking war!" So excited was she that she scarcely noticed the helicopters circling overhead and the sirens wailing ever-nearer. "Come and join us, come and join us over 'ere" she shouted into the night.

"Look, I've got some business, right? I'll be back to help out later, yeah?"

Blokey was on the warpath again and hatred raged in his heart. Vengeance, bloody vengeance: only this could put out the fire that burned in his breast. The bastard Bates had to die. No matter that Blokey had caused him severe injuries already, there could be no rest until the bailiff was six feet under.

Aggie nodded, pulled a pistol from her jacket pocket and fired it into the air three times: BANG. BANG. BANG.

Blokey winced, blagged his way past the barriers into the tower and scurried upstairs. Bleedin' popgun, he thought, stroking his own shooter: the firearm given to him by his grandfather as a souvenir from world war two that now lay hidden down the dice man's right trouserleg. Since his previous visit to Seaton Point the gun had regained its deadly qualities.

Tululah stepped towards the guru. "No-one takes the piss out of me," she murmured dangerously. She'd already proved this point a few minutes earlier by giving Bates the treatment condemning him to a fate worse than death. Stan was now the world's first vampire bailiff.

Guru waved his hand theatrically in an attempt to take control of the vampire's brain. Tululah stepped forward again. The guru looked down at his hand as if it were a piece of faulty equipment.

"Your shitty tricks won't work on me anymore" the vampire laughed. "I've been saving all my powers for you, baybeee..." she sang, advancing still further towards the terrified Malcolm.

He glanced across at the bailiff, hoping that he could manipulate Stan's damaged body and get him to distract Tululah. The bailiff smiled at the guru, revealing two long white fangs. The sound of sirens took over from the punk rock record that had recently finished.

Guru forgot any ideas of a power struggle, did a rugby league-style sideswerve and pegged it out of the flat door. The vampire shrieked a joyous banshee wail and set off after him. Frank gave the baby another beer and lit a fag for her.

Down the stairs flew the guru, panic-stricken and shocked that his powers had failed him. All the way down he could hear the shrieking above him and the click-clack of Tululah's spiked heels. It was lucky that they were impeding her downward progress, because the further he descended, the weaker and slower he felt. He couldn't float anymore, he just ran as fast as his underused legs could carry him.

A quarter of the way up, Blokey cursed himself. Why did he have to live by the bloody dice all the time? He couldn't help himself. He wanted to be spontaneous, but he knew that he had to say something impressive just before he killed the bailiff, and also that the dice would have to choose which one of the six alternatives to say.

Cursing himself again for the delay, he punched the lift door and was shocked when the doors parted. Christ, that doesn't happen very often, he thought to himself. He entered the metal box, took out the shooter and laid it against the far wall. Settling cross-legged on the floor he got out his precious dice and thumped the button for the sixteenth floor. So deep in concentration was he that he didn't hear the wailing and clattering of Guru and Tululah as they charged past outside.

Right, he thought. Roll a one and he'd say 'time to die, sucker'. Two, 'say your prayers fatman'. Three, 'get ready to meet your maker'. Four, 'this place ain't big enough for the both of us, and I ain't the one getting out'. Five, 'this here's a lynching party' and six, 'you're dead, cunt'. Blokey had run out of cowboy clichés.

He rolled a six. "Heh, heh, sorted." The lift doors opened on the sixteenth floor.

"All of you come out, surrender yourselves and you will be treated fairly" the megaphone buzzed. Various insults, raspberries and wanker signs were returned.

"This is your last chance. Otherwise you will leave us with no alternative but to use force."

"Come and try it!" shouted Arthur to resounding cheers.

"Right," muttered chief inspector Chubb. "Remember what they did to our armed response units. Remember what they did to Dimshit and his crew. Remember what they did to Ron Skiddy – he may have been a bloody weirdo but he was still a copper." He nodded at the distraught Smoulder standing next to him in her punk disguise. "OK B-company. Batons ready, CS gas at the ready, GO, GO, GO, do the bastards!!"

The armoured and helmeted riot squad vaulted over the bonnets of the squad cars, keeping an eye out for any piles of dynamite or machine gun snipers that may have been in the vicinity. This time, Maxwell and his comrades gave the outward appearance of being less well prepared. Chubb rubbed his hands together.

"Charge!!" the cops roared.

Blokey strode down the stairs to the fifteenth floor and towards the guru's flat. The door was wide open. He walked straight in.

"Alright Frank." Blokey nodded at his mate. Ignoring Edie and Poppy, he looked across at the bailiff and smiled.

"Not yet" shouted Maxwell. "Wait for it, wait for it... now!!"

A volley of automatic fire ripped into the shocked riot squad, their body armour offering no protection from the lethal ammo. It seemed that the cretins would never learn. Blood and guts flew once again as flesh was torn apart by the hail of bullets, and half a dozen filth fell to the floor.

The sounds of gunfire and screams snapped Blokey out of his ire for a second. Frank and Edie rushed towards the window. "What's going on, Frank?" the old bag cackled, clearly enjoying herself.

Poppy and the bailiff stared thirstily at Blokey, who turned back towards his intended victim. "You're dead, cunt" he spat.

WHOOOSH. Someone had given Joolz the rocket launcher. She flew backwards from the recoil, missing the sight of the missile flying past some of the terrified surviving police and hitting one of the riot vans. KERCHOOM. Deadly shrapnel cut into a group of cops organising the CS gas launchers: the bastards were cut to ribbons. "Fucking hell" Chubb wailed, "they're a fucking army!"

"Ouch!" Blokey screamed as Poppy buried her fangs into his left calf. The room lurched as his gun exploded, BANG, both barrels blasting and bringing plaster down from the ceiling onto the dice man's head. He tried to turn, but unfeasibly strong hands gripped his shoulders and he found himself looking into the blood-red eyes of the bailiff. He sensed himself being lifted from the ground and he felt the searing agony as Poppy swung from his leg; then there was an even more terrible pain in his chest. The last thing that he saw before he died was his own still-beating heart being popped into the mouth of the bailiff who had wrenched it from his body.

Some people were more cut out to be vampires than others. Generally, vampires were invincible and could only be taken out if someone did something very drastic like sticking a stake through particular vital organs. But this rule didn't apply between one vampire and another: those of this creed had their own special methods of settling scores between themselves. It appeared that Stan Bates was a harder vampire than Blokey, whose horribly mutilated body dropped onto the guru's floor allowing the bailiff to get down onto all fours and lap up the blood that gushed forth from the gaping space in the upper part of the dice man's torso.

An exhausted Malcolm reached the exit of Seaton Point to meet the scene of carnage. All kinds of guns were being fired vaguely in the direction of the cops. He could see at least ten dead police stretched out in front of the tower block, and blood was everywhere. Molotovs arched though the air and smashed in a frenzy of flame. Drunken and drug-crazed former-followers staggered around behind and in front of the barricades whooping with maniacal delight.

"Wahoo! This is better than the bloody war!" Arthur shouted in Malcolm's face. Maude noticed one of the injured pigs trying to crawl backwards to the police line. She took aim and gave a yelp of approval as blood spurted from the copper's side and he lay still.

There was a terrible wailing sound behind Malcolm and this reminded him of the business of survival. With no further ado he scrambled through the barricades and went hell for leather into the darkness. Luck was on his side, for the figure in the bushes didn't notice his escape: the alchemist was too busy enjoying the spectacle. Malcolm wasn't a guru anymore; he'd gone back to being a voyeur of life. He'd had enough of the low-life lark, floating about and conjuring up piles of Tennents Super. He was going back to Redditch. At least he could return there with some sense of importance and worldliness, and a few tales to tell -- if anyone would ever believe him. Shortly, he was gone from Hackney for good.

The frenzied Tululah burst out onto the forecourt outside the tower and could see no sign of the guru. "The bastard, he's pegged it" she complained out loud.

Her psychotic wrath could be contained no more. Letting out a yell, she sank her teeth homicidally into the nearest available neck, her erstwhile comrade Maxwell being the unlucky victim: and just when he'd finally acquired the power he'd sought all his life. Life's like that, ain't it? His finger tightened on the trigger of his AK47 in his death-throes and the resultant blast tore Gerry in half.

"Get every available sniper, every sharpshooter we've got." Chubb shook with fear and rage as he barked down the radio. "It's like bloody Apocalypse Now down here."

"Gerry, Gerry old mate." Tears ran down the dark features of Mick the Brick as he cradled the still and bleeding form of his friend in his muscular arms. "I'll be up there to share a can with you me old mucker, soon as I can."

He laid Gerry's body back on the asphalt, stood up and smacked Tululah one straight round the ear. Blood spurted into his face as her fangs came away from Maxwell's ruptured windpipe.

"We've got to stick together, stick together" shouted Aggie, "we mustn't fight amongst ourselves!"

A door hewn into the barricades behind her swang open violently and cracked against her head knocking her unconscious. The bailiff strode out into the warzone, Poppy on his broad shoulders. These bastards all hated him, he knew that. Now he'd realised his power, and every single one of the fuckers would have to suffer. He took an instant dislike to White Magic who was standing nearby, kneed him in the bollocks, grabbed him by the neck and squeezed and twisted until the geezer's whole head shot off in the direction of the bushes. Blood spurted skywards and the bailiff directed the stream into his thirsty mouth. Then Kelly appeared: he'd come out to see what was going on while his mother was asleep. Kelly's suicidal tendencies hadn't abated, and he encountered no difficulties in persuading Stan Bates to give him the treatment just shown to White Magic.

Poppy jumped off the bailiff's shoulders straight at Mick who was struggling with the stunned Tululah.

"Aarghh, me friggin' arse," the brickie screamed as fangs sank into his backside. He reached behind him and plucked the toddler from his rear. Swivelling gracefully, he dropkicked the baby towards the police line. Poppy landed, somewhat dazed, in a pile of dead pigs and started feeding noisily. Confusion reigned as vampires fought punks and vice versa. It seemed that the Nightingale Estate's population of vampires was increasing rapidly. Insurgents further up the line continued shouting at the remaining cops who were still alive but huddled pathetically behind their jam jars.

The alchemist yawned. The show was losing its gloss. He looked at the dismembered head that had just landed next to him, stuck it behind him, sat on it and farted. Suppressing another giggle he started to stroke the wick until gradually it smouldered and caught alight. The flames raced along its length and disappeared down towards the basement.

49 The insurgents were getting increasingly arrogant about the whole situation. Several dozen cops had been wasted, this outnumbering the revolutionary casualties, and House, Tululah and various other nameless insurrectionaries thought that they had it all sewn up. There was the need for them to defend themselves from vampire attacks from the bailiff and the growing army of vampires in general, which distracted them a little from their battle with the cops, but their confidence ran high nevertheless. Vampires were everywhere. Most of them were nominally on the side of the anarchists, but the creatures were proving extremely undisciplined and difficult to organise; even this couldn't stop the rebels from feeling their strength.

However, they soon shat themselves when the army turned up. There were several tanks, the helicopters overhead had been replaced by Hawker-Harrier jump jets and Black Widow stealth bombers, and the regular police armed response units had been superseded in favour of the SAS. The entire might of the British state had been brought to bear against the rising tide of scum that was Seaton Point.

The incandescent and flickering flame hopped, skipped and jumped along the fuse, making its way towards the air-conditioning room and to the base of the lift shaft where the wick of destruction diverged into two separate pathways. The soap bars of vice with which the alchemist had soaked it were effective enough in cranking up the level of evil, but they made the fuse burn slowly and it took a while for the flame to get to the intended epicentres of the explosion.

Frank and Edie had this feeling that something was going on; they knew that they needed to get out of Seaton Point. They left the guru's flat and legged it down the stairs, partly out of fear and partly because they wanted to find out where their Poppy was: the three-week old baby vampire had disappeared. They were the last people to make it out of the tower before the fuse's flame arrived at its final destination, causing a massive explosion to rock the lower floors of the block. Mustard gas began to hiss from its canisters and up through the tower, choking some of the remaining residents.

The tanks rolled onto the outskirts of the Nightingale estate. Any police still surviving withdrew from the scene amid the continuing and relentless hail of petrol bombs and hand grenades. It was time for the big boys to take over.

A short distance away in the bushes, the alchemist jumped up and down in excitement as flames shot from the shattered windows of the lower floors of Seaton Point. He picked up the severed head that had laid beside him and tossed it into the distance triumphantly: everything was going exactly according to plan.

"Hee, hee, hee" he giggled.

Poppy managed to crawl unnoticed past the tanks in the general direction of the bushes. The tower was completely sealed off as various crack army regiments encircled the autonomous zone entirely. Frank and Edie scurried around the inside of the circle, shouting "Poppy! Poppy!;" and then an army sniper shot each of them in the head and they both slumped to the ground. Blood oozed from Frank's wound and he expired immediately, but no crimson liquid leaked out of the hole in Edie's cranium.

Tululah and her mates would have had a mind to get back inside the tower, had the flames not become so forbidding. It had been a long night and they could well have done with some kip; Besides, the British armed forces were putting the shits up the rival scum army and looking rather scary – and the tower block of Seaton Point had been the only place to go.

Many of the scum had finished their tins and were anxious to get back to the guru's flat and replenish their supplies, although a few had exercised some forward planning and taken carrier bags each containing several cans of Tennents Super along with them. Fighting began to break out amongst the drinkers over the remaining tins as it became clear that the fire that was consuming the tower block had rendered the place inaccessible.

Tululah and the rest of the vampires were becoming more and more anxious. Dawn was breaking now, and the sun's rays were starting to itch and irritate their skin – but there was no way of getting back inside as the flames grew ever more fierce and made their way progressively higher up the block. Residents still inside the building who hadn't been taken out by the mustard gas moved onto their balconies and screamed for help as the blaze invaded their flats; but help was not forthcoming. It was becoming more and more uncomfortable for the rioters – the heat from the fire was getting to them and the armed forces were closing in on all sides, decreasing the range of orbit that the insurgents had.

Panic set in amongst the revolutionaries. Stan the bailiff took advantage of the situation by producing a hammer and smashing as many people around the head with it as possible, decimating the confused and brawling rabble. Alkie after alkie bit the dust as Bates delivered one powerful, lethal blow after another; the increasing stinging effect of the sun's rays exacerbated his anger and his desire to take out as many of the little bastards as possible.

"You fucking cunts, I'll take you all on!" he screamed as he waved his hammer about like Thor, the Norse god of thunder.

Edie rose from the ground and dusted herself down. The bullet had gone straight into one side of her skull and out the other, but she was still alive and conscious, as she observed with some regret.

"Goo, goo, goo" gurgled the baby Poppy as she toddled into the bushes and sat beside the alchemist who was dancing a wild jig of delight.

Mick the Brick looked around and saw no sign of the guru. It struck him that he was the only remaining insurrectionary who had any common sense. He racked his brains, wondering how he could take charge of the situation now that Seaton Point was ablaze. The scum were a disorganised mess and were diminishing rapidly in number; conversely, vampires were multiplying by the minute as rioter after rioter was bitten. It didn't look too good.

Further and further up the tower shot the flames. The stench of roasting flesh was perceptible to surrounding nostrils amidst the other burning aromas. Screams rang through the air as dozens and dozens of ordinary council tenants perished in the hellish inferno. The lower floors were becoming increasingly burnt-out and Seaton Point was getting distinctly very unstable: it seemed as though it might well collapse at any moment. Some residents jumped from their balconies to their dooms as a quicker alternative to being roasted alive. Still the rabble outside squabbled over the few remaining beers: each and every pisshead knew that their next can might be the last – ever. An army aeroplane that was circling overhead dropped a little bomb on Seaton Point, just to make sure. The aircraft crew needn't have bothered: nobody was getting out of the tower block alive.

Army snipers began to fire at punks, vampires, pissheads and everyday working-class people at random. The tanks stood by, ready to take any necessary action.

"'Ere darlin'" Mick said to Tululah, "I think we've lost this one. What d'you say about if we go up to those cunts over there and show 'em the white flag? Seems like the only way out, know what I mean?"

Tululah concurred. She was in agonising pain as the sun tore into her flesh. Any possible way out of the situation seemed worth a try under the circumstances.

"Hee, hee, hee!" Poppy giggled.

"You're learning!" said the alchemist. "Now, repeat after me – hee, hee, hee!"

"Hee, hee, hee! Hee, hee, hee!!"

"That's perfect! When I've taken over the world I'm going to give you a top job in the new global administration!" The wizard bounced the baby vampire up and down on his knee: the pair of them were getting along just fine. "You might have to grow up a bit first, but I reckon you've got plenty of potential and I'm going to need a few assistants sooner or later."

Poppy made a gesture, mimicking the opening of a beercan and putting the invisible tin to her lips; then she mimed the act of lighting up a fag. The alchemist got the message and conjured up a few tins of Special Brew, twenty Marlboros and a box of matches. Contentedly, the three-week old baby cracked open a can, swigged on it, got out a fag and lit up.

The pair began to giggle in unison: a harmony in perfect pitch.

"Hee, hee, hee! Hee, hee, hee!"

The blaze was scorching and deadly. Virtually everyone in the block had copped it already, but any last shred of doubt was eliminated when the lower half of the building crumbled and the whole structure toppled to one side, crushing to death House and many of the other insurgents hanging around outside what had been Seaton Point. Huge piles of blazing embers and stuff burned away around the forecourts. The army had already advanced to close off the surrounding tower blocks from the protesters. The fire brigade arrived and hosed down some of the burning rubble, preventing the flames from spreading to the other towers on the estate. And in the nearby tower blocks, residents looked on out of their windows in horror and amazement.

Joolz was wearing a white shirt she'd found at Maxwell's flat and taken a fancy to, but Mick managed to persuade her to take it off and give it to him. She didn't really need the garment anyway because it was hot enough in the vicinity without it. Mick stuck it on a pole and advanced towards the tanks and snipers, waving it about.

"Who's your leader?" he barked. "We give in – we're fucked. Stop having a pop at us and we'll come quietly."

A head poked out from the top of one of the tanks. The soldier pulled out a gun and shot the brickie in the stomach. Mick collapsed and lay on the floor dying. It was pretty clear that he was going up there to share a can or three with Gerry sooner than he'd expected.

Tululah and the rest of the vampires, including the bailiff, continued to writhe on the paving slabs next to the ruins of Seaton Point in unbearable agony. It had turned out to be a nice sunny day and the cheery rays of golden sunlight were having a rather devastating effect on them. If they didn't get indoors soon, they'd shrivel up and waste away. Edie looked at the carnage impassively: and then she had an idea!

A thick layer of forestry suddenly sprang up in between the remaining recalcitrants and the army lines. The layer then expanded outwards, repelling the confused soldiers and those tanks whose occupants had been waiting for the optimum moment to polish off the few remaining rebels who remained upright. The tall trees cast strong shadows across the grey concrete of the Nightingale estate; the ailing vampires crawled across into the shade in order to begin their frantic and lacklustre attempts at recovery.

The alchemist was a little aggrieved to find his view of the spectacle impeded by the forest, but overall he was satisfied with the way that things were panning out: his plan seemed to be working. The monstrous and transparent shapes of the demons from hell loomed over the estate and were evidently preparing to spread their wings of destruction. The alchemist bounced his newly-adopted daughter up and down on his knee once more, sat back and waited.

"BURP!!" belched the extremely inebriated Poppy.

The soldiers were scared quite rigid. They'd never seen thick forests appear in front of them out of nowhere before, and they were more than a little disconcerted at the vibes of evil and eldritch horror emanating from the debris of Seaton Point in ever-increasing quantities. They weren't sure what the fuck to do next. And then, spontaneously disobeying the orders of their superiors relayed to them over their mobile phones, one by one the tanks and crack army regiments began to retreat and the soldiers – by twos, threes and fours – deserted. It appeared in any case that the original cause of the disturbance no longer posed a discernible threat to the British state and that the situation had been overtaken by forces far more powerful than a few anarchists.

And as the fires began, in places, to recede, an object appeared amidst the smouldering embers. A grey and metallic structure that was approximately ten feet by six.

A door became distinct at the front of the metal box and suddenly slid open. And then a figure emerged from the box, walked its way across the surrounding, smoking rubble, and surveyed the scenario around it.

50 Damon the demon wandered out from the ruins of his lift shaft, and at last he knew who he was. At fucking last: he was Damon the demon. For 8,000 years or more – give or take the odd decade or two – he'd been either sleeping, nodding out in a heroin-induced comatose state, or simply twiddling his thumbs in the lift. But throughout all of this he'd really only been waiting for the moment: and now his moment was here. Now, at last, it was time for him to walk the earth; it was time for him to fulfil his immortal destiny as the inevitable ruler of this fucking awful mental coil. Now he was ready for a bit of fun: Damon's moment had finally arrived, for every demon has its day.

He blinked and squinted, in awe of the terrible sunlight, which was a bit of a culture shock after all of that time. Eight thousand years – eight millenia of timelessness; but now it was time.

Damon looked up to face the tower block opposite him: its name was Rathbone Point. All around the base of the block there sat smouldering rubble blasted across from the pitched battle and the blaze earlier, and the form of the tower block space rocket was readily prepared for its launching into deep space. Rathbone Point was a veritable projectile waiting to happen, pre-destined for the distant and irreconcilable stars that lay so far beyond the murky cloudscape overhead.

Then Damon the demon spoke. "The thing that I will miss most about England," he declared in sudden and booming tones, "is the furniture!"

The remnants of the police presence had all but receded now. A few particularly committed cops hid in the depth of the forest that lay between themselves and their adversaries, speaking into walkie-talkies and awaiting further tactical instructions from the local station. However, immediate response was not exactly forthcoming and the army, much to everyone's bemusement, seemed to have completely vanished to a man, without even a khaki and combat-green trace to remind anyone that they had ever been there in the first place.

The police, Damon mused to himself, were the working class hired by the middle class to protect itself from the working class. He thought that he'd probably gleaned this information from a metropolitan police recruitment pamphlet that he'd seen somewhere, but he couldn't be sure as to how, where and when this might have been: it was probably just a small part of one of his heroin-addled and disturbed, disturbing dreams. And anyway, he reflected, he couldn't really blame them: there was no moral that stood out at the end of the long, dark lifetime of the soul. Life was tough and you just had to cope. People didn't do unspeakable things for no good reason, or because they were born just plain old nasty. Most of human life was about nurture, not nature. People's innate humanity usually got annihilated very soon after birth. A few people retained the ability to cling to bits of it, but not many. Life was about survival; all else had never been more than a contemptible middle class fantasy. It was nice to be comfortable for a little while; this was a good trick if and when you could manage it, but it was an option open only to a very few people during the course of human history – and not terribly often.

But all of this was completely beside the point: he was a demon and he didn't give a fuck about anything. Damon scratched his scalp, squeezed the base of a horn and squinted again at the blinding daylight of doom – although the bedazzlement was waning a little now as he grew more accustomed to it.

Poppy was still in the bushes with the alchemist. After making his acquaintance she gave him a sultry, come-on look and began her seduction of the man who could forge heroin-flavoured yoghurt from occult substances. The mystical one was obviously flattered by the evil infant's attentions, and attempted to strike up a conversation:

"Alright baby?" he intoned creepily, without even a hint of irony. "Where's a nice chick like you been all my life, then?"

"Goo, goo, goo" Poppy replied.

"Hee, hee, hee!"

The alchemist picked the baby up and cradled her in his loving arms as he leaned towards her temptatious form, then they began snogging. The liaison went on for some minutes, and then there was a hideous gurgling sound as Poppy broke away from the deathly embrace. The alchemist fell back into the shrubbery of doom, the fingers of his right hand delving into his mouth, grasping at the space where his tongue used to be.

"Goo! Goo! Goo!" Poppy exclaimed greedily before diving headlong into the crotch of the prostrate wizard and ripping away with carefree and unfeeling abandon at the velvet curtain that clad the nutter. Having arrived at the object of her bloody desire, the infant from hell wasted no time in wrenching it from the alchemist's groin and breaking away from the now screaming and dying erstwhile worker of much magic with soap bars and dairy products. She then spread her newly-discovered wings and flapped her way above the bushes and over the trees, chewing and gurgling freely at the mystic's dismembered pork sword, and simply and quite callously left him there to die. And that's exactly what he did.

Edie stumbled across the smouldering bricks and piles of rubble that littered the former floor of the Nightingale's long-since redundant subterranean car park. Hanging in the air now was a rank and somewhat annoying smell of festering decay, brimstone and maybe some treacle. Flying alongside Edie at head-height was the baby vampire, wrapped in swaddling clothes. She chewed the head off a live chicken, raised the remainder of it into the air, tilted her head back and poured the blood from the cadaver down her thirsty gullet as if from an organic drinking chalice. Then she belched, drew her right forearm back and forth across her blood-stained lips smearing the formerly life-giving fluid all over her cheeks, and pulled a can of Special Brew from the front of her nappy to wash it all down with.

A few frightened cops left cowering in the trees tried to pick off the airborne undead alcoholic sproglet by clicking off rounds through the gaps in the thick latticework of branches overhead with their assault rifles, but they soon ran out of bullets. Now they were inadvertently caught in the attentive stare of Damon the demon's third eye, which encountered no problems in seeing through the woods which might just as well have been transparent. He pointed the index finger of his right hand at them, his arm outstretched suggestively. All the way down the arm were blisters, bruises and several boils. Damon snarled in true demonic fashion, one side of his mouth transformed into a frightening and yet at the same time rather fetching Sid Vicious leer. It would have intimidated a few old ladies, that was for sure; that and the horns and the smell of sulphur. There was the crackle of static electricity as a modest bolt of ethereal hellfire shot out from his finger across empty space and straight through the trees like a guided missile. There was a further crackle as the projectile found its intended target, and then a macabre hissing sound as an officer of the lore, as the creative writers of fictitious confessions at Stoke Newington station were sometimes called locally, went instantly into photographic negative behind his tree: his black uniform turned a blinding, brilliant white and his now skeletal features were transformed into a pitch blackness which was accentuated nicely by the piercing intensity of the eye sockets, nasal cavities and gaps between the rotten metropolitan teeth. And then he was just gone.

Two other cops, one standing either side of the space where their mate had just been, opened their mouths together so wide that you would have been able to see their twin epiglotti wobble from a distance of maybe fifteen feet; then they screamed out loud in unison, turned on their heels and scarpered. Realising that their adversaries had gone, the majority of the remaining pissheads and vampires hanging around in the forecourt outside what had once been Seaton Point wandered off through the trees and went down to the Crown.

Damon grinned malevolently and looked down at his German size twelve pink paratrooper boots, then turned slowly around to face the ruin of Seaton Point and discover the identities of his disciples.

"Crikey, mate!" exclaimed Edie, wide eye-socketed.

"Goo, goo, goo" flapped Poppy as she hovered in mid-air. Then Tululah came shambling across.

"Who the fuck are you, mate?" she enquired of the hellish manifestation.

"Sssssssss" Damon hissed back at her. "I am Damon, I'm a demon and we're all off to the red planet!"

"You what?"

"I said, we're all off to the red planet. You know, Mars, the bringer of war and stuff. That's what the Romans thought – I can just about remember the Romans, you know."

"Never mind about that, where have the army got to?"

"You won't have to worry about them anymore – I've dealt with them already. They wouldn't have been around for long anyway: it's armageddon, you see. It's the battle of armageddon and I'm in fucking charge!"

"But I thought armageddon was a mountain in the middle east" Edie suggested, trying to be helpful.

"No, no, that was what **they** wanted you to think – 'the illuminations' or whatever they call themselves. It was an encrypted biblical lie. **This** is the place!"

The vampires Tululah and Stan were beginning to recover now as they basked in the glorious shade of the forest that Edie had created. The hermaphrodite and the bailiff both felt as if they'd just woken up after a bit of a session, feeling a touch of the shakes in their bodies and brains having previously been somewhat fucked-up by the sunshine. Seaton Point, their most recent place of hiding from the holy rays, was now dead and gone and they explained this and their unfortunate daylight allergy to Damon.

"So where were you living before this big piss-up in Seaton Point, then?"

"How did you know about that? Oh, never mind. In the old church over on the other side of the estate there;" Tululah pointed across a pile of old bricks, dust, doors and severed limbs and through some dense black smoke. "Just opposite the park."

"A church? Jesus H. Christ! Ooops! I mean, unholy Lucifer! Just who have I got for my disciples here? Things have certainly been allowed to go to pot over the last few thousand years, I can see that. You're supposed to be fucking vampires, for fuck's sake! There need to be some serious changes made around here. On Mars, I mean. You people..."

"Vampires," Tululah corrected.

"Oh, yes, sorry, you vampires are going to have to be slapped into evil satanic shape!"

"Fuckin' slag," muttered Stan. "Slags and slappers. All the same." He was standing to Tululah's left, staring down at the ground and scuffing one boot compulsively back and forth through the detritus that lay at his feet. He still looked pretty pissed off. "Everyone must be destroyed," he went on.

"Yessss, I absolutely concur with you there, me old son" Damon agreed, "but my children alone must be spared: my followers. We must have fresh seed to begin anew on Mars. We need a new start. This place is a fucking tip!"

"Couldn't agree with you more, man" quipped in a new voice: it was Joolz of the scum army. She'd been scrabbling around in the shite, digging under every last pile of shattered house-bricks in search of wayward tins of Tennents Super, or even a stray bottle of cider – anything! When, exasperated, she'd been just about to give up the hunt for that which powered the spirit and made life worthwhile, Joolz had spotted a demon and a couple of vampires nattering away opposite what had once been the estate's podium. 'Well, that's gotta be worth a try!' she'd reasoned to herself, and she'd wandered on over to them.

"So, who's got anything to drink then?" Joolz said conversationally. Damon the demon and Edie ceased the merry banter they were engaged in and fixed the pisshead with almost identical cheesed-off, who-the-fuck-is-this-idiot? type glares.

"...Errrm," Joolz continued a bit awkwardly, "only that guru geezer's fucked off back to Redditch, ain't 'e? At least that's what he's done as far as I can make out. And he was the one keeping us in the old joy juice, weren't 'e? Know what I mean? Heh, heh, heh..."

Joolz arched her eyebrows and she trailed off, but her forced and stunted laughter didn't cut much ice in hell frozen over with Damon.

"And who, pray, are you exactly?" he asked impatiently.

"Pray?" said Tululah.

"Oh, fuck," Damon answered, "I don't think I'm quite used to all of this business just yet. It's been a while, you know? I need to wake up properly. Anyone got any coffee?"

Fifteen minutes later, Damon, Edie, Joolz, Tululah, a reluctant and still-complaining Stan, and even Poppy were attempting to break into Rathbone Point through its basement entrance at the rear, opposite Clapton Way. It had been haphazardly secured by miserable and badly-paid council employees who didn't seem to have taken any pride in their work whatsoever. A rusting sheet of corrugated iron had been nailed to the old door-frame and it was bent over almost to the point of folding at its top left-hand corner, and pretty loose all around its rather shaky perimeter. But there appeared to be a strange, unmentionable and invisible force that was holding it steadfastly in place. The efforts of the six proved so strenuous that even Damon, the demon from hell, had to remove and discard his pink paratrooper boots in order to facilitate movement. The intrepid crew stood back and stared at the structure before unanimously deciding to take a breather for a few minutes. Joolz ferreted around in one of her crap-encrusted pockets for a dog-end roll-up and finally pulled a short, bent one out with a shaking hand.

"...A-a-anyone got a l-l-light m-man?" she stammered. The DTs were beginning to kick in with a murderous vengeance now.

From his position crouching down low on sinister hoofy haunches, Damon pointed his evil wiry forefinger at her. There was a fiery crackle and Joolz's face lit up with brilliant cobalt colour for a nanosecond. Then she beamed and smiled radiantly with a perfect set of teeth at the assembled crew of the brave new world, who were destined for a new start on Mars.

"Wow!" she exclaimed, "thanks, man, I feel great!" Her roll-up was now a Superkings luxury-length, and it was even lit and smouldering away too.

"S'nothing mate" Damon answered, looking down at his cloven feet, a little bit embarrassed.

"So," Joolz went on, attempting to prolong what she saw as their flirtations for a while longer, "what the fuck have you got on then?"

Damon looked down at himself, and if he could have glowed any more red then he most certainly would have done so right there and then. Aside from the oversized pink paratrooper boots that he'd just taken off, his lithe and supple legs were garbed in skin-tight lycra leopard-print leggings and his upper torso was partially hidden behind a filthy black T-shirt with the sleeves cut off rather roughly. Emblazoned upon its front was the image of a hypodermic syringe, surrounded by the slogan 'GOD'S GIFT' in phosphorescent dayglo green. Damon just shrugged.

"It's just the image, mate" he told her.

"They said you would have to crawl on your belly like a snake for the rest of your days," Edie suggested.

"They said a lot of fucking things," Damon told her.

After some substantial physical efforts that lasted for a further twenty minutes, the sinister sextet finally managed to gain access to the previously impregnable cosmic probe that was Rathbone Point. What lay in wait for them inside wasn't the fleapit that they'd expected but instead a pristine and glittery mirror-tiled corridor reminiscent of Star Trek. The process had eventually been quite simple: Damon had stood back a couple of feet, stared malevolently at the sheet of corrugated iron and whispered thunderously at it: "In, demons, in!!" And the festering metal sheet had come clattering down onto the floor, leaving an eight-feet square space of pure nothingness for them all to step on through into their bright new dawn.

After they'd bounced up a flight of stairs onto the first floor where the initial lift entrances were, Damon felt some strange stirrings of deja-vu upon seeing lift doors again. However, this soon passed as Joolz pushed the 'call down' button, and the luxury aluminium conveyance shortly arrived. They stepped into the vestibule in concert and very soon found themselves alighting onto the bridge of the interstellar star cruiser, Rathbone Point. Damon clicked his fingers and a large viewing-screen lit up in front of them.

"Behold, the future of mankind!" he explained. Tululah just glared at him fiercely. Then she gave Edie another glance. She couldn't quite put her finger on what it was about her that seemed familiar, so she assumed that her mind was playing tricks on her after the recent traumatic events, and resolved not to give the matter any further thought.

Outside the block the entire foundations of the estate shook, at first gently and then more and more violently as the four towers on the estate other than Rathbone and the already-defunct Seaton began to tumble. First Rachel and Sutherland Points, and then the remaining Embley and Farnell came crashing to the ground: but most of them were due for demolition anyway, so it didn't really matter; the council just hadn't quite got around to it yet. The resulting carnage was reminiscent of one of the great Sunday morning estate-clearance parties that had entertained the residents of the borough during the mid-1990s, only all the more spectacular as four blocks were coming down at once instead of merely one. It was fucking mental!

Damon the demon leaned back into a seventies-style swivel chair, his arms folded, grinning broadly away to himself with smug satisfaction. His smack cravings had all but disappeared, superseded by the evil psychic magickal powers which had been gradually returning to him since he'd walked free from his enforced incarceration in the lift, and prior to that in the pit below where Seaton Point had latterly stood. Even the bruises that had marked the underside of his forearms were gone – temporarily. He put it all down to some form of stigmata.

"Well, that ought to sort out the prehistoric site of the thirteenth bunghole!" he proclaimed. "Open for business again! It's DOOMTIME, EVERYBODY!!" Then he just collapsed into these fits of giggles. The others looked at him strangely.

The launching of Rathbone Point from its corporeal base was the initial spur for the opening-up of a direct gateway into Hell, London E5. It was the vibrations what had done it. But now the earth was doomed, and the crew was destined for Mars. Edie was unaware that she was heading towards home. It was armageddon come at last, and it was the last thing ever to go right for Damon the demon.

Somewhere along the journey to the land of little green men with pointy heads, something went wrong. Joolz began to get the DTs and picked a fight with Stan, who was still well edgy from being caught out in the sun earlier. Then Damon, his smack cravings returning much the same as Joolz' DTs, got irritable and brained Joolz to death with a microphone that the film crew from Star Trek had left behind in the sixties. Tululah thought that this was out of order and attacked the demon, and he sorted her out too with a wooden stake and some silver bullets before disposing of the bailiff in a similar manner just for the hell of it. It then finally occurred to Edie that the now deceased Tululah had in fact been no other than her long-lost lover and betrayer Lee Christo, who hadn't even recognised her in her decayed state; all that remained of Edie's heart and spirit snapped with this realisation and she became a mute catatonic. Then Poppy got upset and started to puke all this horrible runny green stuff everywhere.

But what finally happened was that they simply ran out of petrol. Damon the demon had had his day but now his day was over: the clock had struck midnight. But he should have known that something like this was going to happen all along.

Because the final and inescapable truth was that nothing was ever any good, ever.

ALSO AVAILABLE FROM SPARE CHANGE BOOKS...

THE PRIMAL SCREAMER
A NOVEL BY NICK BLINKO. £5.95, 128pp.

THE PRIMAL SCREAMER is a gripping and disturbing account of the author's personal experience of Primal Scream therapy, set against the background of the early 80s anarchist punk scene. Written by Nick Blinko – singer, guitarist and songwriter in acclaimed punk band Rudimentary Peni – this semi-autobiographical novel will be of interest to all punk fans and people concerned with the cutting edge of modern mental health treatments.

"The insights it offers into the punk scene and into the unsettling landscapes of its author's mind are fascinating. The whole book... has a distinct sense of coming from a mind unlike most we are used to" – The Big Issue.

"Nick Blinko is a madman. That's not intended as pejorative opinion but rather a statement of plain fact" – Maximum Rock N Roll.

GOBBING POGOING AND GRATUITOUS BAD LANGUAGE
AN ANTHOLOGY OF PUNK SHORT STORIES. £6.95, 160pp.

Punk fiction by over twenty of the world's leading punk authors including Nick Blinko, Stewart Home, Poppy Z. Brite, Mark Perry, Robert Wyatt, Nikki Sudden and all seven of the authors of Seaton Point. A must for all punks who can read.

"Gobbing tells it like it is... It kind of defines punk as a cider swilling, green mohican wearing kinda thing, which is part of its charm... It runs through the gamut of righteous punk rock activity: mainly drinking, shagging, fighting and being a deviant. Well worth the price of a few cans of Special Brew" – D-Tour.

"A treasure trove of stories, testimonies and commentaries... Greil Marcus eat your heart out" – I-D.

You can order your copies of the above books from Spare Change Books, Box 26, 136-138 Kingsland High Street, London E8 2SN. If you live outside the UK please add on a little bit extra for postage.